A TEXT BOOK OF

OBJECT ORIENTED PROGRAMMING

FOR
SEMESTER – II

SECOND YEAR DEGREE COURSE IN ELECTRONICS /
ELECTRONICS & TELECOMMUNICATION ENGINEERING

Strictly According to New Revised Credit System Syllabus
of Savitribai Phule Pune University
(w.e.f June 2016)

Mrs. SHILPA N. BHOSALE
ME. (Comp. Engg.)
Assistant Professor,
Comp. Engg. Deptt.,
NBN Sinhgad School of Engineering,
Ambegaon (Bk.), PUNE.

Mrs. PRITI P. JORVEKAR - KUMBHAR
ME. (Comp. Engg.)
Assistant Professor,
Comp. Engg. Deptt.,
NBN Sinhgad School of Engineering,
Ambegaon (Bk.), PUNE.

NIRALI PRAKASHAN
ADVANCEMENT OF KNOWLEDGE

N3575

OBJECT ORIENTED PROGRAMMING (SE Elect. / E&TC)　　　ISBN 978-93-86353-07-8

First Edition : **January 2017**

© : **Authors**

Published By :　　　　　　　　　　　**Polyplate**

NIRALI PRAKASHAN

Abhyudaya Pragati, 1312, Shivaji Nagar,
Off J.M. Road, Pune – 411005
Tel - (020) 25512336/37/39, Fax - (020) 25511379
Email : niralipune@pragationline.com

☞ DISTRIBUTION CENTRES

PUNE

Nirali Prakashan : 119, Budhwar Peth, Jogeshwari Mandir Lane, Pune 411002, Maharashtra
Tel : (020) 2445 2044, 66022708, Fax : (020) 2445 1538
Email : bookorder@pragationline.com, niralilocal@pragationline.com

Nirali Prakashan : S. No. 28/27, Dhyari, Near Pari Company, Pune 411041
Tel : (020) 24690204 Fax : (020) 24690316
Email : dhyari@pragationline.com, bookorder@pragationline.com

MUMBAI

Nirali Prakashan : 385, S.V.P. Road, Rasdhara Co-op. Hsg. Society Ltd.,
Girgaum, Mumbai 400004, Maharashtra
Tel : (022) 2385 6339 / 2386 9976, Fax : (022) 2386 9976
Email : niralimumbai@pragationline.com

☞ DISTRIBUTION BRANCHES

JALGAON

Nirali Prakashan : 34, V. V. Golani Market, Navi Peth, Jalgaon 425001,
Maharashtra, Tel : (0257) 222 0395, Mob : 94234 91860

KOLHAPUR

Nirali Prakashan : New Mahadvar Road, Kedar Plaza, 1st Floor Opp. IDBI Bank
Kolhapur 416 012, Maharashtra. Mob : 9850046155

NAGPUR

Pratibha Book Distributors : Above Maratha Mandir, Shop No. 3, First Floor,
Rani Jhanshi Square, Sitabuldi, Nagpur 440012, Maharashtra
Tel : (0712) 254 7129

DELHI

Nirali Prakashan : 4593/21, Basement, Aggarwal Lane 15, Ansari Road, Daryaganj
Near Times of India Building, New Delhi 110002
Mob : 08505972553

BENGALURU

Pragati Book House : House No. 1, Sanjeevappa Lane, Avenue Road Cross,
Opp. Rice Church, Bengaluru – 560002.
Tel : (080) 64513344, 64513355,Mob : 9880582331, 9845021552
Email:bharatsavla@yahoo.com

CHENNAI

Pragati Books : 9/1, Montieth Road, Behind Taas Mahal, Egmore,
Chennai 600008 Tamil Nadu, Tel : (044) 6518 3535,
Mob : 94440 01782 / 98450 21552 / 98805 82331,
Email : bharatsavla@yahoo.com

niralipune@pragationline.com　|　www.pragationline.com

Also find us on 🇫 www.facebook.com/niralibooks

Dedicated to ...

My lovely daughter **'Devanshi'**.

...... *Shilpa N. Bhosale*

Dedicated to ...

My beloved aunty Late. **Ms. Suman Durgadas Jorvekar**.

...... *Priti P. Jorvekar*

PREFACE

It gives us great pleasure in publishing this text book on "**Object Oriented Programming**" for the students of Second Year Degree Course in Electronics / Electronics & Telecommunication Engineering. This book is strictly written according to **New Revised Credit System Syllabus** of Savitribai Phule Pune University (2015 Pattern).

As per the policy of the University, Engineering Syllabi is revised every five years. Last revision was in the year 2012. New revision is coming little earlier, as university has introduced **Online System of Examination** from year 2012.

As per the **New Credit System**, the **Online Examinations** Phase–I will be conducted based on First & Second Units and Phase–II on Third & Fourth Units. The **Online** examinations will have objective types of questions with multiple choices. End Sem. Theory Examination will be based on all the six units and that will be conducted in traditional way and the Theory Course will have 4 credits.

It is our objective to keep the presentation systematic, consistent, intensive and clear presentation of concept through explanatory notes and figures. So we are sure that this book will cater for all your needs for this subject.

Main feature of this book is, **Complete Coverage** of the New Credit System Syllabus with large number of **Worked (Solved) Programs, Examples and Exercises.**

We have given Separate Book of Multiple Choice Questions (MCQ's) which will be very useful to the students especially for Online Examinations.

We would also like to thanks Dr. R. S. Prasad, Principal, NBN Sinhgad School of Engineering, Ambegaon (Bk) Pune, for their valuable guidance and timely reliving us for performing this task.

We take this opportunity to express our sincere thanks to Shri. Dineshbhai Furia, Shri. Jignesh Furia, Mrs. Nirali Verma and Shri. M. P. Munde and entire team of Nirali Prakashan namely Mrs. Deepali Lachake (Co-ordinator), who really have taken keen interest and untiring efforts in publishing this text.

The advice and suggestions of our esteemed readers to improve the text are most welcomed, and will be highly appreciated.

Pune   **Authors**

SYLLABUS

Unit I : Introduction to Object Oriented Programming   (6 Lectures)

Principles of OOP: Software crisis, Software evolution, OOP paradigm, Basic Concepts of OOP, Benefits & applications of OOP. Beginning with C++: What is C++, Applications of C++, A Simple C++ Program, More C++ statements. Moving from C to C++: Declaration of variable, Reference variables, Scope resolution operator, Member dereferencing operator, memory management operators. Functions in C++: Function prototyping, Call by reference.

Unit II : Concepts of Object Oriented Programming with C++   (6 Lectures)

Classes & Objects: Specifying a class, Defining member functions, A C++ program with class, Making an outside function inline, Nesting of member function, Private member function, Arrays within class, Member allocation for objects, Arrays of objects, Objects as function arguments. Constructors & Destructors: Constructors, Parameterized constructors, Multiple constructors in a class, Constructors with default arguments. Operator overloading concept: Use of operator overloading, defining operator overloading, Binary operator overloading. Introduction to Inheritance: Concept and types of Inheritance, Defining derived classes, Single inheritance, Making a private member inheritable, multilevel inheritance.

Unit III : Java Fundamentals   (6 Lectures)

Evolution of Java, Comparison of Java with other programming languages, Java features, Java Environment, Simple Java Program, Java Tokens, Java Statements, Constants, variables, data types. Declaration of variables, Giving values to variables, Scope of variables, arrays, Symbolic constants, Typecasting, Getting values of variables, Standard default values, Operators, Expressions, Type conversion in expressions, Operator precedence and associativity, Mathematical functions, Control statements- Decision making & branching, Decision making & looping.

Unit IV : Classes, Methods and Objects in Java   (6 Lectures)

Class Fundamentals, Declaring Objects, Assigning Object reference variables, Methods, Constructors, The This keyword, Garbage collection, finalize method, Overloading methods, using objects as parameters, Argument passing, returning objects, Recursion, access control, static, final, arrays, strings class, Command line arguments.

Unit V : Inheritance, Packages and Interfaces   (6 Lectures)

Inheritance basics, Using Super, Creating Multilevel hierarchy, Constructors in derived class, Method overriding, Dynamic method dispatch, Using Abstract classes, Using final with inheritance, Object class, Packages, Access protection, Importing packages, Interfaces: Define, implement and extend. Default interface methods, Use static method in interface.

Unit VI : Multithreading, Exception handling and Applets   (6 Lectures)

Introduction to multithreading: Introduction, Creating thread and extending thread class. Concept of Exception handling: Introduction, Types of errors, Exception handling syntax, Multiple catch statements. I/O basics, Reading console inputs, Writing Console output. Applets: Concepts of Applets, differences between applets and applications, life cycle of an applet, types of applets, creating a simple applet.

CONTENTS

INTRODUCTION TO OBJECT ORIENTED PROGRAMMING

1.1 PRINCIPLES OF OOP

The Objects Oriented Programming (OOP) is constructed over four major principles:

- Encapsulation,
- Data Abstraction,
- Polymorphism and
- Inheritance.

1.1.1 Encapsulation

- Encapsulation means that the internal representation of an object is generally hidden from view outside of the object's definition. Typically, only the object's own methods can directly inspect or manipulate its fields.

- Encapsulation is the hiding of data implementation by restricting access to accessors and mutators.

- An **accessor** is a method that is used to ask an object about itself. In OOP, these are usually in the form of properties, which have a *get* method, which is an accessor method. However, accessor methods are not restricted to properties and can be any public method that gives information about the state of the object.

- A **Mutator** is a public method that is used to modify the state of an object, while hiding the implementation of exactly how the data gets modified. It's the *set* method that lets the caller modify the member data behind the scenes.

- Hiding the internals of the object protects its integrity by preventing users from setting the internal data of the component into an invalid or inconsistent state. This type of data protection and implementation protection is called *Encapsulation*. A benefit of encapsulation is that it can reduce system complexity.

1.1.2 Abstraction

- Data abstraction and encapuslation are closely tied together, because a simple definition of data abstraction is the development of classes, objects, types in terms of their interfaces and functionality, instead of their implementation details. Abstraction denotes a model, a view, or some other focused representation for an actual item.

- "An abstraction denotes the essential characteristics of an object that distinguish it from all other kinds of object and thus provide crisply defined conceptual boundaries, relative to the perspective of the viewer." — G. Booch
- In short, data abstraction is nothing more than the implementation of an object that contains the same essential properties and actions we can find in the original object we are representing.

1.1.3 Inheritance

- Inheritance is a way to reuse code of existing objects, or to establish a subtype from an existing object, or both, depending upon programming language support. In classical inheritance where objects are defined by classes, classes can inherit attributes and behavior from pre-existing classes called base classes, superclasses, parent classes or ancestor classes. The resulting classes are known as derived classes, subclasses or child classes. The relationships of classes through inheritance gives rise to a hierarchy.

Subclasses and Superclasses

- A subclass is a modular, derivative class that inherits one or more properties from another class (called the superclass). The properties commonly include class data variables, properties, and methods or functions. The superclass establishes a common interface and foundational functionality, which specialized subclasses can inherit, modify, and supplement. The software inherited by a subclass is considered reused in the subclass.
- In some cases, a subclass may customize or redefine a method inherited from the superclass. A superclass method which can be redefined in this way is called a virtual method.

1.1.4 Polymorphism

- Polymorphism means one name, many forms. Polymorphism manifests itself by having multiple methods all with the same name, but slightly different functionality.

There are 2 basic types of polymorphism.

- Overridding, also called run-time polymorphism. For method overloading, the compiler determines which method will be executed, and this decision is made when the code gets compiled.
- Overloading, which is referred to as compile-time polymorphism. Method will be used for method overriding is determined at runtime based on the dynamic type of an object.

1.2 SOFTWARE CRISIS

Developments in software technology continue to be dynamic. New tools and techniques are announced in quick succession. This has forced the software engineers and industry to continuously look for new approaches to software design and development, and they are becoming more and more critical in view of the increasing complexity of software systems as well as the highly competitive nature of the industry. These rapid advances appear to have created a situation of crisis within the industry. The following issues need to be addressed to face the crisis:

- How to represent real-life entities of problems in system design?

- How to design system with open interfaces?

- How to ensure reusability and extensibility of modules?

- How to develop modules that are tolerant of any changes in future?

- How to improve software productivity and decrease software cost?

- How to improve the quality of software?

- How to manage time schedules?

1.3 SOFTWARE EVOLUTION

- Ernest Tello, a well known writer in the field of artificial intelligence, compared the evolution of software technology to the growth of the tree. Like a tree, the software evolution has had distinct phases "layers" of growth.

- These layers were building up one by one over the last five decades as shown in Fig. 1.1, with each layer representing and improvement over the previous one. However, the analogy fails if we consider the life of these layers. In a software system, each of the layers continues to be functional, whereas in the case of trees, only the uppermost layer is functional.

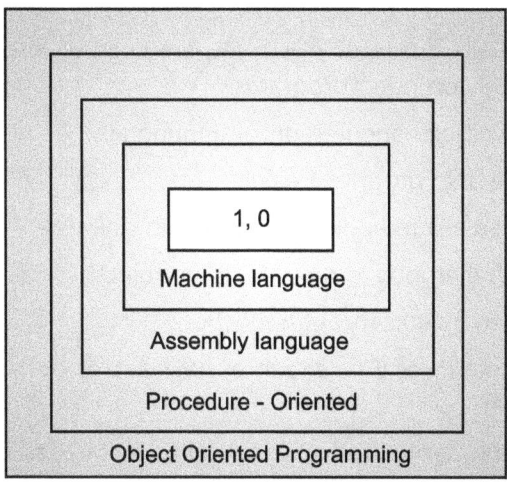

Fig. 1.1 : Software evolution

- Alan Kay, one of the promoters of the object-oriented paradigm and the principal designer of Smalltalk, has said: "As complexity increases, architecture dominates the basic materials". To build today's complex software it is just not enough to put together a sequence of programming statements and sets of procedures and modules; we need to incorporate sound construction techniques and program structures that are easy to comprehend implement and modify.

- With the advent of languages such as C, structured programming became very popular and was the main technique of the 1980's. Structured programming was a powerful tool that enabled programmers to write moderately complex programs fairly easily. However, as the programs grew larger, even the structured approach failed to show the desired result in terms of bug-free, easy-to- maintain, and reusable programs.

- Object Oriented Programming (OOP) is an approach to program organization and development that attempts to eliminate some of the pitfalls of conventional programming methods by incorporating the best of structured programming features with several powerful new concepts. It is a new way of organizing and developing programs and has nothing to do with any particular language. However, not all languages are suitable to implement the OOP concepts easily.

1.4 OOP PARADIGM

- Object-oriented programming (OOP) is a programming paradigm based on the concept of "objects", which may contain data, in the form of fields, often known as attributes; and code, in the form of procedures, often known as methods.

- Object–oriented programming (OOP) is a programming paradigm based upon objects (having both data and methods) that aims to incorporate the advantages of modularity and reusability.

- Objects which are usually instances of classes, are used to interact with one another to design applications and computer programs.

The important features of object–oriented programming are:

- Bottom–up approach in program design

- Programs organized around objects, grouped in classes

- Focus on data with methods to operate upon object's data

- Interaction between objects through functions

- Reusability of design through creation of new classes by adding features to existing classes(Inheritance)

- Some examples of object–oriented programming languages are C++, Java, Smalltalk, Delphi, C#, Perl, Python, Ruby, and PHP.

- Grady Booch has defined object–oriented programming as "a method of implementation in which programs are organized as cooperative collections of objects, each of which represents an instance of some class, and whose classes are all members of a hierarchy of classes united via inheritance relationships".

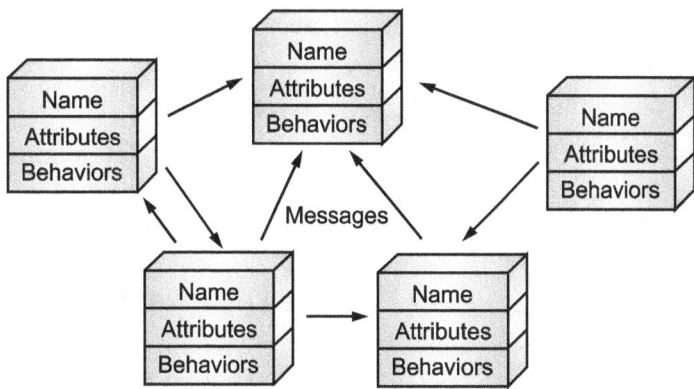

Fig. 1.2: Structure of object oriented programming

1.5 BASIC CONCEPTS OF OBJECT ORIENTED PROGRAMMING

- The prime purpose of C++ programming was to add object orientation to the C programming language, which is in itself, one of the most powerful programming languages.

- The core of the pure object–oriented programming is to create an object, in code, that has certain properties and methods. While designing C++ modules, we try to see whole world in the form of objects. For example, a car is an object which has certain properties such as color, number of doors, and the like. It also has certain methods such as accelerate, brake, and so on.

- Basics of Object Oriented Programming includes,
    1. Object
    2. Class
    3. Data Members and Member Function
    4. Data Encapsulation
    5. Data Abstraction
    6. Inheritance
    7. Polymorphism
    8. Information Hiding
    9. Dynamic Binding
    10. Message Passing.

Basics Concepts of Object Oriented Programming are as follows

1. Object

- Object is the run time entity in Object oriented programming.
- Objects are the fundamentals block, object is associated with data and functions which defines meaningful operations on that object.

- Object is the instance of class. When program is executed the Object interact by sending messages to one another.
- Object may represent a person, place, bank account etc
- A class provides the blueprints for objects, so object is created from a class.
- We declare objects of a class declaration that we declare variables of basic types.

  Following statements declare two objects of class Student

  Student Student1;   // Declare Student1 of type Student

  Student Student2;   // Declare Student2 of type Student
- Both the objects Student1 and Student2 will have their own copy of data members.

2. Class

- A class is any functional entity which defines its properties and functions. For example: Human Being class having body parts and performing various actions.

Syntax of Class Definition

```
class ClassName
{
    Access specifier:
    Data members;
    Member Functions()
{ }
};
```

Example, we have made a simple class named Student with appropriate data members and functions

```
class Student
{
    public:
    int rollno;
    string name;
    void read();
};
```

3. Data Members and Member Function

- Class is a collection of data members and member functions.
- Data members are the attributes of the class. Data members are the variables declared in the class.

- Member functions are the functions, which have declaration inside the class definition and its works on the data members of the class.

- Member function performs various operations on data members and execute some logic on them which defines the behaviour.

- The definition of member functions can be inside or outside the definition of class.

- If the member functions are defined inside then class definition it can be defined directly, but If the member functions are defined outside the class, then we must use the scope resolution: operator along with class name and function name.

4. Data Encapsulation

- It is also called as data binding.

- Data encapsulation is the mechanism of wrapping up data and function in single unit.

  Example: Class, Encapsulation is all about binding the data members and member functions together in class.

- It is the mechanism that associates the code and data, manipulate into a single unit and keep them safe from misuse and external interference.

5. Data Abstraction

- Abstraction refers to showing only the essential features of the application and hiding the all background details and explanation.

- In C++, classes provide methods to the outside world to access and use the data variables, but the variables are hidden from direct access. This can be done by different access specifiers.

6. Inheritance

- Inheritance is basically used for reusability purpose. It is way to reuse once written code again and again.

- The class which is inherited is called base class and the class which inherits is called derived class. So when, a derived class inherits a base class, the derived class can use all the functions which are defined in base class, hence making code reusable.

- It is the mechanism of deriving new class from the existing one.

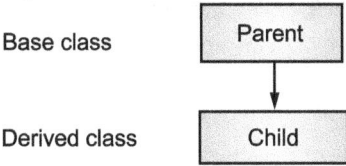

Fig. 1.3: Inheritance

7. Polymorphism

- Polymorphism used to create functions with same name but different arguments, which will perform differently. That is function with same name, functioning in different way.

- Ability to take more than one form is classed as Polymorphism.

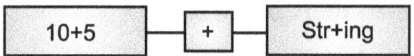

| 10+5 | + | Str+ing |

Fig. 1.4: Polymorphism

- Consider in above Fig. 1.4, operation addition is used for 2 purposes, one will generate a sum of two number and another will concatenate the two different strings.

8. Information Hiding

- Information hiding is the primary criteria of system modularization and It should be concerned with hiding the critical decisions of OOP designing.

- Information hiding isolates the end users from the requirement of intimating knowledge of the design for the usage of a module.

- Information hiding concept restricts direct exposure of data.

- Data is accessed indirectly using safe mechanism, methods in case of programming object.

    For Example: In Bike, we have no access to the piston directly, we can use 'start button' to run the piston. If a bike manufacturer allows direct access to piston, it would be very difficult to control actions on the piston.

9. Dynamic Binding

- Dynamic binding is the process of linking of the code associated with a procedure call at the run time.

10. Message Passing

- Message Passing is sending and receiving of information by the objects same as people exchange information. So, this helps in building systems that simulate real life.

    Following are the basic steps in message passing.

    ➤ Creating classes that define objects and its behaviour

    ➤ Creating objects from class definitions

    ➤ Establishing communication among objects

In OOPs, Message Passing involves specifying the name of objects, the name of the function, and the information to be sent.

Example

    Student .result(name);

    Where, Student is the object

    result is Message

    name is information

1.6 BENEFITS OF OBJECT ORIENTED PROGRAMMING

Object–oriented programming is commonly used to manage software systems. however, OOP technology offers several advantages.

- **Reusability:** In OOP's programs functions and modules that are written by a user can be reused by other users without any modification.
- **Inheritance:** Through this we can eliminate redundant code and extend the use of existing classes.
- **Data Hiding:** The programmer can hide the data and functions in a class from other classes. It helps the programmer to build the secure programs.
- **Reduced Complexity of a Problem:** The given problem can be viewed as a collection of different objects. Each object is responsible for a specific task. The problem is solved by interfacing the objects. This technique reduces the complexity of the program design.
- **Easy to Maintain and Upgrade:** OOP makes it easy to maintain and modify existing code as new objects can be created with small differences to existing ones.
- **Message Passing:** The technique of message communication between objects makes the interface with external systems easier.
- **Modifiability:** It is easy to make minor changes in the data representation or the procedures in an Object Oriented Program. Changes inside a class do not affect any other part of a program, since the only public interface that the external world has to change a class is through the use of methods.

The Typical Programmer's Advantages are

- Multiple–inheritance, where classes can inherit from multiple super classes.
- Multi–method dispatch, where operations can be specialized not just on a single object, but on any of the arguments for the operation, or any combination of those arguments.
- Method combination, in which the means by which several applicable operations to a particular set of arguments can be combined, is itself an object–oriented specification, definable by the programmer.
- Operations that can specialize on particular instances of classes, rather than on just the broad class of the arguments.
- Shared class variables (slots, attributes) that are shared by all instances of a class, in addition to instance variables which are unique to each instance.
- Specification of the creation operation for instances of a class as an object–oriented program, definable by the programmer.
- The behaviour of operations on objects (methods) are themselves defined as first–class objects, which can be specialized by the programmer.
- Access to classes themselves as first–class objects. The objects which define the behaviour of classes are themselves classes, usable directly by the programmer.

1.7 APPLICATIONS OF OBJECT ORIENTED PROGRAMMING

Applications of OOP are beginning to gain importance in many areas. The most important application is user interface design. Real business systems are more complex and contain many attributes and methods, but OOP applications can simplify a complex problem.

- **Real Time System**

A real time system is a system that give output at given instant and its parameters changes at every time. A real time system is nothing but a dynamic system. Dynamic means the system that changes every moment based on input to the system. OOP approach is very useful for Real time system because code changing is very easy in OOP system and it leads toward dynamic behaviour of OOP codes thus more suitable to real time system.

- **Simulation and Modelling**

System modelling is another area where criteria for OOP approach is countable. Representing a system is very easy in OOP approach because OOP codes are very easy to understand and thus is preferred to represent a system in simpler form.

- **Hypertext and Hypermedia**

Hypertext and hypermedia is another area where OOP approach is spreading its legs. Its ease of using OOP codes that makes it suitable for various media approaches.

- **Decision Support System**

Decision support system is an example of Real time system that too very advance and complex system. More details are explained in real time system.

- **CAM/CAE/CAD System**

Computer has wide use of OOP approach. This is due to time saving in writing OOP codes and dynamic behaviour of OOP codes.

- **Office Automation System**

Automation system is just a part or type of real time system. Embedded systems make it easy to use OOP for automated system.

- **AI and Expert System**

It is mixed system having both hypermedia and real time system.

1.8 BEGINNING WITH C++

1.8.1 What is C++?

- C++ is an object oriented programming (OOP) language, developed by Bjarne Stroustrup, and is an extension of C language. It is therefore possible to code C++ in a "C style" or "object-oriented style." In certain scenarios, it can be coded in either way and is thus an effective example of a hybrid language.

- C++ is a general purpose object oriented programming language. It is considered to be an intermediate level language, as it encapsulates both high and low level language features. Initially, the language was called 'C with classes' as it had all properties of C language with an additional concept of 'classes'. However, it was renamed to C++ in 1983.

- C++ is one of the most popular languages primarily utilized with system/application software, drivers, client-server applications and embedded firmware.

- The main highlight of C++ is a collection of pre-defined classes, which are data types that can be instantiated multiple times. The language also facilitates declaration of user defined classes. Classes can further accommodate member functions to implement specific functionality. Multiple objects of a particular class can be defined to implement the functions within the class. Objects can be defined as instances created at run time. These classes can also be inherited by other new classes which take in the public and protected functionalities by default.

- C++ includes several operators such as comparison, arithmetic, bit manipulation, logical operators etc. One of the most attractive features of C++ is that it enables the overloading of certain operators such as addition.

- A few of the essential concepts within C++ programming language include polymorphism, virtual and friend functions, templates, namespaces and pointers.

1.8.2 Applications of C++

- **Games:** C++ overrides the complexities of 3D games, optimizes resource management and facilitates multiplayer with networking. The language is extremely fast, allows procedural programming for CPU intensive functions and provides greater control over hardware, because of which it has been widely used in development of gaming engines. For instance, the science fiction game Doom 3 is cited as an example of a game that used C++ well and the Unreal Engine, a suite of game development tools, is written in C++.

- **Graphic User Interface (GUI) Based Applications:** Many highly used applications, such as Image Ready, Adobe Premier, Photoshop and Illustrator, are scripted in C++.

- **Web Browsers:** With the introduction of specialized languages such as PHP and Java, the adoption of C++ is limited for scripting of websites and web applications. However, where speed and reliability are required, C++ is still preferred. For instance, a part of Google's back-end is coded in C++, and the rendering engine of a few open source projects, such as web browser Mozilla Firefox and email client Mozilla Thunderbird, are also scripted in the programming language.

- **Advance Computations and Graphics:** C++ provides the means for building applications requiring real-time physical simulations, high performance image processing and mobile sensor applications. Maya 3D software, used for integrated 3D modeling, visual effects and animation, is coded in C++.

- **Database Software:** C++ and C have been used for scripting MySQL, one of the most popular database management software. The software forms the backbone of a variety of database-based enterprises, such as Google, Wikipedia, Yahoo and YouTube etc.

- **Operating Systems:** C++ forms an integral part of many of the prevalent operating systems including Apple's OS X and various versions of Microsoft Windows, and the erstwhile Symbian mobile OS.

- **Enterprise Software:** C++ finds a purpose in banking and trading enterprise applications, such as those deployed by Bloomberg and Reuters. It is also used in development of advanced software, such as flight simulators and radar processing.

- **Medical and Engineering Applications:** Many advanced medical equipments, such as MRI machines, use C++ language for scripting their software. It is also part of engineering applications, such as high-end CAD/CAM systems.

- **Compilers:** A host of compilers including Apple C++, Bloodshed Dev-C++, Clang C++ and MINGW make use of C++ language.

C and its successor C++ are leveraged for diverse software and platform development requirements, from operating systems to graphic designing applications. Further, these languages have assisted in the development of new languages for special purposes like C#, Java, PHP, Verilog etc. As updating of these languages, particularly C++, continues on a periodic basis, their utilization for robust applications is likely to expand as well.

1.8.3 Syntax and Structure of C++ Program

In this section, we will discuss one simple and basic C++ program to print "Welcome to C++".

First C++ program

```
include <iostream>
using namespace std;
int main()
{
    cout << "Welcome to C++";
}
```

Line 1: Header files are included at the beginning like in C program. In C++, iostream is a header file which provides us with input and output streams. Header files contained predeclared function libraries, which can be used by users.

Line 2: Using namespace std tells the compiler to use standard namespace. Namespace collects identifiers used for class, object and variables. NameSpace can be used by two ways in a program, either by the use of using statement at the beginning, like we did in above mentioned program or by using name of namespace as prefix before the identifier with scope resolution (::) operator. Example: std::cout << "B";

Line 3: int main() is the function which holds the executing part of program its return type is int.

Line 4: cout << is used to print anything on screen, same as printf in C language. cin and cout are same as scanf and printf, only difference is that you do not need to mention format specifiers like, %d for int etc, in cout and cin.

1.8.4 How to Compile and Execute C++ Program ?

- g++ is your friendly Gnu C++ compiler. g++ does not handle templates well, but you can use them.

- You can compile and run C++ program from the Linux prompt as follows:

  % g++ helloworld.cpp

- This creates an executable called "a.out". You can run it by typing

   % ./a.out

- Since no executable name was specified to g++, a.out is chosen by default. Use the "–o" option to change the name:

   % g++ –o helloworld helloworld.Cpp

Creates an executable called "helloworld".

1.8.5 Comments

- In C++ for single line comments use // .

  cout<<"single line";   // This is single line comment

- In C++ for multiple line comment, enclose the comment between /* and */

  /*this is

  a multiple line

  comment */

1.8.6 Uses of Classes

- Classes name must start with capital letter, and they contain data members and member functions.

```
class Abc
{
    int i;              //data Member
    void display()      //Member Function
```

```
{
   cout<<"Inside Member Function";
 }
}; // Class ends here
int main()
{
   Abc obj;      // Creatig Abc class's object obj
   obj.display();  //Calling member function using class object obj
}
```

- This is how class is defined, its object is created and the member functions are used.
- Variables can be declared anywhere in the entire program, but must be declared, before they are used.

1.8.7 Cin: Extracting Input from User Using Keyboard

- In C++ Extraction operator is used to accept value from the user.
- User can able to accept value from user and that value gets stored inside value container i.e. Variable.

Syntax: Get Value from User

```
cin >> variable;
Include <iostream> header file is used when we are using cin.
#include<iostream>// ANSI Standard
using namespace std;
```

- cin is used for accepting data from the keyboard. The operator >> called as extraction operator or get from operator.
- The extraction operator can be overloaded. Extraction operator is similar to the scanf() operation in C.
- cin is the object of istream class. Data flow direction is from input device to variable.

Program 1.1: Accepting Input from User

```
#include<iostream>
using namespace std;
int main()
{
   int number1;
   int number2;
```

```
  cout<<"Enter First Number: ";
  cin>>number1;              //accept first number
  cout<<"Enter Second Number: ";
  cin>>number2;              //accept first number
  cout<<"Addition : ";
  cout<<number1+number2;       //Display Addition
  return 0;
}
```

Output :

Enter First Number: 10

Enter Second Number: 10

Addition: 20

1.8.8 Cout: Display Output to User Using Screen (Monitor)

- In C++ Insertion operator is used to display value to the user. The value may be some message in the form of string or variable.

Syntax: Display Value to User

```
cout << variable;
Include <iostream> header file to use cin.
#include<iostream>// ANSI Standard
using namespace std;
```

- cout is used for displaying data on the screen. The operator << called as insertion operator or put to operator.
- The Insertion operator can be overloaded. Insertion operator is similar to the printf() operation in C.
- cout is the object of ostream class. Data flow direction is from variable to output device.

Program 1.2: Displaying Output on Screen

```
#include<iostream>
using namespace std;
int main()
{
  int number1;
  int number2;
  cout<<"Enter First Number: ";
```

```
/* Display the message to tell the user to do appropriate action */
cin>>number1;
cout<<"Enter Second Number: ";
/* Display the message to tell the user to do appropriate action */
cin>>number1;
cin>>number2;
cout<<"Addition : ";
cout<<number1+number2;  //Display Result
return 0;
}
```

Output :

Enter First Number: 8

Enter Second Number: 8

Addition: 16

1.9 MOVING FROM C TO C++

Need of Object Oriented Programming

• Object oriented Programming is required because there were certain limitations in earlier approaches. To understand what OOP does we need to understand the limitations of traditional programming languages.

1.9.1 Procedure Oriented Programming

• A program in a procedural language is a list of instruction where each statement tells the computer to do something. It focuses on procedure (function) and algorithm is needed to perform the derived computation.

• When program become larger, it is divided into function and each function has clearly defined purpose as shown in Fig. 1.5. Dividing the program into functions and module is one of the cornerstone of structured programming.

Example : C, FORTRAN.

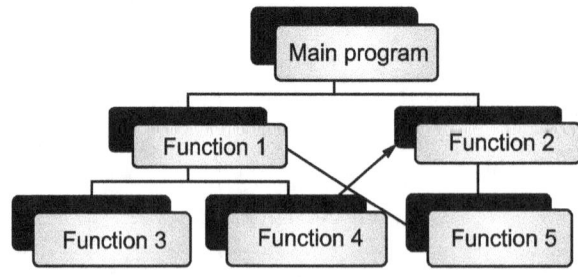

Fig. 1.5 : Structure of procedure oriented programming

Characteristics of Procedural Oriented Programming

- It focuses on process rather than data.

- It takes a problem as a sequence of things to be done such as reading, calculating and printing. Hence, a number of functions are written to solve a problem.

- A program is divided into a number of functions and each function has clearly defined purpose.

- Most of the functions share global data.

- Data moves openly around the system from function to function.

Limitations of Procedural Oriented Programming (Structured Programming)

- It emphasis on doing things. Data is given a second class status even through data is the reason for the existence of the program.

- Since every function has complete access to the global variables, the new programmer can corrupt the data accidentally by creating function. Similarly, if new data is to be added, all the function needed to be modified to access the data.

- It is often difficult to design because the components function and data structure do not model the real world. For example, in designing graphics user interface, we think what functions, what data structures are needed rather than which menu, menu item and soon.

- It is difficult to create new data types. The ability to create the new data type of its own is called extensibility. Structured programming languages are not extensible.

- To overcome the limitation of Procedural oriented programming languages, Object oriented programming languages were developed.

Difference Between Procedure Oriented Programming (POP) and Object Oriented Programming (OOP)

	Procedure Oriented Programming	Object Oriented Programming
Approach	POP follows Top Down approach.	OOP follows Bottom Up approach.
Divided Into	In POP, program is divided into small parts called functions.	In OOP, program is divided into parts called objects.

Contd...

Importance	In POP, Importance is not given to data but to functions as well as sequence of actions to be done.	In OOP, Importance is given to the data rather than procedures or functions because it works as a real world.
Access Specifiers	POP does not have any access specifier.	OOP has access specifiers named Public, Private, Protected, etc.
Data Moving	In POP, Data can move freely from function to function in the system.	In OOP, objects can move and communicate with each other through member functions.
Expansion	To add new data and function in POP is not so easy.	OOP provides an easy way to add new data and function.
Data Access	In POP, Most functions uses Global data for sharing that can be accessed freely from function to function in the system.	In OOP, data can not move easily from function to function, it can be kept public or private so we can control the access of data.

1.9.2 Declaration of Variable

- Variable is the name of memory location allocated by the compiler depending upon the data type of the variable.
- Variable can be declared in multiple ways each with different memory requirements and functioning.
- Data type must be given to each variable declaration, on which the memory assigned to the variable depends on data type.

Example: int i=10; //declared and initialized.

Variable Declaration and Initialization

- Variable must be declared before they are used. Usually it is preferred to declare them at the starting of the program. In C++ they can be declared in the middle of program too, but must be done before using them.

Example :

```
int i;          // declared but not initialised
char c;
int i, j, k;    // Multiple declaration
Initialization means assigning value to an already declared variable,
int i;          // declaration
i = 10;         // initialization
```

Initialization and declaration can be done in one single step also,

int i=10;   //initialization and declaration in same step

int i=10, j=11;

1.9.3 Scope of Variables

- All the variables have their area of functioning, and out of that boundary they do not hold their value, this boundary is called scope of the variable.

- Variable scope is divided into two main types,

    1. Global Variables

    2. Local Variables

1. Global Variables

- Global variables are declared at the top of the program and can be accessed anywhere in the entire program.

- Global variables are those, which are once declared and can be used throughout the lifetime of the program by any class or any function.

- They must be declared outside the main() function.

- If only declared, they can be assigned different values at different time in program lifetime. But even if they are declared and initialized at the same time outside the main() function, then also they can be assigned any value at any point in the program.

Example :

```
include <iostream>
using namespace std;
int g;          // Global variable declared
int main()
{
    int a,b;
    a=10;
    b=20;
    g=a+b;
    cout<<g;
    return 0;
}
```

2. Local Variables

- The variables declared inside the definition of a function are local.

- They only exist inside the function body once, the function returns the variable that no longer exist.

- Local variables are the variables which exist only between the curly braces, in which its declared.

- Outside that, they are unavailable and leads to compile time error.

Example :

```
include <iostream>
using namespace std;
int main()
{
    int a,b,c; // Local variable declared
    a=10;
    b=20;
    c=a+b;
    cout<<c;
    return 0;
}
```

1.9.4 Reference Variables

- A reference variable is an alias, that is, another name for an already existing variable. Once a reference is initialized with a variable, either the variable name or the reference name may be used to refer to the variable.

Creating References in C++

- Think of a variable name as a label attached to the variable's location in memory. You can then think of a reference as a second label attached to that memory location. Therefore, you can access the contents of the variable through either the original variable name or the reference. For example, suppose we have the following example:

```
int   i = 17;
```

We can declare reference variables for i as follows.

```
int&   r = i;
```

Read the & in these declarations as reference. Thus, read the first declaration as "r is an integer reference initialized to i" and read the second declaration as "s is a double reference initialized to d.".

Following example makes use of references on int and double:

Program 1.3 :

```cpp
#include <iostream>
 using namespace std;
 int main ()
{
  // declare simple variables
  int   i;
  double d;
  // declare reference variables
  int&   r = i;
  double& s = d;
   i = 5;
  cout << "Value of i : " << i << endl;
  cout << "Value of i reference : " << r  << endl;
  d = 11.7;
  cout << "Value of d : " << d << endl;
  cout << "Value of d reference : " << s  << endl;
    return 0;
}
```

Output :

Value of i : 5

Value of i reference : 5

Value of d : 11.7

Value of d reference : 11.7

References are usually used for function argument lists and function return values. So following are two important subjects related to C++ references which should be clear to a C++ programmer:

Concept	Description
References as parameters	C++ supports passing references as function parameter more safely than parameters.
Reference as return value	You can return reference from a C++ function like a any other data type can be returned.

1.9.5 Scope Resolution Operator in C++

- In computer programming, scope is an enclosing context where values and expressions are associated. The scope resolution operator helps to identify and specify the context to which an identifier refers, particularly by specifying a namespace. The specific uses vary across different programming languages with the notions of scoping. In many languages the scope resolution operator is written "::".

- In C++, scope resolution operator is **::**. It is used for following purposes.

Program 1.4 : To Access a Global Variable when there is a Local Variable with Same Name.

```
// C++ program to show that we can access a global variable
// using scope resolution operator :: when there is a local
// variable with same name
#include<iostream>
using namespace std;
 int x;  // Global x
 int main()
{
 int x = 10; // Local x
 cout << "Value of global x is " << ::x;
 cout << "\nValue of local x is " << x;
 return 0;
}
```

Output:

Value of global x is 0
Value of local x is 10

Program 1.5 : To Define a Function Outside a Class.

```
// C++ program to show that scope resolution operator :: is used
// to define a function outside a class
#include<iostream>
using namespace std;
 class A
{
public:
   // Only declaration
```

```cpp
   void fun();
};
 // Definition outside class using ::
void A::fun()
{
   cout << "fun() called";
}
 int main()
{
   A a;
   a.fun();
   return 0;
}
```

Output:

fun() called

Program 1.6 : To Access a Class's Static Variables.

```cpp
// C++ program to show that :: can be used to access static
// members when there is a local variable with same name
#include<iostream>
using namespace std;

class Test
{
   static int x;
public:
   static int y;

   // Local parameter 'a' hides class member
   // 'a', but we can access it using ::
   void func(int x)
```

```
    {
        // We can access class's static variable
        // even if there is a local variable
        cout << "Value of static x is " << Test::x;

        cout << "\nValue of local x is " << x;
    }
};
// In C++, static members must be explicitly defined
// like this
int Test::x = 1;
int Test::y = 2;

int main()
{
    Test obj;
    int x = 3;
    obj.func(x);

    cout << "\nTest::y = " << Test::y;

    return 0;
}
```

Output:

Value of static x is 1

Value of local x is 3

Test: : y = 2;

4. In Case of Multiple Inheritance:

If same variable name exists in two ancestor classes, we can use scope resolution operator to distinguish.

Program 1.7 : Use of Scope Resolution Operator in Multiple Inheritance.

```cpp
#include<iostream>
using namespace std;
 class A
{
protected:
   int x;
public:
   A() { x = 10; }
};
class B
{
protected:
   int x;
public:
   B() { x = 20; }
};
 class C: public A, public B
{
public:
   void fun()
   {
     cout << "A's x is " << A::x;
     cout << "\nB's x is " << B::x;
   }
};
 int main()
{
   C c;
   c.fun();
   return 0;
}
```

Output:

A's x is 10

B's x is 20

1.9.6 Member Dereferencing Operator

- Dereferencing a pointer means getting the value that is stored in the memory location pointed by the pointer. The operator * is used to do this, and is called the dereferencing operator.
- It is possible to access the value of variables pointed by the pointer variables using pointer. This is performed by using the Dereference operator in C++ which has the notation *.

The general syntax of the Dereference operator is as follows:

*pointer_variable

In this example, pointer variable denotes the variable defined as pointer. The * placed before the pointer_variable denotes the value pointed by the pointer_variable.

Example:

exforsys = 100;

test = exforsys;

x = &exforsys;

y=*x;

In the above example, the assignment takes place as below:

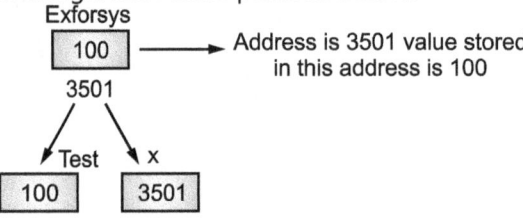

That is

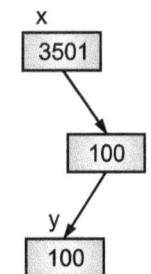

In the above example, the exforsys is an integer variable having the value of 100 stored in memory address location 3501.

The variable exforsys is assigned to the variable test in the second statement:

test = exforsys;

The value of the variable exforsys is 100 and is then copied to the variable test.

In the third statement, the address of the variable exforsys denoted by reference operator &exforsys is assigned to the variable x as:

x = &exforsys;

The address of the variable 3501 and not the contents of the variable exforsys is then copied into the variable x.

The fourth statement makes use of the deference operator:

y=*x

This means that the value pointed to by the pointer variable x gives the value 100 to y.

Some Points for the Programmer to Note:

- The programmer must note that the x refers to the address 3501 whereas *x refers to the value stored in the address 3501 namely 100.

- The reference operator is denoted by & and deference operator denoted by * . Both differ in their meaning and functionality. The reference operator denotes the address of. The dereference operator denotes the value pointed by. In short, a deference variable can be denoted as referenced.

- If the programmer wants to define more than two pointer variables, then comma operator may be used in this instance. The programmer must carefully place pointer symbol * before each pointer variable.

- For instance, if the user wishes to define two integer pointer variables, e1 and e2, this can be done as follows:

  int *e1,*e2;

If the programmer declares:

  int *e1,e2;

This means that e1 is a pointer variable pointing to integer data type but e2 is only an integer data type and not a pointer type. The programmer must ensure to place * before each pointer variable.

The dereferencing or indirect addressing is performed using the indirection operator * used to access the value stored in an address.

The defining of pointer variable:

  int* exf;

The definition of pointer variable as in the above case is the pointer variable exf.

It is also possible to assign value to pointer variable using indirection operator. This gives the same effect as working with variables.

Example:

```
#include <iostream>
using namespace std;
void main()
```

```
{
    int example,test;
    int* exforsys;
    exforsys=&example;
    example=200;
    test=200;
    *exforsys=100;
    test=*exforsys;
    cout << *exforsys << endl << test;
}
```

Output :

100

100 press any key to continue

In the above example, the pointer variable exforsys points to integer variable example and takes the address of the variable example as:

test and example have initial values of 200.

The statement:

*exforsys=100

Sets the value of the variable pointed by pointer variable exforsys as 100. This is equivalent to setting example=100.

The assignment is as follows:

Example test

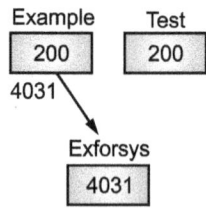

The statement

test=*exforsys;

sets the value of variable test with the value pointed by the pointer variable exforsys which is 100 as seen in the above example. Test also becomes 100 and the assignment becomes:

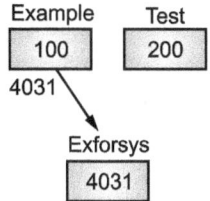

Both results are displayed having the value 100.

1.9.7 Memory Management Operators

Need for Memory Management Operators

- The concept of arrays has a block of memory reserved. The disadvantage with the concept of arrays is that the programmer must know, while programming, the size of memory to be allocated in addition to the array size remaining constant.

- In programming, there may be scenarios where programmers may not know the memory needed until run time. In this case, the programmer can opt to reserve as much memory as possible, assigning the maximum memory space needed to tackle this situation. This would result in wastage of unused memory spaces. Memory management operators are used to handle this situation in C++ programming language.

- In 'C' language, we have studied the function malloc(), calloc(), and realloc() to allocate memory dynamically at run-time in the program. am. The free() function is used to release the resources allocated by these functions. C++ allows us to use these functions. In additional, C++ provides operators which help us to allocate and release the memory in easy way than these functions. These new operators are new and delete. The new operator creates an object and delete destroys the object. These operators are easy in writing as compared to malice() and calloc(). The syntaxes for new and delete are illustrated with suitable programs.

Following are the advantages of new operator over the function malloc():

- The new operator itself calculates the size of the object without the use of sizeof() operator.

- It returns the pointer type. The programmers need not take care of its type casting.

- The new operator allocates memory and initializes the object at once.

The new and delete operators are simple in syntax. They can be overloaded.

1. new Operator

- Format of new operator is as follows:

pointer memory variable = new operator — data type[size];

- Here, pointer memory variable is a pointer to the data type. The new operator allocates memory of specified type and returns back the starting address to the pointer memory variable. Here, the element size is optional and used when the allocation of memory space is required for user-defined data types such as arrays, classes, and structures. If the new operator fails to allocate the memory it returns NULL, which can be used to detect failure or success of new operator.

Examples:

1. pv = new int;

2. int *pv = new int (50);

3. *p = new int [3]

- In example (1), pv is a pointer variable of integer type. Once allocated, the pv contains the starting address. In example (2), 50 is assigned to pointer variable pv. In example (3), memory for 3 integers, that is, 6 bytes are assigned to pointer variable p. The example of new operator with arrays are as follows:

pv= new int [5] [2]; // valid

pv= new int [8][k][2] // invalid

pv= new int [ ] [2] [2] // invalid

Program 1.8 : Illustrate the Simple Example of New Operator.

```
#include<conio.h>
#include<iostream.h>
int main()
{
int *x;
clrscr();
x=new int[10]; if(x==NULL) cout«"\nMemory is not allocated":
 else
cout«"\nMemory is allocated" :
return 0;
}
```

Output :

Memory is allocated

Explanation: In the above program, x is an integer pointer variable. The new operator allocates memory required for 10 integers, i.e. 20 bytes to pointer x as each integer occupies 2 bytes. new operator is used to replace the sizeof() operator.

2. delete Operator

The delete operator frees the memory allocated by the new operator. This operator is used when the memory allocated is no longer used in the program. The following syntax is used for the delete operator.

Syntax Example

1. delete <pointer memory a) delete p;

   variable>

2. delete [element size] b) delete [5]p or delete Hp;

   <pointer memory variable>

In example (1), the delete operator releases the memory allocated to pointer p. Example (2) is advantageous when we want to free the dynamically allocated memory of array. The new C++ compilers do not require element size.

Program 1.9 : Illustrate the Simple Example of New Operator.

```
#include<conio.h>
#include<iostream.h>
int main()
{
int *x;
clrscr();
x=new int[10];
if(x==NULL)
cout<<"\nMemory is not allocated";
else
cout<<"\nMemory is allocated";
delete x;
return 0;
```

Output :

Memory is allocated

Explanation: The above program shows allocation of memory by using new operator. The delete operator frees the memory allocated by the new operator.

Program 1.10 : To Allocate Memory using New Operator.

```
#include<iostream. h>
#include<conio.h>
void main()
{
clrscr();
int *p= new int[3],k; // Memory allocation for 3 integers for (k=0;k<3;k++)
{
cout«"\nEnter a Number :";
cin»*p;
p++; // Pointing to next location
}
p-=3; // Back to starting location
cout«"\n Entered numbers with their address are :\n"; for (k=0;k<3;k++)
{
cout«"\n\t"«*p «"\t"«(unsigned)p; // type casting
p++; }
P-=3;
delete p;
}
```

Output:

Enter a Number : 7 Enter a Number : 9 Enter a Number : 8 Entered numbers with their address are :

7 3658

9 3660

3662

Explanation: In the above program, p is an integer pointer variable. The new operator allocates memory required for three integers, i.e. 6 bytes to pointer p. The first for loop reads integer through the keyboard and stores the number at memory location pointed by p as shown in Fig. 1.6. Each time, pointer p is incremented and it shows the next location of its type. The second for loop displays the number by applying the same logic. Before that the pointer is again set to the starting location by decrementing by 3. The delete operator releases the memory allocated by the new operator. Fig. 1.6 shows the memory allocation of the different variable.

In the output of the program, only starting memory location numbers are displayed.

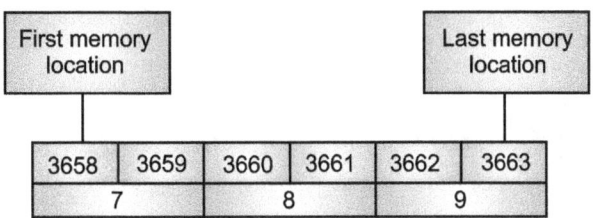

Fig. 1.6 : Memory allocated by the different variables

3. sizeof()

The sizeof() operator is used to return size occupied in bytes in memory by the variable. The sizeof() operator in C++ displays different values as compared to C. The following program illustrates this.

Program 1.11 : Display Number of Bytes Occupied by Char Data Type.

```
#include<iostream.h>

#include<conio.h>

void main()

{

clrscr();

cout<<sizeof(`a');

}
```

Output :

1

Explanation: In the above program, a character constant is used, sizeof() operator. The size determined is 1 byte. The same program 'C' will display the size 2 bytes, because C and C++ reacts differently with data types. In C, 'a' character is considered as integer. Hence the size displayed is 2 whereas in C++, it is considered as a character.

The size is the space occupied in memory in bytes by the variable. It depends upon the data type of variable. Fig. 1.7 describes the space occupied in the memory by the variable integer and float.

Example:

int x = 5;

float f = 3.14;

The integer variable occupies two bytes and float variable occupies four bytes in memory.

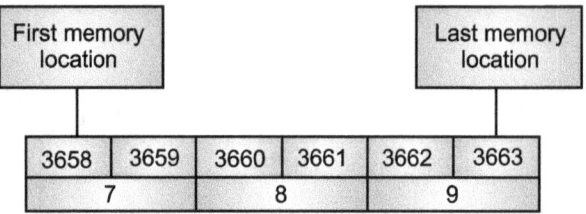

Fig. 1.7 : Memory allocated by the different variables

1.10 FUNCTIONS IN C++

- A function is a group of statements that together perform a task. Every C++ program has at least one function, which is main(), and all the most trivial programs can define additional functions.

- You can divide up your code into separate functions. How you divide up your code among different functions is up to you, but logically the division usually is so each function performs a specific task.

- A function declaration tells the compiler about a function's name, return type, and parameters. A function definition provides the actual body of the function.

- The C++ standard library provides numerous built–in functions that your program can call. For example, function strcat() to concatenate two strings, function memcpy() to copy one memory location to another location and many more functions.

- A function is known with various names like a method or a sub–routine or a procedure etc.

Defining a Function

The general form of a C++ function definition is as follows:

```
return_type function_name( parameter list )
{
   body of the function
}
```

A C++ function definition consists of a function header and a function body. Here are all the parts of a function:

Return Type: A function may return a value. The return_type is the data type of the value the function returns. Some functions perform the desired operations without returning a value. In this case, the return_type is the keyword void.

Function Name: This is the actual name of the function. The function name and the parameter list together constitute the function signature.

Parameters: A parameter is like a placeholder. When a function is invoked, you pass a value to the parameter. This value is referred to as actual parameter or argument. The parameter list refers to the type, order, and number of the parameters of a function. Parameters are optional; that is, a function may contain no parameters.

Function Body: The function body contains a collection of statements that define what the function does.

Example :

Following is the source code for a function called max(). This function takes two parameters num1 and num2 and returns the maximum between the two:

```
// function returning the max between two numbers
int max(int num1, int num2)
{
  // local variable declaration
  int result;
  if (num1 > num2)
    result = num1;
  else
    result = num2;
  return result;
}
```

1.10.1 Functions Prototype / Function Declarations

- In computer programming, a function prototype or function interface is a declaration of a function that specifies the function's name and type signature C Parity, parametertypes, and return type), but omits the function body. The term is particularly used in C and C++. While a function definition specifies how the function does what it does (the "implementation"), a function prototype merely specifies its interface, i.e. what data types go in and come out of it.

- In a prototype, parameter names are optional (and in C/C++ have function prototype scope, meaning their scope ends at the end of the prototype), however, the type is necessary along with all modifiers (e.g. if it is a pointer or a const parameter).

- A function declaration tells the compiler about a function name and how to call the function. The actual body of the function can be defined separately.

A function declaration has the following parts:

```
return_type function_name( parameter list );
```

For the above defined function max(), following is the function declaration:

int max(int num1, int num2);

Parameter names are not important in function declaration only their type is required, so following is also valid declaration:

int max(int, int);

- Function declaration is required when you define a function in one source file and you call that function in another file. In such case, you should declare the function at the top of the file calling the function.

Calling a Function:/Accessing Function

- While creating a C++ function, you give a definition of what the function has to do. To use a function, you will have to call or invoke that function.
- When a program calls a function, program control is transferred to the called function. A called function performs defined task and when its return statement is executed or when its function–ending closing brace is reached, it returns program control back to the main program.
- To call a function, you simply need to pass the required parameters along with function name, and if function returns a value, then you can store returned value. For example:

Program 1.12 : Function

```
#include <iostream>
using namespace std;
// function declaration
int max(int num1, int num2);
int main ()
{
  // local variable declaration:
  int a = 100;
  int b = 200;
  int ret;
  // calling a function to get max value.
  ret = max(a, b);
  cout << "Max value is : " << ret << endl;
  return 0;
}
// function returning the max between two numbers
int max(int num1, int num2)
{
  // local variable declaration
```

```
 int result;
 if (num1 > num2)
    result = num1;
 else
    result = num2;
 return result;
}
```

- I kept max() function along with main() function and compiled the source code. While running final executable, it would produce the following result:

Max value is : 200

Function Arguments

If a function is to use arguments, it must declare variables that accept the values of the arguments. These variables are called the formal parameters of the function.

The formal parameters behave like other local variables inside the function and are created upon entry into the function and destroyed upon exit.

While calling a function, there are two ways that arguments can be passed to a function:

Table 1.1 : Function Argument

Call Type	Description
Call by value	This method copies the actual value of an argument into the formal parameter of the function. In this case, changes made to the parameter inside the function have no effect on the argument.
Call by pointer	This method copies the address of an argument into the formal parameter. Inside the function, the address is used to access the actual argument used in the call. This means that changes made to the parameter affect the argument.
Call by reference	This method copies the reference of an argument into the formal parameter. Inside the function, the reference is used to access the actual argument used in the call. This means that changes made to the parameter affect the argument.

By default, C++ uses call by value to pass arguments. In general, this means that code within a function cannot alter the arguments used to call the function and above mentioned example while calling max() function used the same method.

C++ Function Call by Value

The call by value method of passing arguments to a function copies the actual value of an argument into the formal parameter of the function. In this case, changes made to the parameter inside the function have no effect on the argument.

By default, C++ uses call by value to pass arguments. In general, this means that code within a function cannot alter the arguments used to call the function. Consider the function swap() definition as follows.

Program 1.13: Function

```
// function definition to swap the values.
void swap(int x, int y)
{
  int temp;
  temp = x; /* save the value of x */
  x = y;   /* put y into x */
  y = temp; /* put x into y */
  return;
}
```

Now, let us call the function swap() by passing actual values as in the following example:

```
#include <iostream>
using namespace std;
// function declaration
void swap(int x, int y);
int main ()
{
  // local variable declaration:
  int a = 100;
  int b = 200;
  cout << "Before swap, value of a :" << a << endl;
  cout << "Before swap, value of b :" << b << endl;
  // calling a function to swap the values.
  swap(a, b);
  cout << "After swap, value of a :" << a << endl;
  cout << "After swap, value of b :" << b << endl;
  return 0;
}
```

Output :

Before swap, value of a : 100

Before swap, value of b : 200

After swap, value of a : 100

After swap, value of b : 200

Which shows that there is no change in the values though they had been changed inside the function.

C++ Function Call by Pointer

The call by pointer method of passing arguments to a function copies the address of an argument into the formal parameter. Inside the function, the address is used to access the actual argument used in the call. This means that changes made to the parameter affect the passed argument.

To pass the value by pointer, argument pointers are passed to the functions just like any other value. So accordingly you need to declare the function parameters as pointer types as in the following function swap(), which exchanges the values of the two integer variables pointed to by its arguments.

```
// function definition to swap the values.
void swap(int *x, int *y)
{
   int temp;
   temp = *x; /* save the value at address x */
   *x = *y; /* put y into x */
   *y = temp; /* put x into y */
   return;
}
```

To check the more detail about C++ pointers, kindly check C++ Pointers chapter.

For now, let us call the function swap() by passing values by pointer as in the following

Program 1.14 : C++Function Call by Pointer

```
#include <iostream>
using namespace std;
// function declaration
void swap(int *x, int *y);
int main ()
{
   // local variable declaration:
   int a = 100;
   int b = 200;
   cout << "Before swap, value of a :" << a << endl;
   cout << "Before swap, value of b :" << b << endl;
   /* calling a function to swap the values.
    * &a indicates pointer to a ie. address of variable a and
    * &b indicates pointer to b ie. address of variable b.
```

```
*/
swap(&a, &b);
cout << "After swap, value of a :" << a << endl;
cout << "After swap, value of b :" << b << endl;
return 0;
}
```

When the above code is put together in a file, compiled and executed, it produces the following result:

Before swap, value of a :100

Before swap, value of b :200

After swap, value of a :200

After swap, value of b :100

1.10.2 C++ Function Call by Reference

The call by reference method of passing arguments to a function copies the reference of an argument into the formal parameter. Inside the function, the reference is used to access the actual argument used in the call. This means that changes made to the parameter affect the passed argument.

To pass the value by reference, argument reference is passed to the functions just like any other value. So accordingly you need to declare the function parameters as reference types as in the following function swap(), which exchanges the values of the two integer variables pointed to by its arguments.

```
// function definition to swap the values.
void swap(int &x, int &y)
{
  int temp;
  temp = x; /* save the value at address x */
  x = y;   /* put y into x */
  y = temp; /* put x into y */
  return;
}
```

For now, let us call the function swap() by passing values by reference as in the following example:

Program 1.15: C++Function Call by Reference

```
#include <iostream>
using namespace std;
// function declaration
```

```
void swap(int &x, int &y);
int main ()
{
   // local variable declaration:
   int a = 100;
   int b = 200;
   cout << "Before swap, value of a :" << a << endl;
   cout << "Before swap, value of b :" << b << endl;
   /* calling a function to swap the values using variable reference.*/
   swap(a, b);
   cout << "After swap, value of a :" << a << endl;
   cout << "After swap, value of b :" << b << endl;
   return 0;
}
```

When the above code is put together in a file, compiled and executed, it produces the following result:

Before swap, value of a :100
Before swap, value of b :200
After swap, value of a :200
After swap, value of b :100

Default Values for Parameters

When you define a function, you can specify a default value for each of the last parameters. This value will be used if the corresponding argument is left blank when calling to the function.

This is done by using the assignment operator and assigning values for the arguments in the function definition. If a value for that parameter is not passed when the function is called, the default given value is used, but if a value is specified, this default value is ignored and the passed value is used instead. Consider the following example:

Program 1.16: Default Values for Parameter

```
#include <iostream>
using namespace std;
int sum(int a, int b=20)
{
   int result;
   result = a + b;
   return (result);
}
```

```
int main ()
{
  // local variable declaration:
  int a = 100;
  int b = 200;
  int result;
  // calling a function to add the values.
  result = sum(a, b);
  cout << "Total value is :" << result << endl;
  // calling a function again as follows.
  result = sum(a);
  cout << "Total value is :" << result << endl;
  return 0;
}
```

When the above code is compiled and executed, it produces the following result:

Total value is :300

Total value is :120

EXERCISE

1. Explain Principles of OOP.
2. Explain the difference between Procedure Oriented Programming and Object Oriented Programming.
3. What are the different Software crises?
4. Explain in brief Software evolution.
5. What is C++?
6. Explain Applications of C++.
7. Explain OOP paradigm.
8. Explain Basic Concepts of OOP.
9. What are the different Benefits of OOP?
10. Explain Applications of OOP.
11. How to create reference variable in C++? Explain with example.
12. What is function prototyping? Explain with example.
13. Explain following terms with example
    (a) Scope resolution operator,
    (b) Member dereferencing operator,
    (c) Memory management operators.

CONCEPTS OF OBJECT ORIENTED PROGRAMMING WITH C++

2.1 CLASSES AND OBJECTS

2.1.1 Specifying a Class

• A class is any functional entity which defines its properties and functions. For example– Human Being class having body parts and performing various actions.

Syntax :

```
class ClassName
{
Access specifier:
Data members;
Member Functions()
{ }
};
```

Example : We have made a simple class named Student with appropriate data members and functions

```
class Student
{
public:
int rollno;
string name;
void read();
};
```

2.1.2 Object

- Object is the run time entity in object oriented programming.
- Objects are the fundamentals block, object is associated with data and functions which defines meaningful operations on that object.
- Object is the instance of class. When program is executed the object interact by sending messages to one another.
- Object may represent a person, place, bank account etc.
- A class provides the blueprints for objects, so object is created from a class.
- We declare objects of a class declaration that we declare variables of basic types.
- Following statements declare two objects of class Student:

Student Student1;   // Declare Student1 of type Student

Student Student2;   // Declare Student2 of type Student

Both the objects Student1 and Student2 will have their own copy of data members.

2.1.3 Defining Member Functions

- A member function of a class is a function that has its definition or its prototype within the class definition like any other variable. It operates on any object of the class of which it is a member, and has access to all the members of a class for that object.
- Let us take previously defined class to access the members of the class using a member function instead of directly accessing them.

```
class Box {
  public:
    double length;         // Length of a box
    double breadth;        // Breadth of a box
    double height;         // Height of a box
    double getVolume(void);  // Returns box volume
};
```

- Member functions can be defined within the class definition or separately using scope resolution operator :: Defining a member function within the class definition declares the function inline, even if you do not use the inline specifier. So either you can define getVolume() function as below:

```
class Box {
  public:
    double length;     // Length of a box
```

```
    double breadth;     // Breadth of a box
    double height;      // Height of a box
    double getVolume(void) {
      return length * breadth * height;
    }
};
```

- If you like you can define same function outside the class using scope resolution operator :: as follows:

```
double Box::getVolume(void)
{
  return length * breadth * height;
}
```

- Here, only important point is that you would have to use class name just before :: operator. A member function will be called using a dot operator (.) on an object where it will manipulate data related to that object only as follows:

```
Box myBox;        // Create an object


myBox.getVolume();  // Call member function for the object
```

Program 2.1 : To Set and Get the Value of Different Class Members in a Class using above Concepts.

```
#include <iostream>
using namespace std;
class Box
{
  public:
    double length;      // Length of a box
    double breadth;     // Breadth of a box
    double height;      // Height of a box
    // Member functions declaration
    double getVolume(void);
    void setLength( double len );
    void setBreadth( double bre );
```

```cpp
      void setHeight( double hei );
};
// Member functions definitions
double Box::getVolume(void) {
   return length * breadth * height;
}
void Box::setLength( double len ) {
   length = len;
}
void Box::setBreadth( double bre ) {
   breadth = bre;
}
void Box::setHeight( double hei ) {
   height = hei;
}
// Main function for the program
int main( ) {
   Box Box1;              // Declare Box1 of type Box
   Box Box2;              // Declare Box2 of type Box
   double volume = 0.0; // Store the volume of a box here
   // box 1 specification
   Box1.setLength(6.0);
   Box1.setBreadth(7.0);
   Box1.setHeight(5.0);
   // box 2 specification
   Box2.setLength(12.0);
   Box2.setBreadth(13.0);
   Box2.setHeight(10.0);
   // volume of box 1
   volume = Box1.getVolume();
```

```
  cout << "Volume of Box1 : " << volume <<endl;
  // volume of box 2
  volume = Box2.getVolume();
  cout << "Volume of Box2 : " << volume <<endl;
  return 0;
}
```

Output :

Volume of Box1 : 210

Volume of Box2 : 1560

2.1.4 A C++ program with class

Program 2.2 : C++ Program to Display Student Information using Class

```
#include<iostream>
using namespace std;
class student
{
private:
char name[20],regd[10],branch[10];
int sem;
public:
void input();
void display();
};
void student::input()
{
cout<<"Enter Name:";
cin>>name;
cout<<"Enter Regdno.:";
cin>>regd;
cout<<"Enter Branch:";
cin>>branch;
cout<<"Enter Sem:";
```

```
cin>>sem;
}
void student::display()
{
cout<<"\nName:"<<name;
cout<<"\nRegdno.:"<<regd;
cout<<"\nBranch:"<<branch;
cout<<"\nSem:"<<sem;
}
int main()
{
student s;
s.input();
s.display();
}
```

Output:

Enter Name:Bikash

Enter Regdno.:123

Enter Branch:CS

Enter Sem:5

Sample Output

Name:Bikash

Regdno.:123

Branch:CS

Sem

2.1.5 C++ Inline Functions

- Inline function is like normal function proceed by inline keyword, In inline function, compiler places a copy of the code of that function at each point where the function is called at compile time.

- C++ inline function is powerful concept that is commonly used with classes. Any change to an inline function could require all clients of the function to be recompiled because compiler would need to replace all the code once again otherwise it will continue with old functionality.

- To inline a function, place the keyword inline before the function name and define the function before any calls are made to the function. The compiler can ignore the inline qualifier in case defined function is more than a line.

- A function definition in a class definition is an inline function definition, even without the use of the inline specifier.

Disadvantages of Function

When a function is called, it takes a lot of time to execute a series of instructions. Function takes lot of time to execute following actions:

- Jumping to function
- Saving the registers
- Pushing arguments into stack
- Returning to calling function

Syntax :

```
Inline return_type function_name(formal parameters)
{
//function body
}
```

Program 2.3 : Use of Inline Function to Return Max of Two Numbers.

```cpp
#include <iostream>
using namespace std;

inline int Max(int x, int y)
{
   return (x > y)? x : y;
}
// Main function for the program
int main( )
{
   cout << "Max (20,10): " << Max(20,10) << endl;
   cout << "Max (0,200): " << Max(0,200) << endl;
   cout << "Max (100,1010): " << Max(100,1010) << endl;
   return 0;
}
```

Output :

Max (20,10): 20

Max (0,200): 200

Max (100,1010): 1010

Advantages of Inline Function

- Shorter execution time
- Time saving
- Reduces context switch overhead
- No variables push/pop on the stack overhead.

Disadvantages of Inline Function

- Increases length of the file.
- If the function is expanded inline in the header file and function size is large, it may become unreadable.

2.1.6 Nesting of Member Function

A member function of a class can be called only by an object of that class using a dot operator. However, there is an exception to this. A member function can be called by using its name inside another member function of the same class. This is known as nesting of member functions.

Program 2.4 : Nesting of Member Functions

```
#include <iostream>
using namespace std;
class comparing
{
        int m,n;
    public:
        void input(void);
        void display(void);
        int larger(void);
};
 void comparing :: input(void)
{
cout << "Enter the two numbers to be compared \n";
```

```
cin >> m >> n;
}
 void comparing :: display(void)
{
cout << "The larger number among the entered values is :" << larger() << endl;
}
 int comparing :: larger(void)
{
if (m >= n)
{
return (m);
}
else {
return (n);
}
}
 int main ()
 {
comparing x;
x.input();
x.display();
return 0;
}
```

Output:

Enter the two numbers to be compared

    5

    6

The larger number among the entered values is :6

2.1.7 Private Member Function

- Data hiding is one of the important features of Object Oriented Programming which allows preventing the functions of a program to access directly the internal representation of a class type. The access restriction to the class members is specified by the labeled public, private, and protected sections within the class body. The keywords public, private, and protected are called access specifiers.

- A class can have multiple public, protected, or private labeled sections. Each section remains in effect until either another section label or the closing right brace of the class body is seen. The default access for members and classes is private.

Syntax :

```
class Base
{
    public:
    // public members go here
    protected:
    // protected members go here
    private:
    // private members go here
};
```

- A private member variable or function cannot be accessed, or even viewed from outside the class. Only the class and friend functions can access private members.

- By default, all the members of a class would be private, for example in the following class width is a private member, which means until you label a member, it will be assumed a private member:

Example :

```
class Box
{
    double width;
    public:
        double length;
        void setWidth( double wid );
        double getWidth( void );
};
```

- Practically, we define data in private section and related functions in public section so that they can be called from outside of the class as shown in the following program.

Program 2.5 :

```cpp
#include <iostream>
using namespace std;
class Box
{
  public:
    double length;
    void setWidth( double wid );
    double getWidth( void );
    private:
    double width;
};
// Member functions definitions
double Box::getWidth(void)
{
  return width ;
}
void Box::setWidth( double wid )
{
  width = wid;
}
// Main function for the program
int main( )
{
  Box box;
  // set box length without member function
  box.length = 10.0; // OK: because length is public
  cout << "Length of box : " << box.length <<endl;
  // set box width without member function
```

```
// box.width = 10.0; // Error: because width is private
box.setWidth(10.0);  // Use member function to set it.
cout << "Width of box : " << box.getWidth() <<endl;
return 0;
}
```

Output :

Length of box : 10

Width of box : 10

2.1.8 Arrays within Class

- The array can be used within a class as a member. For example:

Example 1 :

```
class XYZ
{
    int a[10];
    public:
}
```

Example 2 :

```
class abc
{
int a[5][6];
public:
```

- Arrays can be declared as the members of a class. The arrays can be declared as private, public or protected members of the class.

- To understand the concept of arrays as members of a class, consider this example.

Program 2.6 : A Program to Demonstrate the Concept of Arrays as Class Members

```
#include<iostream>
using namespace std;
const int size=5;
class student
{
int roll_no;
```

```cpp
int marks[size];
public:
void getdata ();
void tot_marks ();
} ;
void student :: getdata ()
{
cout<<"\nEnter roll no: ";
Cin>>roll_no;
for(int i=0; i<size; i++)
{
cout<<"Enter marks in subject"<<(i+1)<<": ";
cin>>marks[i] ;
}
void student :: tot_marks() //calculating total marks
{
int total=0;
for(int i=0; i<size; i++)
total+ = marks[i];
cout<<"\n\nTotal marks "<<total;
}
int main()
student stu;
stu.getdata() ;
stu.tot_marks() ;
return 0;
}
```

Output :

Enter roll no: 101

Enter marks in subject 1: 67

Enter marks in subject 2 : 54

Enter marks in subject 3 : 68

Enter marks in subject 4 : 72

Enter marks in subject 5 : 82

Total marks = 343

- In this example, an array 'marks' is declared as a private member of the class student for storing a student's marks in five subjects. The member function tot_marks () calculates the total marks of all the subjects and displays the value.

- Similar to other data members of a class, the memory space for an array is allocated when an object of the class is declared. In addition, different objects of the class have their own copy of the array. Note that the elements of the array occupy contiguous memory locations along with other data members of the object. For instance, when an object stu of the class student is declared, the memory space is allocated for both roll no. and marks.

2.1.9 Memory Allocation for Objects

- A good understanding of how dynamic memory really works in C++ is essential to becoming a good C++ programmer. Memory in your C++ program is divided into two parts:

  ➤ **The Stack:** All variables declared inside the function will take up memory from the stack.

  ➤ **The Heap:** This is unused memory of the program and can be used to allocate the memory dynamically when program runs.

- Many times, you are not aware in advance how much memory you will need to store particular information in a defined variable and the size of required memory can be determined at run time.

- You can allocate memory at run time within the heap for the variable of a given type using a special operator in C++ which returns the address of the space allocated. This operator is called new operator.

- If you are not in need of dynamically allocated memory anymore, you can use delete operator, which de-allocates memory previously allocated by new operator.

The new and delete operators

- There is following generic syntax to use new operator to allocate memory dynamically for any data-type.

new data-type;

- Here, data-type could be any built-in data type including an array or any user defined data types include class or structure. Let us start with built-in data types. For example, we can define a pointer to type double and then request that the memory be allocated at execution time. We can do this using the new operator with the following statements:

```
double* pvalue = NULL; // Pointer initialized with null
pvalue = new double;   // Request memory for the variable
```

- The memory may not have been allocated successfully, if the free store had been used up. So, it is good practice to check if new operator is returning NULL pointer and take appropriate action as below:

```
double* pvalue = NULL;
if( !(pvalue = new double ))
{
  cout << "Error: out of memory." <<endl;
  exit(1);
}
```

- The malloc() function from C, still exists in C++, but it is recommended to avoid using malloc() function. The main advantage of new over malloc() is that new doesn't just allocate memory, it constructs objects which is prime purpose of C++.

- At any point, when you feel a variable that has been dynamically allocated is not anymore required, you can free up the memory that it occupies in the free store with the delete operator as follows:

```
delete pvalue;      // Release memory pointed to by pvalue
```

Program 2.7 :

```
#include <iostream>
using namespace std;
int main ()
{
  double* pvalue = NULL; // Pointer initialized with null
  pvalue = new double;   // Request memory for the variable

  *pvalue = 29494.99;    // Store value at allocated address
  cout << "Value of pvalue : " << *pvalue << endl;
  delete pvalue;         // free up the memory.
  return 0;
}
```

Output :

Value of pvalue : 29495

Dynamic Memory Allocation for Arrays

- Consider you want to allocate memory for an array of characters, i.e., string of 20 characters. Using the same syntax what we have used above we can allocate memory dynamically as shown below:

```
char* pvalue = NULL;  // Pointer initialized with null
pvalue = new char[20]; // Request memory for the variable
```

- To remove the array that we have just created the statement would look like this:

```
delete [] pvalue;       // Delete array pointed to by pvalue
```

Following is the syntax of new operator for a multi-dimensional array as follows:

```
int ROW = 2;
int COL = 3;
double **pvalue = new double* [ROW]; // Allocate memory for rows

// Now allocate memory for columns
for(int i = 0; i < COL; i++) {
    pvalue[i] = new double[COL];
}
```

The syntax to release the memory for multi-dimensional will be as follows:

```
for(int i = 0; i < COL; i++)
{
    delete[] pvalue[i];
}
delete [] pvalue;
```

Dynamic Memory Allocation for Objects

- Objects are no different from simple data types. For example, consider the following code where we are going to use an array of objects to clarify the concept:

Program 2.8 :

```
#include <iostream>
using namespace std;
class Box
```

```cpp
{
  public:
    Box()
{
      cout << "Constructor called!" <<endl;
    }
    ~Box()
{
      cout << "Destructor called!" <<endl;
    }
};
int main( )
{
  Box* myBoxArray = new Box[4];
  delete [] myBoxArray; // Delete array
  return 0;
}
```

If you were to allocate an array of four Box objects, the Simple constructor would be called four times and similarly while deleting these objects, destructor will also be called same number of times.

Output :

Constructor called!

Constructor called!

Constructor called!

Constructor called!

Destructor called!

Destructor called!

Destructor called!

Destructor called!

2.1.10 Array of Objects

- As an array can be of any data type including struct, we can also have arrays of variables that are of the type class. Such variables are called arrays of objects.

Syntax: class-name object-name

Example: example e; // example is class name and e is object

Program 2.9 : Array of Objects

```
#include <iostream.h>
const int MAX =100;
class Details
{
private:
int salary;
float roll;
public:
void getname( )
{
cout << "\n Enter the Salary:";
cin >> salary;
cout << "\n Enter the roll:";
cin >> roll;
}
void putname( )
{
cout << "Employees" << salary <<
"and roll is" << roll << '\n';
}
};
void main()
{
Details det[MAX];
int n=0;
```

```
char ans;
do{
cout << "Enter the Employee Number::" << n+1;
det[n++].getname;
cout << "Enter another (y/n)?: " ;
cin >> ans;
} while ( ans != 'n' );
for (int j=0; j<n; j++)
{
cout << "\nEmployee Number is:: " << j+1;
det[j].putname( );
}
}
```

Output :

Enter the Employee Number:: 1

Enter the Salary:20

Enter the roll:30

Enter another (y/n)?: y

Enter the Employee Number:: 2

Enter the Salary:20

Enter the roll:30

Enter another (y/n)?: n

2.1.11 Objects as Function Arguments

- Objects as function arguments are similar to variables, object can be passed to functions. The following are the three methods to pass an argument to a function:

    (i) Pass-by-Value : A copy of object (actual object) is sent to function and assigned to the object of callee function (formal object). Both actual and formal copies of objects are stored at different memory locations. Hence, changes made in formal object are not reflected to actual object.

    (ii) Pass-by-Reference : Address of object is implicitly sent to function.

    (iii) Pass-by-Address : Address of the object is explicitly sent to function.

- In pass-by-reference and pass-by-address methods, an address of actual object is passed to the function. The formal argument is reference/pointer to the actual object. Hence, changes made in the object are reflected to actual object. These two methods are useful because an address is passed to the function and duplicating of object is prevented.

- The following examples illustrate both the methods of passing objects to the function as an argument.

Program 2.10 : To Pass Objects to the Function by Pass-by-Value Method.

```
#include<iostream.h>
 #include<conio.h>
class life
{
int mfgyr;
int expyr;
int yr;
public :
void getyrs ()
{
cout<<" \nManufacture Year :
cin>>>mfgyr;
cout<<" \n Expiry Year : " ;
cin>>>expyr;
}
void period ( life) ;
} ;
void life : : period (life yl)
{
yr=y1.expyr-yl.mfgyr;
cout<<"Life of the product : " <<yr <<" Years" ;
}
int main ()
{
clrscr () ;
```

```
life a1;
a1 .getyrs () ;
a1 .period (a1) ;
return 0;
}
```

Output :

Manufacture Year : 1999

Expiry Year : 2002

Life of the product : 3 Years

Explanation: In the above program, the class life is declared with three member integer variables. The function getrys() reads the integers through the keyboard. The function period() calculates the difference between the two integers entered. In the function main(), al is an object to the class life. The object al calls the function getyrs(). Immediately after this, the same object (al) is passed to the function period(). The function period() calculates the difference between two integers (dates) using the two data members of the same class. Thus, an object can be passed to the function. To pass an object by reference, the prototype of function period() should be as follows:

```
void period ( life &);
```

Program 2.11 : To Pass Objects to the Function Pass-by-Address Method.

```
#include<iostream.h>
#include<conio.h>
class life
{
int mfgyr;
int expyr; int yr;
public :
void getyrs ( )
{
 cout<<" \nManufacture Year : " ;
 cin>>mfgyr;
 cout<<" \n Expiary Year : " ;
 cin>>>expyr;
}
```

```
void period ( life*);
};
void life : : period (life *y1)
{
yr=y1->expyr-y1->mfgyr;
 cout<<"Life of the product : " <<yr;
}
int main ()
{
clrscr ();
 life a1;
a1 .getyrs ();
a1 .period(&a1);
return 0;
}
```

Output :

Manufacture Year : 1999

Expiry Year : 2002

Life of the product : 3 Years

Explanation: The above program is same as previous one. In this program, the object a1 is passed by address. Consider the following statements,

    (a) void period (life*);

    (b) a1 .period (&a1);

    (c) Yr=y1 ->expyr-y1 ->mfgyr;

The statement (a) is the prototype of the function period(). In this statement, the deference operator (*) indicates that the function will accept address of the actual argument. The statement (b) is used to pass the address of the argument to the function period(). The statement (c) is used to access the member variables of the class. When an object is a pointer to the class members, then its elements are accessed by using arrow (->) operator. In this case, use of a dot operator (.) is invalid.

2.2 CONSTRUCTORS AND DESTRUCTORS

2.2.1 Constructors

- A class constructor is a special member function of a class that is executed whenever we create new objects of that class.

- A constructor will have exact same name as the class and it does not have any return type at all, not even void.

- Constructors can be very useful for setting initial values for data variables.

Characteristics of Constructors

- Constructors are called automatically when the objects are created.

- All objects of the class having a constructor are initialized before some use.

- Constructors should be declared in the public section for availability to all the functions.

- Constructors does not have any return type not even void.

- These cannot be inherited, but a derived class can call the base class constructor.

- These cannot be static.

- Default and copy constructors are generated by the compiler wherever required. Generated constructors are public.

- A constructor can call member functions of its class.

- Constructor can be used to create new objects of its class type by using the syntax.

Name_of_the_class (expresson_list)

For example,

Employee obj3 = obj2; // see program 10.5

Or even

     Employee obj3 = employee (1002, 35000); //explicit call

- The make implicit calls to the memory allocation and deallocation operators new and delete.

- These cannot be virtual.

- A class constructor is a special member function of a class that is executed whenever we create new objects of that class.

- A constructor will have exact same name as the class and it does not have any return type at all, not even void. Constructors can be very useful for setting initial values for certain member variables.

- Following example explains the concept of constructor:

```
class A
{
int x;
public:
 A(); //Constructor
};
```

- While defining a contructor, you must remember that the name of constructor will be same as the name of the class, and contructors never have return type.
- Constructors can be defined either inside the class definition or outside class definition using class name and scope resolution :: operator.

```
class A
{
int i;
public:
 A(); //Constructor declared
};
A::A()  // Constructor definition
{
i=1;
}
```

Following example explains the concept of constructor:

Program 2.12 : Constructor

```
#include <iostream>
using namespace std;
class Line
{
  public:
    void setLength( double len );
    double getLength( void );
    Line();  // This is the constructor
```

```
  private:
     double length;
};
// Member functions definitions including constructor
Line::Line(void)
{
   cout << "Object is being created" << endl;
}
void Line::setLength( double len )
{
   length = len;
}
double Line::getLength( void )
{
   return length;
}
// Main function for the program
int main( )
{
  Line line;
  // set line length
  line.setLength(6.0);
  cout << "Length of line : " << line.getLength() <<endl;
  return 0;
}
```

Output :

Length of line : 6

Types of Constructors

Constructors are of three types

1.   Default Constructor
2.   Parametrized Constructor
3.   Copy Constructor

1. Default Constructor

Default constructor is the constructor which doesn't take any argument. It has no parameter.

Syntax :

```
class_name ()
{ Constructor Definition }
```

Program 2.13 : Default Constructors

```
class Cube
{
int side;
public:
Cube()
 {
  side=10;
 }
};
int main()
{
Cube c;
cout << c.side;
}
```

Output :

10

- In this case, as soon as the object is created the constructor is called which initializes its data members.
- A default constructor is so important for initialization of object members, that even if we do not define a constructor explicitly, the compiler will provide a default constructor implicitly.

Program 2.14 :

```
class Cube
{
 int side;
};
```

```
int main()
{
Cube c;
cout << c.side;
}
```

Output :

0

- In this case, default constructor provided by the compiler will be called which will initialize the object data members to default value, that will be 0 in this case.

2. Parameterized Constructor

- These are the constructors with parameter. Using this Constructor, you can provide different values to data members of different objects, by passing the appropriate values as argument.

Program 2.15 : Parameterized Constructors

```
class Cube
{
int side;
public:
Cube(int x)
 {
   side=x;
 }
};
int main()
{
Cube c1(10);
Cube c2(20);
Cube c3(30);
cout << c1.side;
cout << c2.side;
cout << c3.side;
}
```

Output :

10 20 30

- By using parameterized constructor in above case, we have initialized 3 objects with user defined values. We can have any number of parameters in a constructor.

3. Copy Constructor

- The copy constructor is a constructor which creates an object by initializing it with an object of the same class, which has been created previously. The copy constructor is used to:

  ➢ Initialize one object from another of the same type.

  ➢ Copy an object to pass it as an argument to a function.

  ➢ Copy an object to return it from a function.

- If a copy constructor is not defined in a class, the compiler itself defines one. If the class has pointer variables and has some dynamic memory allocations, then it is a must to have a copy constructor. The most common form of copy constructor is shown here:

```
classname (const classname andobj) {
  // body of constructor
}
```

- Here, obj is a reference to an object that is being used to initialize another object.

Program 2.16 : Copy Constructors

```
#include <iostream>
using namespace std;
class Line
{
  public:
    int getLength( void );
    Line( int len );          // simple constructor
    Line( const Line andobj); // copy constructor
    ~Line();                  // destructor
  private:
    int *ptr;
};
```

```cpp
// Member functions definitions including constructor
Line::Line(int len)
{
    cout << "Normal constructor allocating ptr" << endl;
    // allocate memory for the pointer;
    ptr = new int;
    *ptr = len;
}
Line::Line(const Line andobj)
{
    cout << "Copy constructor allocating ptr." << endl;
    ptr = new int;
    *ptr = *obj.ptr; // copy the value
}
Line::~Line(void)
{
    cout << "Freeing memory!" << endl;
    delete ptr;
}
int Line::getLength( void )
{
    return *ptr;
}
void display(Line obj)
{
    cout << "Length of line : " << obj.getLength() <<endl;
}
// Main function for the program
int main( )
```

```
{
  Line line(10);
  display(line);
  return 0;
}
```

Output :

Normal constructor allocating ptr

Copy constructor allocating ptr

Length of line: 10

Freeing memory!

Freeing memory!

These examples illustrate how copy constructors work and why they are required sometimes.

Implicit Copy Constructor

- Let us consider the following example:

Program 2.17 : Implicit Copy Constructor

```
#include <iostream>
class Person {
public:
  int age;
  explicit Person(int a)
    : age(a)
  {
  }
};
int main()
{
  Person timmy(10);
  Person sally(15);
  Person timmy_clone = timmy;
  std::cout << timmy.age << " " << sally.age << " " << timmy_clone.age << std::endl;
  timmy.age = 23;
  std::cout << timmy.age << " " << sally.age << " " << timmy_clone.age << std::endl;
}
```

Output :

10 15 10

23 15 10

- As expected, timmy has been copied to the new object, timmy_clone. While timmy's age was changed, timmy_clone's age remained the same. This is because they are totally different objects.

- The compiler has generated a copy constructor for us, and it could be written like this:

```
Person(const Personand other)

  : age(other.age) // calls the copy constructor of the age

{

}
```

- So, when do we really need a user–defined copy constructor? The next section will explore that question.

- User–defined copy constructor

- Now, consider a very simple dynamic array class like the following:

Program 2.18 : User–defined Copy Constructor

```
#include <iostream>

class Array

{

public:

  int size;

  int* data;

  explicit Array(int sz)

    : size(sz), data(new int[size])

  {

  }

  ~Array()

  {

    if (data != NULL) delete[] this->data;

  }

};
```

```
int main()
{
   Array first(20);
   first.data[0] = 25;
   {
      Array copy = first;
      std::cout << first.data[0] << " " << copy.data[0] << std::endl;
   }   // (1)
   first.data[0] = 10;   // (2)
}
```

Output :

25 25

Segmentation fault

Constructor Overloading :

- Just like other member functions, constructors can also be overloaded. Infact, when you have both default and parameterized constructors defined in your class, you are having overloaded constructors, one with no parameter and other with parameter.

- You can have any number of Constructors in a class that differ in parameter list.

Program 2.19 : Constructor Overloading

```
class Student
{
int rollno;
string name;
public:
Student(int x)
{
 rollno=x;
 name="None";
}
Student(int x, string str)
```

```
{
 rollno=x ;
 name=str ;
 }
};
int main()
{
 Student A(10);
 Student B(11,"Ram");
}
```

- In above case, we have defined two constructors with different parameters, hence overloading the constructors.

- One more important thing, if you define any constructor explicitly, then the compiler will not provide default constructor and you will have to define it yourself.

- In the above case if we write Student S; in main(), it will lead to a compile time error, because we haven't defined default constructor, and compiler will not provide its default constructor because we have defined other parameterized constructors.

2.2.2 Multiple Constructors in a Class

- Similar to functions, it is also possible to overload constructors. In the previous examples, we declared single constructors without arguments and with all arguments. A class can contain more than one constructor. This is known as constructor overloading. All constructors are defined with the same name as the class they belong to. All the constructors contain different number of arguments. Depending upon the number of arguments, the compiler executes appropriate constructor. Table 2.1 describes object declaration and appropriate constructor to it. Consider the following example:

```
class num
{
private: int a;
float b;
char c;
public:
a) num (int m, float j , char k);
b) num (int m, float j);
```

c) num();

d) class num x (4,5.5,'A');

e) class num y (1,2.2);

f) class num z;

}

Table 2.1 : Overloaded Constructors

Constructor Declaration	Object Declaration
(a) num (int m, float j, char k);	(d) num x (4,5.5, 'A');
(b) num (int m, float j);	(e) num y (1,2.2);
(c) num();	(f) num z;

- In the above example, the statements (a), (b), and (c) are constructor declarations and (d), (e), and (0 are the object declarations. The compiler decides which constructor to be called depending on the number of arguments present with the object.

- When object x is created, the constructor with three arguments is called because the declaration of an object is followed by three arguments. For object y, constructor with two arguments is called and lastly the object z, which is without any argument, is candidate for constructor without argument.

Program 2.20 : Multiple Constructors for the Single Class

```
#includeciostream.h>

#include<conio.h>

class num

{

private: int a; float b; char c; public:

num(int m, float j , char k);

num (int m, float j);

num();

void show()

{

cout«"\n\ta."«a«"b="«b«"c="«c;

}

};
```

```
num:: num (int m, float j , char k)
cout«"\n Constructor with three arguments"; a=m;
b=j; c=k;
}
num:: num (int m, float j)

cout«"\n Constructor with two arguments"; a=m;
b=j; c=";
}
num:: num()
{
cout«"\n Constructor without arguments"; a=b=c=NULL;
}
main()
{
clrscr();
class num x(4,5.5,'A');
x.show();
class num y(1,2.2);
y.show();
class num z;
z.show();
return 0;
}
```

Output :

Constructor with three arguments

a= 4 b= 5.5 c= A

Constructor with two arguments

a= 1 b= 2.2 c=

Constructor without arguments

a= 0 b= 0 c=

Explanation: In the above program, three constructors are declared. The first constructor is with three arguments, second with two, and third without any argument. While creating objects, arguments are passed. Depending on number of arguments, compiler decides on the constructor to be called. In this program, x, y, and z are three objects created. The x object passes three arguments, the y object passes two arguments, and the z object passes no arguments. The function show() is used to display the contents of the class members.

Program 2.21 :

```cpp
#include<iostream.h>
#include<conio.h>
class date_time
{
int d,m,y,hrs,min,sec;
public:
date_time(int i,int j,
int k,int a,int b,int c);
date_time();
void print()
{
cout<<"\nDate="<<d<<"Month="
<<m<<"Year="<<y<<endl;
cout<<"\n Hour="<<hrs<<"Minutes="
<<min<<"seconds="<<sec;
}
};
date_time::date_time
(int i,int j,int k,int a,int b,int c)
{
d=i;
m=j;
y=k;
hrs=a;
min=b;
```

```
sec=c;
}
date _time::date_time()
{
cout«"\nEnter Date Month Year (dd/mm/yy):";
cin»d»m»y;
cout«"\nEnter Hours Minutes Seconds
(hr:min:sec):";
cin»hrs»min»sec;
}
int main()
{
clrscr();
date_time n(1,1,2012,14,45,21);
n.print();
cout«"\n- - - - - - - - - - - - - - - - - - - - - - - - - - - -
       - ";date_time m;- - - - - - - - - - - - - - - - - - - - - - -
cout«"\n - - - - - - - - - - - - - - - - - - - - - - - - - - - - -
-----------";
m.print();
 return 0;
}
```

Output :

Date =1 Month =1 Year =2012

Hour = 14 Minutes = 45 seconds =21

Enter Date Month Year (dd/mm/yy):4 4 2012

Enter Hours Minutes Seconds (hr:min:sec):23 45 12

Date = 4 Month = 4 Year =2012

Hour = 23 Minutes = 45seconds =12

Explanation: The program has two constructors. The first constructor has six parameters. Six arguments are passed through the object to the first constructor.

The second constructor takes the date and time details entered through keyboard.

2.2.3 Constructors with Default Arguments

- Constructors With Default Arguments Similar to functions, it is also possible to declare constructors with default arguments. Consider the following example:

power(int 9,int 3);

- In the above example, the default value for the first argument is nine and two for second.

power p1 (3);

- In this statement, object p1 is created and 9 raise to 3 expression n is calculated. Here, one argument is absent hence default value 9 is taken, and its third power is calculated. Consider the following example on the above discussion:

Program 2.22 : To Declare Default Arguments in a Constructor. Obtain the Power of the Number.

```
#include<iostream.h>
#include<conio.h>
#includecmath.h>
 class power
{
private: int num;
int power;
int ans;
public: power(int n=9,int p=3); // declaration of constructor with default arguments
void show()
{
cout«"\n"«num «"raise to"«power «"is" «ans;
}
};
power:: power (int n,int p ) {
num=n;
power=p;
ans=pow(n,p);
}
```

```
main()
{
Clrscr();
class power pl,p2(5);
pl.show();
p2.show();
 return 0;
}
```

Output :

9 raise to 3 is 729

5 raise to 3 is 125

Explanation: In the above program, the class power is declared. It has three integer member variables and one member function show().The show() function is used to display the values of member data variables. The constructor of class power is declared with two default arguments. In the function main(), p1 and p2 are two objects of class power. The p1 object is created without argument. Hence, the constructor uses default arguments in pow() function. The p2 object is created with one argument. In this call of constructor, the second argument is taken as default. Both the results are shown in output.

2.2.4 Destructors

- A destructor is a special member function of a class that is executed whenever an object of it's class goes out of scope or whenever the delete expression is applied to a pointer to the object of that class.
- A destructor will have exact same name as the class prefixed with a tilde (~) and it can neither return a value nor can it take any parameters. Destructor can be very useful for releasing resources before coming out of the program like closing files, releasing memories etc.
- Following example explains the concept of destructor

Program 2.23 : Concept of Destructor

```
#include <iostream>
using namespace std;
class Line
{
  public:
    void setLength( double len );
```

```cpp
      double getLength( void );
      Line();   // This is the constructor declaration
      ~Line();  // This is the destructor: declaration
   private:
      double length;
};
// Member functions definitions including constructor
Line::Line(void)
{
   cout << "Object is being created" << endl;
}
Line::~Line(void)
{
   cout << "Object is being deleted" << endl;
}
void Line::setLength( double len )
{
   length = len;
}
double Line::getLength( void )
{
   return length;
}
// Main function for the program
int main( )
{
   Line line;
   // set line length
   line.setLength(6.0);
   cout << "Length of line : " << line.getLength() <<endl;
   return 0;
}
```

Output :

Object is being created

Length of line : 6

Object is being deleted

2.3 OPERATOR OVERLOADING CONCEPT

- C++ allows you to specify more than one definition for a function name or an operator in the same scope which is called function overloading and operator overloading respectively.

- An overloaded declaration is a declaration that had been declared with the same name as a previously declared declaration in the same scope except that both declarations have different arguments and obviously different implementation.

- When you call an overloaded function or operator the compiler determines the most appropriate definition to use by comparing the argument types you used to call the function or operator with the parameter types specified in the definitions. The process of selecting the most appropriate overloaded function or operator is called overload resolution.

2.3.1 Operator Overloading

- Operator overloading is an important concept in C++. It is a type of polymorphism in which an operator is overloaded to give user defined meaning to it.

- Overloaded operator is used to perform operation on user-defined data type.

- For example '+' operator can be overloaded to perform addition on various data types like for Integer, String (concatenation of strings) etc.

cout<<"This is Test String";

where,

      cout- object of ostream class

      << overloaded insertion operator

      This is Test String- string

- Almost any operator can be overloaded in C++. However, there are few operators which can not be overloaded. Operator that are not overloaded are follows:
    - Scope operator -::
    - Sizeof
    - Member selector - .
    - Member pointer selector - *
    - Ternary operator - ?:

Operator Overloading Syntax :

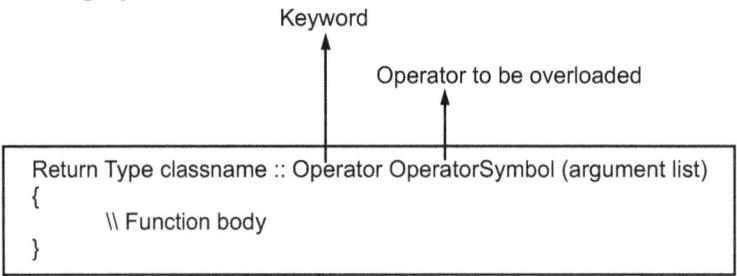

Implementing Operator Overloading

- Operator overloading can be done by implementing a function which can be:
  1. Member Function
  2. Non-Member Function
  3. Friend Function
- Operator overloading function can be a member function if the left operand is an object of that class, but if the left operand is different, then Operator overloading function must be a non-member function.
- Operator overloading function can be made friend function if it needs access to the private and protected members of class.

Restrictions on Operator Overloading

Following are some restrictions to be kept in mind while implementing operator overloading.

- Precedence and Associativity of an operator cannot be changed.
- Numbers of Operands cannot be changed. Unary operator remains unary, binary remains binary etc.
- No new operators can be created, only existing operators can be overloaded.
- Cannot redefine the meaning of a procedure. You cannot change how integers are added.

Following is the list of operators which can be overloaded:

Table 2.2: Overloadable/Non-overloadable Operators

+	−	*	/	%	^
&	|	~	!	,	=
<	>	<=	>=	++	--
<<	>>	==	!=	&&	||
+=	-=	/=	%=	^=	&=
|=	*=	<<=	>>=	[ ]	( )
->	->*	new	new [ ]	delete	delete [ ]

Following is the list of operators, which can not be overloaded:

: :	.*	.	?:

There are Two Types of Operator Overloading

1. Unary Operator Overloading
2. Binary Operator Overloading

2.3.2 Overloading Binary Operators

- The binary operators take two arguments and following are the examples of Binary operators.

- You use binary operators very frequently like addition (+) operator, subtraction (–) operator and division (/) operator.

Program 2.24 : How Addition (+) Operator can be Overloaded. Similar Way, You can Overload Subtraction (–) and Division (/) Operators.

```
#include <iostream>
using namespace std;
class Box
{
  double length;
  double breadth;
  double height;
public:
  double getVolume(void)
  {
    return length * breadth * height;
  }
  void setLength( double len )
  {
    length = len;
  }
  void setBreadth( double bre )
  {
    breadth = bre;
  }
```

```cpp
    void setHeight( double hei )
    {
       height = hei;
    }
    // Overload + operator to add two Box objects.
    Box operator+(const Box & b)
    {
       Box box;
       box.length = this->length + b.length;
       box.breadth = this->breadth + b.breadth;
       box.height = this->height + b.height;
       return box;
    }
};
// Main function for the program
int main( )
{
   Box Box1;            // Declare Box1 of type Box
   Box Box2;            // Declare Box2 of type Box
   Box Box3;            // Declare Box3 of type Box
   double volume = 0.0;    // Store the volume of a box here
   // box 1 specification
   Box1.setLength(6.0);
   Box1.setBreadth(7.0);
   Box1.setHeight(5.0);
   // box 2 specification
   Box2.setLength(12.0);
   Box2.setBreadth(13.0);
   Box2.setHeight(10.0);
```

```
// volume of box 1
volume = Box1.getVolume();
cout << "Volume of Box1: " << volume <<endl;
// volume of box 2
volume = Box2.getVolume();
cout << "Volume of Box2: " << volume <<endl;
// Add two object as follows:
Box3 = Box1 + Box2; //+ Overloded operator function called.
// volume of box 3
volume = Box3.getVolume();
cout << "Volume of Box3: " << volume <<endl;
return 0;
}
```

Output :

Volume of Box1: 210

Volume of Box2: 1560

Volume of Box3: 5400

2.4 INHERITANCE

- Inheritance allows us to define a class in terms of another class, which makes it easier to create and maintain an application. This also provides an opportunity to reuse the code functionality and fast implementation time.

- When creating a class, instead of writing completely new data members and member functions, the programmer can designate that the new class should inherit the members of an existing class. This existing class is called the base class, and the new class is referred to as the derived class.

2.4.1 Base Class

- Base class is parent class of a derived class.

- Base classes may be used to create other classes.

- A class that is used to create another class is called the Base class.

- Base class is also called a Super class.

2.4.2 Derived Class

- A class that was created based on a previously existing class that is base class is called as Derived class.
- A derived class inherits all the member variables and methods of the base class from which it is derived.
- It is also called a derived type.

The general form of defining a derived class is

```
class derived-class-name : visibility-mode base-class-name
{
.....//
.....// members of derived class
.....//
};
```

- A class can be derived from more than one classes, which means it can inherit data and functions from multiple base classes.
- To define a derived class, we use a class derivation list to specify the base classes.

  ➢ The colon indicates that the derived-class-name is derived from the base-class-name.

  ➢ The visibility-mode is optional and, if present, may be either private or public.

  ➢ The default visibility-mode is private.

  ➢ Visibility mode specifies whether the features of the base class are privately derived or publicly derived.

Table 2.3 : Visibility of Inherited Members

Base Class Visibility	Derived Class Visibility		
	Public Derivation	Private Derivation	Protected Derivation
Private →	Not inherited	Not inherited	Not inherited
Protected →	Protected	Private	Protected
Public →	Public	Private	Protected

2.4.3 Member Access Control and Inheritance

- A derived class can access all the non-private members of its base class. Thus base-class members that should not be accessible to the member functions of derived classes should be declared private in the base class.

- We can summarize the different access types according to who can access them in the following Table 2.4.

Table 2.4 : Access Specifier

Access	Public	Protected	Private
Same class	Yes	Yes	Yes
Derived classes	Yes	Yes	No
Outside classes	Yes	No	No

- A derived class inherits all base class methods with the following exceptions
  - ➢ Constructors, destructors and copy constructors of the base class.
  - ➢ Overloaded operators of the base class.
  - ➢ The friend functions of the base class.
- When deriving a class from a base class, the base class may be inherited through public, protected or private inheritance.
- We hardly use protected or private inheritance, but public inheritance is commonly used. While using different type of inheritance, following rules are applied
  - ➢ **Public:** A public member is accessible from anywhere outside the class but within a program. When deriving a class from a public base class, public members of the base class become public members of the derived class and protected members of the base class become protected members of the derived class. A base class's private members are never accessible directly from a derived class, but can be accessed through calls to the public and protected members of the base class.
  - ➢ **Protected:** When deriving from a protected base class, public and protected members of the base class become protected members of the derived class.
  - ➢ **Private:** A private member variable or function cannot be accessed, or even viewed from outside the class. Only the class and friend functions can access private members. When deriving from a private base class, public and protected members of the base class become private members of the derived class.

2.4.4 Types of Inheritance

In C++, there are five different types of Inheritance.

1. Single Inheritance
2. Multiple Inheritance
3. Hierarchical Inheritance
4. Multilevel Inheritance
5. Hybrid Inheritance

1. Single Inheritance

- In single level inheritance, there is only one base class and has only one derived class.
- It is the simplest form of inheritance.

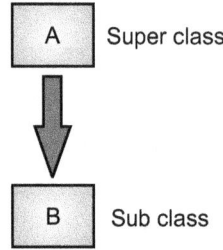

Fig. 2.1 : Single inheritance

Syntax of Single Level Inheritance :

```
class A
{
};
class B: public A
{
};
```

Program 2.25 : Payroll System Using Single Inheritance

```
#include<iostream.h>
#include<conio.h>
class emp
{
  public:
    int eno;
    char name[20],des[20];
    void get()
    {
        cout<<"Enter the employee number:";
        cin>>eno;
        cout<<"Enter the employee name:";
        cin>>name;
```

```cpp
        cout<<"Enter the designation:";
        cin>>des;
    }
};
class salary:public emp
{
    float bp,hra,da,pf,np;
  public:
    void get1()
    {
        cout<<"Enter the basic pay:";
        cin>>bp;
        cout<<"Enter the Humen Resource Allowance:";
        cin>>hra;
        cout<<"Enter the Dearness Allowance :";
        cin>>da;
        cout<<"Enter the Profitablity Fund:";
        cin>>pf;
    }
    void calculate()
    {
        np=bp+hra+da-pf;
    }
    void display()
    {
cout<<eno<<"\t"<<name<<"\t"<<des<<"\t"<<bp<<"\t"<<hra<<"\t"<<da<<"\t"<<pf<<"\t"<<np<<"\n";
    }
};
void main()
```

```
{
    int i,n;
    char ch;
    salary s[10];
    clrscr();
    cout<<"Enter the number of employee:";
    cin>>n;
    for(i=0;i<n;i++)
    {
            s[i].get();
            s[i].get1();
            s[i].calculate();
    }
cout<<"\ne_no \t e_name\t des \t bp \t hra \t da \t pf \t np \n";
    for(i=0;i<n;i++)
    {
            s[i].display();
    }
    getch();
}
```

Output :

Enter the Number of employee:1

Enter the employee No: 150

Enter the employee Name: Seema

Enter the designation: Manager

Enter the basic pay: 5000

Enter the HR allowance: 1000

Enter the Dearness allowance: 500

Enter the profitability Fund: 300

E.No	E.nam	des	BP	HRA	DA	PF	NP
150	Seema	Manager	5000	1000	500	300	6200

2. Multiple Inheritance

- In this type of inheritance, a single derived class may inherit from two or more than two base classes.

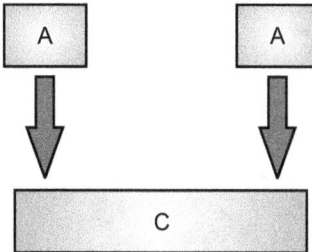

Fig. 2.2 : Multiple inheritance

Syntax of Multiple Inheritance :

```
class A
{
};
class B
{
};
class C: public B, public A
{
};
```

Program 2.26 : Students Details Using Multiple Inheritance

```
#include<iostream.h>
#include<conio.h>
class student
{
   protected:
     int rno,m1,m2;
   public:
          void get()
          {
                  cout<<"Enter the Roll no :";
                  cin>>rno;
```

```cpp
                cout<<"Enter the two marks   :";
                cin>>m1>>m2;
        }
};
class sports
{
  protected:
    int sm;                 // sm = Sports mark
  public:
        void getsm()
        {
         cout<<"\nEnter the sports mark :";
         cin>>sm;
        }
};
class statement:public student,public sports
{
  int tot,avg;
  public:
  void display()
        {
         tot=(m1+m2+sm);
         avg=tot/3;
         cout<<"\n\n\tRoll No  : "<<rno<<"\n\tTotal    : "<<tot;
         cout<<"\n\tAverage    : "<<avg;
        }
};
void main()
{
  clrscr();
  statement obj;
  obj.get();
```

```
  obj.getsm();
  obj.display();
  getch();
}
```

Output :

Enter the Roll no: 100

Enter two marks

90

80

Enter the Sports Mark: 90

Roll No: 100

Total: 260

Average: 86.66

3. Hierarchical Inheritance

- In this type of inheritance, multiple derived classes inherit from a single base class.

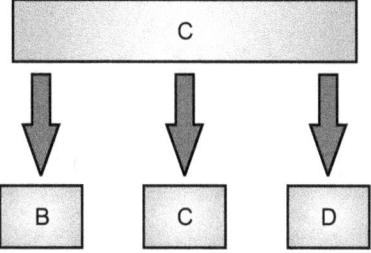

Fig. 2.3 : Hierarchical inheritance

Syntax of Hierarchical Inheritance :

```
class A
{
};
class B: public A
{
};
class C: public A
{
};
```

```
class D: public A
{

};
```

Program 2.27 : C++ Program to Create Employee and Student inheriting from Person using Hierarchical Inheritance

```cpp
#include <iostream>
#include <conio.h>
using namespace std;
class person
{
    char name[100],gender[10];
    int age;
    public:
        void getdata()
        {
            cout<<"Name: ";
            fflush(stdin);  /*clears input stream*/
            gets(name);
            cout<<"Age: ";
            cin>>age;
            cout<<"Gender: ";
            cin>>gender;
        }
        void display()
        {
            cout<<"Name: "<<name<<endl;
            cout<<"Age: "<<age<<endl;
            cout<<"Gender: "<<gender<<endl;
        }
};
```

```cpp
class student: public person
{
    char institute[100], level[20];
    public:
        void getdata()
        {
            person::getdata();
            cout<<"Name of College/School: ";
            fflush(stdin);
            gets(institute);
            cout<<"Level: ";
            cin>>level;
        }
        void display()
        {
            person::display();
            cout<<"Name of College/School: "<<institute<<endl;
            cout<<"Level: "<<level<<endl;
        }
};
class employee: public person
{
    char company[100];
    float salary;
    public:
        void getdata()
        {
            person::getdata();
            cout<<"Name of Company: ";
            fflush(stdin);
```

```
        gets(company);
        cout<<"Salary: Rs.";
        cin>>salary;
    }
    void display()
    {
        person::display();
        cout<<"Name of Company: "<<company<<endl;
        cout<<"Salary: Rs."<<salary<<endl;
    }
};
int main()
{
    student s;
    employee e;
    cout<<"Student"<<endl;
    cout<<"Enter data"<<endl;
    s.getdata();
    cout<<endl<<"Displaying data"<<endl;
    s.display();
    cout<<endl<<"Employee"<<endl;
    cout<<"Enter data"<<endl;
    e.getdata();
    cout<<endl<<"Displaying data"<<endl;
    e.display();
    getch();
    return 0;
}
```

Output :

Student

Enter data

Name: John Wright

Age: 21

Gender: Male

Name of College/School: Abc Academy

Level: Bachelor

Displaying data

Name: John Wright

Age: 21

Gender: Male

Name of College/School: Abc Academy

Level: Bachelor

Employee

Enter data

Name: Mary White

Age: 24

Gender: Female

Name of Company: Xyz Consultant

Salary: $29000

Displaying data

Name: Mary White

Age: 24

Gender: Female

Name of Company: Xyz Consultant

Salary: $29000

4. Multi Level Inheritance

- In multi level inheritance, there will be a chain of inheritance with a class derived from only one parent and will have only one child class.

- In this type of inheritance, the derived class inherits from a class, which in turn inherits from some other class. The Super class for one, is sub class for the other.

- It is also called as Levels of Inheritance.

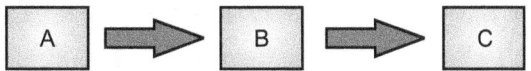

Fig. 2.4 : Multi Level Inheritance

Syntax of Multi Level Inheritance :

```
class A
{
};
class B: public A
{
};
class C: public B
{
};
```

Program 2.28 :

```
#include <iostream.h>
class mm
{
  protected:
  int rollno;
 public:
  void get_num(int a)
  {
    rollno = a;
  }
  void put_num()
  {
    cout << "Roll Number Is:\n"<< rollno << "\n";
  }
};
class marks : public mm
{
  protected:
  int sub1;
  int sub2;
  public:
  void get_marks(int x,int y)
  {
    sub1 = x;
```

```cpp
    sub2 = y;
  }
  void put_marks(void)
  {
    cout << "Subject 1:" << sub1 << "\n";
    cout << "Subject 2:" << sub2 << "\n";
  }
};
class res : public marks
{
 protected:
  float tot;
 public:
  void disp(void)
  {
   tot = sub1+sub2;
   put_num();
   put_marks();
   cout << "Total:"<< tot;
  }
};
int main()
{
  res std1;
  std1.get_num(5);
  std1.get_marks(10,20);
  std1.disp();
  return 0;
}
```

Output :

Roll Number is:

5

Subject 1: 10

Subject 2: 20

Total: 30

5. Hybrid Inheritance

- Hybrid Inheritance is combination of Hierarchical and Mutilevel Inheritance.

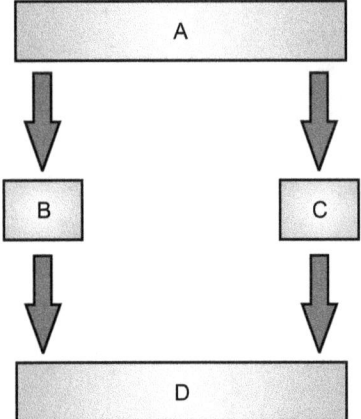

Fig. 2.5 : Hybrid Inheritance

Syntax of Hybrid Inheritance :

```
class A
{
};
class B:public A
{
};
class C: public A
{
};
class D: public B, public C
{
};
```

Program 2.29 : C++ Program for Hybrid Inheritance

```
#include<iostream.h>
#include<conio.h>
class stu
{
protected:
    int rno;
public:
    void get_no(int a)
```

```
        {
           rno=a;
        }
         void put_no(void)
        {
            cout<<"Roll no"<<rno<<"\n";
        }
};
class test: public stu
{
    protected:
    float part1,part2;
  public:
  void get_mark(float x,float y)
  {
     part1=x;
     part2=y;
  }
  void put_marks()
  {
   cout<<"Marksobtained:";
   cout<<"part1="<<part1<<"\n"<<"part2="<<part2<<"\n";
  }
};
class sports
{
    protected:
    float score;
public:
 void getscore(float s)
 {
     score=s;
 }
void putscore(void)
```

```
{
    cout<<"sports:"<<score<<"\n";
}
};
class result: public test, public sports
{
    float total;
public:
    void display(void);
};
void result::display(void)
{
    total=part1+part2+score;
    put_no();
    put_marks();
    putscore();
    cout<<"Total Score="<<total<<"\n";
}
int main()
{
    clrscr();
    result stu;
    stu.get_no(123);
    stu.get_mark(27.5,33.0);
    stu.getscore(6.0);
    stu.display();
    return 0;
}
```

Output :

Roll no 123

Marks obtained : part1=27.5

Part2=33

Sports=6

Total score = 66.5

2.4.5 Making a Private Member Inheritable

- Private derivation means that the base class has been inherited privately.
- Public members of the base class are private within the derived class.
- Protected members of the base class are private within the derived class.

- private members of the base class stay private within the base class.
- These are only visible within the base class.

The General syntax of using inheritance with private member is :

```
class base_class_name
{
-----
-----
}
class derived_class_name : private base_class_name
{
----
----
}
```

Let us see an example to explain how can private members inherited from one class to another.

Program 2.30 :

```
#include<iostream>
using namespace std;
class Parent
{
  public:
   void func_public()
   {
     cout << "Public function of base class Parent is called.\n";
   }
  private:
   void func_private()
   {
     cout << "Private function of base class Parent is called.\n";
   }
  protected:
   void func_protected()
   {
     cout << "Protected function of base class Parent is called.\n";
   }
};
```

```
class Child : private Parent
{
  public:
   void function()
   {
     func_public();
     // Correct. Now Child class's private function is called

     func_protected();
     // Correct. Now Child class's private function is called
     func_private();
     // Error. Now its calling Parent's private function
   }
};

int main()
{
  Child obj;
  obj.function();
  return 0;
}
```

Explanation: Here, the derived class Child has been derived from base class Parent. The derived class Child has inherited the public function and protected function will be private to the Child class from the Parent Class but private function will remain private in the base class Parent and gives an error while calling it from the Child class.

EXERCISE

1. What is a class?
2. How to define member function?
3. What is multilevel inheritance?
4. What is the need of inheritance?
5. Explain Inline function.
6. What are the types of inheritance? Describe each in detail.
7. What is operator overloading?
8. Explain the syntax of binary operator overloading.
9. Explain Constructor with an example.
10. Explain Arrays of objects.
11. Explain Parameterized constructors.

Unit III

JAVA FUNDAMENTALS

3.1 JAVA

- Java is a programming language and a platform. Java is a high level, robust, secured and object-oriented programming language.

- **Platform:** Any hardware or software environment in which a program runs, is known as a platform. Since Java has its own runtime environment (JRE) and API, it is called platform.

3.1.1 Where it is used?

There are many devices where Java is currently used. Some of them are as follows:

- Desktop applications such as acrobat reader, media player, antivirus etc.

- Web applications such as irctc.co.in, Javatpoint.com etc.

- Enterprise applications such as banking applications

- Mobile

- Embedded system

- Smart card

- Robotics

- Games etc.

3.1.2 Types of Java Applications

There are mainly four types of applications that can be created using Java programming:

1. **Standalone Application:**

It is also known as desktop application or window-based application. An application that we need to install on every machine such as media player, antivirus etc. AWT and Swing are used in Java for creating standalone applications.

2. **Web Application:**

An application that runs on the server side and creates dynamic page, is called web application. Currently, servlet, jsp, struts, jsf etc. technologies are used for creating web applications in Java.

3. Enterprise Application:

An application that is distributed in nature, such as banking applications etc. It has the advantage of high level security, load balancing and clustering. In Java, EJB is used for creating enterprise applications.

4. Mobile Application:

An application that is created for mobile devices. Currently Android and Java ME are used for creating mobile applications.

3.2 HISTORY OF JAVA

- The history of Java starts from Green Team. Java team members also known as Green Team, initiated a revolutionary task to develop a language for digital devices such as set-top boxes, televisions etc.

- For the green team members, it was an advance concept at that time. But, it was suited for internet programming. Later, Java technology as incorporated by Netscape.

- Currently, Java is used in internet programming, mobile devices, games, e-business solutions etc. There are given the major points that describes the history of Java.

- James Gosling, Mike Sheridan, and Patrick Naughton initiated the Java language project in June 1991. The small team of sun engineers called Green Team.

- Originally designed for small, embedded systems in electronic appliances like set-top boxes.

- Firstly, it was called "Greentalk" by James Gosling and file extension was .gt. After that, it was called Oak and was developed as a part of the Green project.

- Why Oak? Oak is a symbol of strength and chosen as a national tree of many countries like U.S.A., France, Germany, Romania etc.

- In 1995, Oak was renamed as "Java" because it was already a trademark by Oak Technologies.

- Why they chose Java name for Java language? The team gathered to choose a new name. The suggested words were "dynamic", "revolutionary", "Silk", "jolt", "DNA" etc. They wanted something that reflected the essence of the technology: revolutionary, dynamic, lively, cool, unique, and easy to spell and fun to say.

- According to James Gosling, "Java was one of the top choices along with Silk". Since Java was so unique, most of the team members preferred Java.

- Java is an island of Indonesia where first coffee was produced called Java coffee.

- Originally developed by James Gosling at Sun Microsystems which is now a subsidiary of Oracle Corporation and released in 1995.

- In 1995, Time magazine called Java one of the Ten Best Products of 1995.

- JDK 1.0 released in January 23, 1996.

3.2.1 Java Version History

There are many Java versions that has been released. Current stable release of Java is Java SE 8.

- JDK Alpha and Beta (1995)
- JDK 1.0 (23rd Jan, 1996)
- JDK 1.1 (19th Feb, 1997)
- J2SE 1.2 (8th Dec, 1998)
- J2SE 1.3 (8th May, 2000)
- J2SE 1.4 (6th Feb, 2002)
- J2SE 5.0 (30th Sep, 2004)
- Java SE 6 (11th Dec, 2006)
- Java SE 7 (28th July, 2011)
- Java SE 8 (18th March, 2014)
- Java SE 8-31 CPU (20th Jan, 2015)
- Java SE 8 – 71 CPU (19th Jan, 2016)
- Java SE8 – 111 CPU (18th Oct, 2016)

3.3 C++ VS JAVA

There are many differences and similarities between C++ programming language and Java. A list of top differences between C++ and Java are given below:

Content	C++	Java
Platform-independent	C++ is platform-dependent.	Java is platform-independent.
Mainly used for	C++ is mainly used for system programming.	Java is mainly used for application programming. It is widely used in window, web-based, enterprise and mobile applications.
Goto statement	C++ supports goto statement.	Java doesn't support goto statement.
Multiple inheritance	C++ supports multiple inheritance.	Java doesn't support multiple inheritance through class. It can be achieved by interfaces in Java.
Operator Overloading	C++ supports operator overloading.	Java doesn't support operator overloading.

...Contd.

Pointers	C++ supports pointers. You can write pointer program in C++.	Java supports pointer internally. But you can't write the pointer program in Java. It means Java has restricted pointer support in Java.
Compiler and Interpreter	C++ uses compiler only.	Java uses compiler and interpreter both.
Call by Value and Call by reference	C++ supports both call by value and call by reference.	Java supports call by value only. There is no call by reference in Java.
Structure and Union	C++ supports structures and unions.	Java doesn't support structures and unions.
Thread Support	C++ doesn't have built-in support for threads. It relies on third-party libraries for thread support.	Java has built-in thread support.
Virtual Keyword	C++ supports virtual keyword so that we can decide whether or not override a function.	Java has no virtual keyword. We can override all non-static methods by default. In other words, non-static methods are virtual by default.
unsigned right shift >>>	C++ doesn't support >>> operator.	Java supports unsigned right shift >>> operator that fills zero at the top for the negative numbers. For positive numbers, it works same like >> operator.

3.4 JAVA FEATURES

There are many features of Java. The Java features given below are simple and easy to understand.

- Simple and Small
- Object-Oriented
- Platform independent

- Secured
- Robust
- Architecture neutral
- Portable
- High Performance
- Distributed
- Multithreaded
- **Simple and Small:**
  - ➤ Java language is simple because syntax is based on C++ so easier for programmers to learn it after C++.
  - ➤ Java is easily programmable, with a minimum of training, since it is based on C++.
  - ➤ It enabling construction of compact software that can run 'stand-alone' even on small machines.
- **Object – Oriented:**
  - ➤ An object-oriented design enables the development of small, modular, self-contained units, each of which could later be used as building block for any specific application.
  - ➤ It also facilitates a clean definition of interfaces and allows 'plug-and-play' features, where in reusable software components can be distributed easily across diverse hardware platforms.
  - ➤ Programmers can even attach their applications and data together, and bundle the combination as a single entity.
  - ➤ To be truly considered as 'object oriented' a programming language should support a minimum of four characteristics.
    - **(i) Encapsulation :** Implements information hiding and modularity that is abstraction.
    - **(ii) Polymorphism :** The same message sent to different objects results in behavior that is dependent on the nature of the object receiving the message.
    - **(iii) Inheritance :** You define new classes and behavior based on existing classes to obtain code re-use and code organization.
    - **(iv) Dynamic Binding :** Objects could come from anywhere possibly across the network. You need to be able to send messages to objects without having to know their specific type at the time you write your code. Dynamic binding provides maximum flexibility while a program is executing.

- **Platform Independent:**

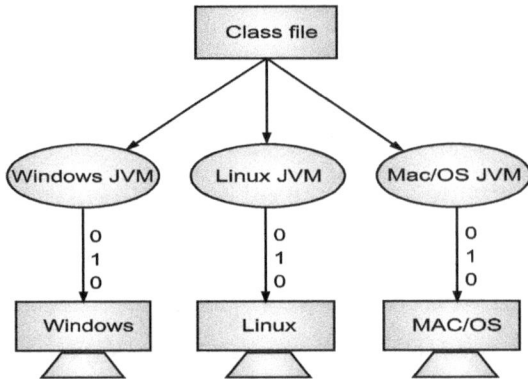

Fig. 3.1 Platform independency

➤ A platform is the hardware or software environment in which a program runs.

➤ There are two types of platforms software-based and hardware-based. Java provides software-based platform.

➤ The Java platform differs from most other platforms in the sense that it is a software-based platform that runs on the top of other hardware-based platforms. It has two components:

(a) Runtime Environment

(b) API (Application Programming Interface)

➤ Java code can be run on multiple platforms e.g. Windows, Linux, Sun Solaris, Mac/OS etc.

➤ Java code is compiled by the compiler and converted into bytecode. This bytecode is a platform-independent code because it can be run on multiple platforms i.e. Write Once and Run Anywhere.

- **Secured:**

Java is secured because:

(a) No explicit pointer

(b) Java Programs run inside virtual machine sandbox

➤ **Classloader:** Adds security by separating the package for the classes of the local file system from those that are imported from network sources.

➤ **Bytecode Verifier:** Checks the code fragments for illegal code that can violate access right to objects.

➤ **Security Manager:** Determines what resources a class can access such as reading and writing to the local disk.

➤ These security features are provided by Java language. Some security can also be provided by application developer through SSL, JAAS, Cryptography etc.

- **Robust:**
  - ➤ Robust simply means strong. Java uses strong memory management. There are lack of pointers that avoids security problem. There is automatic garbage collection in Java.
  - ➤ There is exception handling and type checking mechanism in Java. All these points makes Java robust.
  - ➤ Java programs are robust because explicit memory manipulations by the programmer are prevented.
- **Architecture-Neutral:**
  - ➤ There is no implementation dependent features e.g. size of primitive type is fixed.
  - ➤ In C programming, int data type occupies 2 bytes of memory for 32-bit architecture and 4 bytes of memory for 64-bit architecture. But in Java, it occupies 4 bytes of memory for both 32 and 64 bit architectures.
  - ➤ The Java Compiler generates an architecture-neutral object file, 'generic' Byte Code instructions, which have nothing to do with a particular computer architecture. This compiled code is executable on any processor, given the presence of the Java run-time system, which will translate it into native machine code on the fly.
  - ➤ The same version of the software runs on all platforms, independent of any CPU or hardware architecture, across networks.
- **Portable:**
  - ➤ We may carry the Java bytecode to any platform.
- **High-Performance:**
  - ➤ Java is faster than traditional interpretation since byte code is "close" to native code still somewhat slower than a compiled language (e.g. C++).
- **Distributed:**
  - ➤ We can create distributed applications in Java. RMI and EJB are used for creating distributed applications.
  - ➤ We may access files by calling the methods from any machine on the internet.
- **Multi-Threaded:**
  - ➤ A thread is like a separate program, executing concurrently. We can write Java programs that deal with many tasks at once by defining multiple threads.
  - ➤ The main advantage of multi-threading is that it doesn't occupy memory for each thread. It shares a common memory area. Threads are important for multi-media, web applications etc.

3.5 JAVA ENVIRONMENT

- JVM (Java Virtual Machine) is an abstract machine. It is a specification that provides runtime environment in which Java bytecode can be executed.

- JVMs are available for many hardware and software platforms i.e. JVM is platform dependent.

- JVM is:
  - ➢ **A specification** where working of Java Virtual Machine is specified. But implementation provider is independent to choose the algorithm. Its implementation has been provided by Sun and other companies.
  - ➢ **An implementation** Its implementation is known as JRE (Java Runtime Environment).
  - ➢ **Runtime Instance** Whenever you write Java command on the command prompt to run the Java class, an instance of JVM is created.
- The JVM performs following operation:
  - ➢ Loads code
  - ➢ Verifies code
  - ➢ Executes code
  - ➢ Provides runtime environment
- JVM provides definitions for the:
  - ➢ Memory area
  - ➢ Class file format
  - ➢ Register set
  - ➢ Garbage-collected heap
  - ➢ Fatal error reporting etc.

3.5.1 Internal Architecture of JVM

Let's understand the internal architecture of JVM. It contains class loader, memory area, execution engine etc.

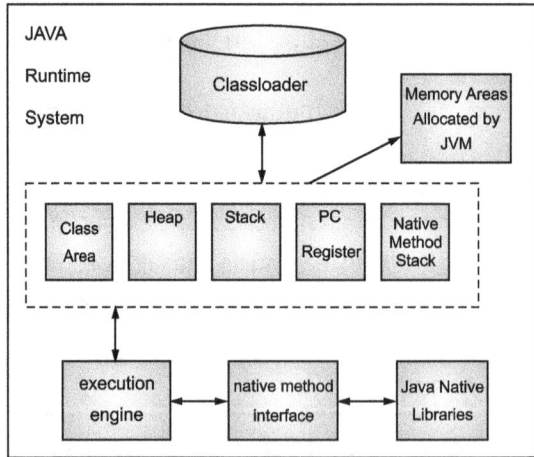

Fig. 3.2 : Internal architecture of JVM

- **Classloader:**

  Classloader is a subsystem of JVM that is used to load class files.

- **Class(Method) Area:**

  Class(Method) Area stores per-class structures such as the runtime constant pool, field and method data, the code for methods.

- **Heap:**

  It is the runtime data area in which objects are allocated.

- **Stack:**

  Java Stack stores frames. It holds local variables and partial results, and plays a part in method invocation and return. Each thread has a private JVM stack, created at the same time as thread. A new frame is created each time a method is invoked. A frame is destroyed when its method invocation completes.

- **Program Counter Register:**

  It contains the address of the Java virtual machine instruction currently being executed.

- **Native Method Stack:**

  It contains all the native methods used in the application.

- **Execution Engine:**

It contains:

  - ➤ **A virtual processor**
  - ➤ **Interpreter:** Read bytecode stream then execute the instructions.
  - ➤ **Just-In-Time(JIT) compiler:** It is used to improve the performance. JIT compiles parts of the byte code that have similar functionality at the same time, and hence reduces the amount of time needed for compilation.

3.6 SIMPLE JAVA PROGRAM

- In this topic, we will learn how to write the simple program of Java. We can write a simple hello Java program easily after installing the JDK.

- To create a simple Java program, you need to create a class that contains main method. Let's understand the requirement first.

3.6.1 Requirement for Hello Java Example

- For executing any Java program, you need to

  Install the JDK if you don't have installed it, download the JDK and install it.

  Set path of the jdk/bin directory. http://www.Javatpoint.com/how-to-set-path-in-Java.

  Create the Java program compile and run the Java program.

3.6.2 Creating Hello Java Example

Let's create the hello Java program:

```
class Simple
{
public static void main(String args[])
 {
    System.out.println("Hello Java");
 }
}
```

Save this file as Simple.Java

To Compile: Javac Simple.Java

To Execute: Java Simple

Output: Hello Java

3.6.3 Explanation of First Java Program

- **class** keyword is used to declare a class in Java.
- **public** keyword is an access modifier which represents visibility, it means it is visible to all.
- **static** is a keyword, if we declare any method as static, it is known as static method. The core advantage of static method is that there is no need to create object to invoke the static method. The main method is executed by the JVM, so it doesn't require to create object to invoke the main method. So, it saves memory.
- **void** is the return type of the method, it means it doesn't return any value.
- **main** represents startup of the program.
- **String[] args** is used for command line argument..
- **System.out.println()** is used print statement. here System is the class, out is the object of class system and println() is the function which is used to print the text.

There are many ways to write a Java program. The modifications that can be done in a Java program are given below:

(1) By changing sequence of the modifiers, method prototype is not changed.

Let's see the simple code of main method.

- Static public void main(String args[])

(2) Subscript notation in Java array can be used after type, before variable or after variable.

Let's see the different codes to write the main method.

- Public static void main(String[] args)

- Public static void main(String []args)

- Public static void main(String args[])

(3) You can provide var-args support to main method by passing 3 ellipses (dots)

Let's see the simple code of using var-args in main method. Public static void main (String... args)

(4) Having semicolon at the end of class in Java is optional.

Let's see the simple code.

```
class A
{
    static public void main(String... args)
    {
    System.out.println("hello Java4");
    }
};
```

3.6.4 Internal Details of Hello Java Program

- In the previous topic, we have learned about the first program, how to compile and how to run the first Java program. Here, we are going to learn, what happens while compiling and running the Java program. Moreover, we will see some question based on the first program.

What Happens at Compile Time?

- At compile time, Java file is compiled by Java compiler and converts the Java code into bytecode.

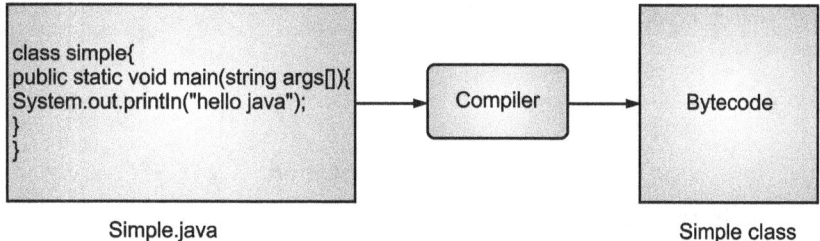

Simple.java   Simple class

Fig. 3.3 : Internal details of hello Java program

What Happens at Runtime?

- At runtime, following steps are performed:

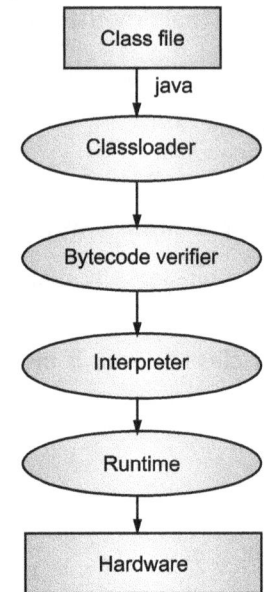

Fig. 3.4 Java runtime execution steps

- **Classloader:**

Classloader is the subsystem of JVM that is used to load class files.

- **Bytecode Verifier:**

Bytecode Verifier checks the code fragments for illegal code that can violate access right to objects.

- **Interpreter:**

Interpreter read bytecode stream then execute the instructions.

Can you save a Java source file by other name than the class name?

Yes, if the class is not public. It is explained in the Fig. 3.5 given below:

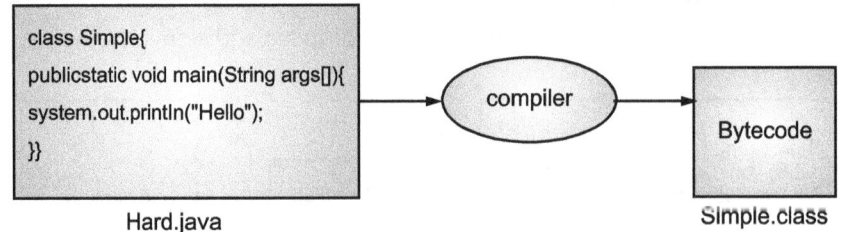

Fig. 3.5 : Java compilation

To Compile: Javac Hard.Java

To Execute: Java Simple

Can you have multiple classes in a Java source file?

Yes, like the Fig. 3.6 given below illustrates:

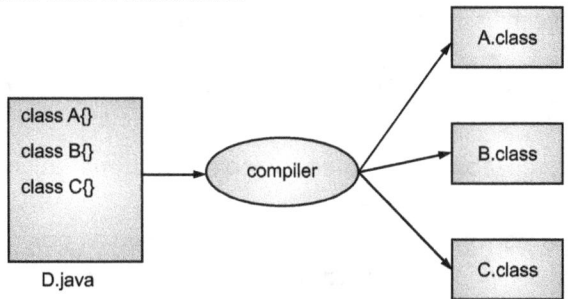

Fig. 3.6 : Example of multiple classes in a Java source file

3.7 JAVA OOPS CONCEPTS

- Object Oriented Programming is a paradigm that provides many concepts such as inheritance, data binding, polymorphism etc.
- Simula is considered as the first object-oriented programming language. The programming paradigm where everything is represented as an object, is known as truly object-oriented programming language.
- Smalltalk is considered as the first truly object-oriented programming language.
- Object-Oriented Programming is a methodology or paradigm to design a program using classes and objects. It simplifies the software development and maintenance by providing some concepts:
  - ➤ Object
  - ➤ Class
  - ➤ Inheritance
  - ➤ Polymorphism
  - ➤ Abstraction
  - ➤ Encapsulation

Object

- Object is a real word entity such as pen, chair, table etc. Any entity that has state and behavior is known as an object.
- For example: chair, pen, table, keyboard, bike etc. It can be physical and logical.

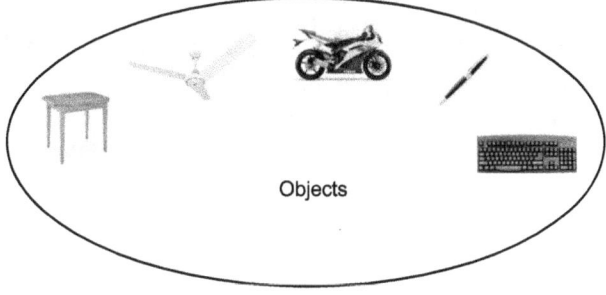

Fig. 3.7 Object

Class
- It is a User defined entity.
- Collection of objects is called class. It is a logical entity.

Inheritance
- When one object acquires all the properties and behaviours of parent object is called as inheritance.
- It provides code reusability. It is used to achieve runtime polymorphism.

Polymorphism
- When one task is performed by different ways known as polymorphism.
- For example: to convince the customer differently, to draw something e.g. shape or rectangle etc.
- In Java, we use method overloading and method overriding to achieve polymorphism.
- Another example can be to speak something e.g. cat speaks meaw, dog barks woof etc.

Abstraction
- Hiding internal details and showing functionality is known as abstraction.
- For example: phone call, we don't know the internal processing.
- In Java, we use abstract class and interface to achieve abstraction.

Encapsulation
- Binding or wrapping code and data together into a single unit is known as encapsulation.
- For example: capsule, it is wrapped with different medicines.

Fig. 3.8: Capsule

- A Java class is the example of encapsulation. Java bean is the fully encapsulated class because all the data members are private here.

3.8 JAVA TOKENS

- Tokens are the various Java program elements which are identified by the compiler.
- A token is the smallest element of a program that is meaningful to the compiler.
- Tokens are the smallest unit of program there are five types of tokens.
  1. Reserve Word or Keywords
  2. Identifier
  3. Literals
  4. Operators
  5. Separators

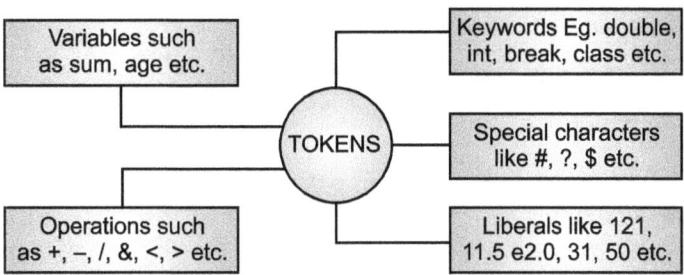

Fig. 3.9: Java tokens

- When you compile a program, the compiler scans the text in your source code and extracts individual tokens. While tokenizing the source file, the compiler recognizes and subsequently removes whitespaces (spaces, tabs, newline and form feeds) and the text enclosed within comments.

Example:

```
Public class Hello
{
    Public static void main(String args[])
    {
        System.out.println("Hello Java");
    }
}
```

- The source code contains tokens such as public, class, Hello, {, public, static, void, main, (, String, [], args, {, System, out, println, (, "Hello Java", }, }.

- The resulting tokens are compiled into Java bytecodes that is capable of being run from within an interpreted Java environment.

- Token are useful for compiler to detect errors.

- When tokens are not arranged in a particular sequence, the compiler generates an error message.

3.9 JAVA STATEMENTS

- A statement forms a complete unit of execution. The following types of expressions can be made into a statement by terminating the expression with a semicolon (;).

  (a) Assignment expressions

  (b) Any use of ++ or --

  (c) Method invocations

  (d) Object creation expressions

- Such statements are called expression statements.
- Here are some examples of expression statements.

  // assignment statement

  Value = 240;

  // increment statement

  Value++;

  // method invocation statement

  System.out.println("Hello World!");

  // object creation statement

  Bicycle myBike = new Bicycle();

- In addition to expression statements, there are two other kinds of statements: (i) declaration statements and (ii) control flow statements.
- A declaration statement declares a variable.

Example:

  // declaration statement

  double Value =240;

- Control flow statements regulate the order in which statements get executed.

3.10 CONSTANTS

- A constant in Java is used to map an exact and unchanging value to a variable name.
- Constants are used in programming to make code a bit more robust and human readable.

Example:

  public static final int MAX_UNITS = 25;

3.11 VARIABLES

- Variable is name of reserved area allocated in memory. In other words, it is a name of memory location.
- It is a combination of "vary + able" that means its value can be changed.
- int data=50;//Here data is variable

Types of Variable :

There are three types of variables in Java:

(1) Local variable

(2) Instance variable

(3) Static variable

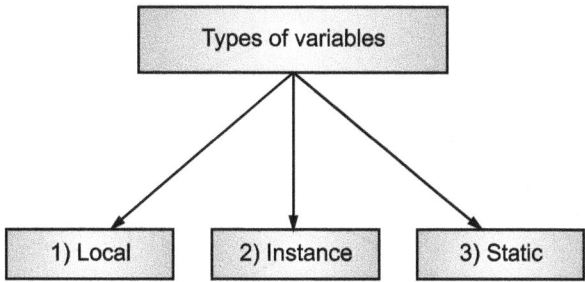

Fig. 3.10 Types of Variable

(1) Local Variable

A variable which is declared inside the method is called local variable.

(2) Instance Variable

A variable which is declared inside the class but outside the method, is called instance variable. It is not declared as static.

(3) Static Variable

A variable that is declared as static is called static variable. It cannot be local.

Example to Understand the Types of Variables in Java

```
class A
{
    int data=50;//instance variable
    static int m=100;//static variable
    void method()
    {
        int n=90;//local variable
    }
}   //end of class
```

3.12 DATA TYPES IN JAVA

Data types represent the different values to be stored in the variable. In Java, there are two types of data types:

(1) Primitive data types

(2) Non-primitive data types

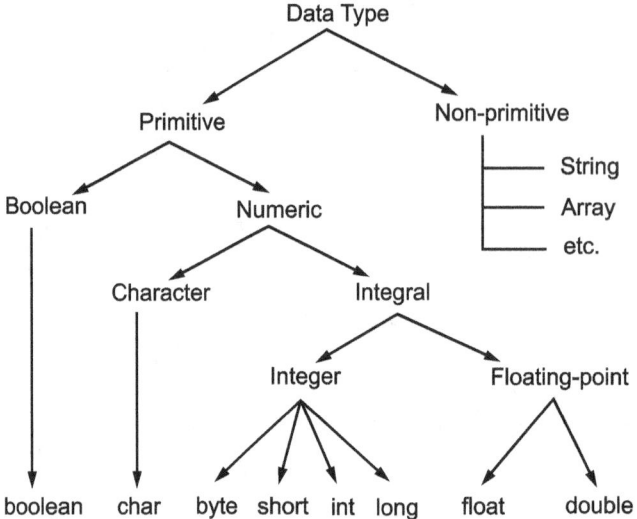

Fig. 3.11 : Data types in Java

Table 3.1 shows datatypes with default value and size.

Table 3.1 : Datatypes with default value and size

Data Type	Default Value	Default size
boolean	false	1 bit
char	'\u0000'	2 byte
byte	0	1 byte
short	0	2 byte
int	0	4 byte
long	0L	8 byte
float	0.0f	4 byte
double	0.0d	8 byte

Why Char Uses 2 Byte in Java and What is \u0000?

- It is because Java uses Unicode system than ASCII code system. The \u0000 is the lowest range of Unicode system.

Unicode System:

- Unicode is a universal international standard character encoding that is capable of representing most of the world's written languages.

3.12.1 Primitive Data Types

- Primitive data types are those whose variables allows us to store only one value but they never allows us to store multiple values of same type.

- This is a data type whose variable can hold maximum one value at a time.

Example:

```
int a; // valid
a=10; // valid
a=10, 20, 30; // invalid
```

Here "a" store only one value at a time because it is primitive type variable.

3.12.2 User Defined Data Types

- User defined data types are those which are developed by programmers by making use of appropriate features of the language.
- User defined data types related variables allows us to store multiple values either of same type or different type or both.
- This is a data type whose variable can hold more than one value of dissimilar type, in Java it is achieved using class concept.
- In Java both derived and user defined data type combined name as reference data type.
- In C language, user defined data types can be developed by using struct, union, enum etc.
- In Java programming, user defined datatype can be developed by using the features of classes and interfaces.

Example:

```
Student s = new Student();
```

- In Java we have eight data type which are organized in four groups. They are

  (1) Integer category data types

  (2) Character category data types

  (3) Float category data types

  (4) Boolean category data types

(1) Integer Category Data Types:

- These category data types are used for storing integer data in the main memory of computer by allocating sufficient amount of memory space.
- Integer category data types are divided into four types which are given in following Table 3.2.

Table 3.2 : Integer Category Data Types in Java

Data Type	Size	Range	
1	Byte	1	+ 127 to -128
2	Short	2	+ 32767 to -32768
3	Int	4	+ x to - (x+1)
4	Long	8	+ y to - (y+1)

(2) Character Category Data Types:

- A character is an identifier which is enclosed within single quotes.

- In Java to represent character data, we use a data type called char. This data type takes two bytes since it follows Unicode character set.

Table 3.3 : Character Category Datatypes

Data Type	Size(Byte)	Range
Char	2	232767 to -32768

- Java support more than 18 international languages so Java take 2 bytes for characters, because for 18 international language 1 byte of memory is not sufficient for storing all characters and symbols present in 18 languages.

- Java supports Unicode but C support ASCII code. In ASCII code only English language are present, so for storing all English letters and symbols 1 byte is sufficient.

- Unicode character set is one which contains all the characters which are available in 18 international languages and it contains 65536 characters.

(3) Float Category Data Types:

- Float category data type are used for representing float values. This category contains two data types, they are in the given table 3.4.

Table 3.4 : Float Category Data Types

Data Type	Size	Range	Number of Decimal Places
Float	4	+2147483647 to -2147483648	8
Double	8	+ 9.223*1018	16

(4) Boolean Category Data Types:

- Boolean category data type is used for representing or storing logical values is true or false.

- In Java programming to represent Boolean values or logical values, we use a data type called Boolean.

- Boolean data type takes zero bytes of main memory space because Boolean data type of Java implemented by Sun Micro System with a concept of flip - flop.

- A flip - flop is a general purpose register which stores one bit of information (one true and zero false).

Table 3.5 : Boolean Category Data Type

Data Type	Default Value	Default size
boolean	false	1 bit

3.12.3 Differences between Primitive Data Types and User Defined Data Types

- Primitive data types are also known as basic data types. Those data types which are not derived from others. For e.g. int , float, double etc. are known as primitive data types .

- User defined datatypes are data types whose name can be defined by users. For e.g. struct(structure) ,pointers ,enums etc .

- Primitive data types include integer, character, float etc which are defined already inside the language i.e, user can use these data types without defining them inside the language.

- User defined data types are the data types which user has to define while or before using them. For e.g. in C language, structure and union are used as user-defined data types.

3.12.4 Signed Vs. Unsigned Data Type

- Java does not support unsigned data types.

- The byte, short, int and long are all signed data types.

- For a signed data type, half of the range of values stores positive number and half for negative numbers, as one bit is used to store the sign of the value.

- For example, a byte takes 8 bits; its range is -128 to 127. If you were to store only positive numbers in a byte, its range would have been 0 to 255.

- Java has some static methods in wrapper classes to support operations treating the bits in the signed values as if they are unsigned integers.

- The following code shows how to get the value stored in a byte as an unsigned integer:

Program 3.1 : Signed and Unsigned Integer

```
public class Main
{
  public static void main(String[] args)
    {
        byte b = -10;
        int x = Byte.toUnsignedInt(b);
        System.out.println("Signed value in byte  = " + b);
        System.out.println("Unsigned value in  byte  = " + x);
    }
}
```

Output:

Signed value in byte =-10

Unsigned value in byte = 246

3.13 DECLARATION OF VARIABLES

- All variables must be declared before they can be used.

- How to declare a variable ?
  1. Choose the type you need.
  2. Choose a name for the variable.
  3. Use the following format for a declaration statement:
        datatype variable identifier;
  4. You may declare more than one variable of the same type by separating the variable names with commas.
        int age, weight, height;
  5. You may initialize a variable (place a value into the variable location) in a declaration statement.
        double mass = 3.45;

- When you declare a variable, Java reserves memory locations of sufficient size to store the variable type. The actual data values will be stored in these memory locations.

- Variables that are not initialized are NOT empty. If you do not initialize your variables, they will contain garbage values left over from the program that last used the memory they occupy, until such time as the program places a value at that memory location.

- Java will allow you to declare a variable anywhere in the program as long as the variable is declared before you use it.

- A good programming practice is to declare variables near the top of the program. Declaring variables in this manner makes for easier readability of the program.

3.14 GIVING VALUE TO VARIABLES

- Giving value to variable means assigning value to declared variable.

Example:

```
public class VarTry
{
   public static void main(String[] argv)
   {
      int i;// declares integer variable named i
      i = 9; // gives i the value 9
```

```
        System.out.println(i);// print the value of i to the screen
    }
}
```

- As shown in above program, The line i = 9 gives the value 9 to variable i. This is known as assigning a value to a variable -- i is assigned the value 9.

- It means that the space in the computer's memory associated with i now holds this value.

- The first time a variable is assigned a value, it is said to be initialised. The = symbol is known as the assignment operator.

- It is also possible to declare a variable and assign it a value in the same line, so instead of int i and then i = 9 you can write int i = 9 all in one go.

- If you have more than one variable of the same type you can also declare them together e.g.

    int i, j;   // or

    int i=1, j, k=2;

3.15 SCOPE OF VARIABLES

- Scope of a variable is the part of the program where the variable is accessible. Like C/C++, in Java, scope of a variable can be determined at compiler time and independent of function call stack.

- Java programs are organized in the form of classes. Every class is part of some package.

Some Important Points about Variable Scope in Java:

- In general, a set of curly brackets { } defines a scope.

- In Java, we can usually access a variable as long as it was defined within the same set of brackets as the code we are writing or within any curly brackets inside of the curly brackets where the variable was defined.

- Any variable defined in a class outside of any method can be used by all member methods.

- When a method has same local variable as a member, this keyword can be used to reference the current class variable.

- For a variable to be read after the termination of a loop, It must be declared before the body of the loop.

Java scope rules can be covered under following categories.

1. Member Variables (Class Level Scope)

These variables must be declared inside class, outside any function. They can be directly accessed anywhere in class.

Example:

```
public class Test
{
    // All variables defined directly inside a class
    // are member variables
    int a;
    private String b
    void method1() {....}
    int method2() {....}
    char c;
}
```

We can declare class variables anywhere in class, but outside methods.

Access specified of member variables doesn't effect scope of them within a class.

Member variables can be accessed outside a class with following rules

Modifier	Package	Subclass	World
Public	Yes	Yes	Yes
Protected	Yes	Yes	No
Default (no modifier)	Yes	No	No
Private	No	No	No

2. Local Variables (Method Level Scope)

- Variables declared inside a method have method level scope and can't be accessed outside the method.

```
public class Test
{
    void method1()
    {
        // Local variable (Method level scope)
        int x;
    }
}
```

Local variables don't exist after method's execution is over.

3. Loop Variables (Block Scope)

- A variable declared inside pair of brackets "{" and "}" in a method has scope within the brackets only.

Example: Consider following program with for loop.

```
class Test
{
   public static void main(String args[])
   {
      for (int x=0; x<4; x++)
      {
         System.out.println(x);
      }


      // Will produce error
      System.out.println(x);
   }
}
```

Output:

11: error: cannot find symbol

    System.out.println(x);   ^

The right way of doing above is,

```
// Above program after correcting the error
class Test
{
   public static void main(String args[])
   {
      int x;
      for (x=0; x<4; x++)
      {
         System.out.println(x);
      }
```

```
    System.out.println(x);
  }
}
```

Output:

    0
    1
    2
    3
    4

3.16 ARRAY

- Array is a collection of similar type of elements that have contiguous memory location.

- Java array is an object that contains elements of similar data type. It is a data structure where we store similar elements. We can store only fixed set of elements in a Java array.

- Array in Java is an index based, first element of the array is stored at 0 index.

- Instead of declaring individual variables, such as number0, number1, ..., and number99, you declare one array variable such as numbers and use numbers[0], numbers[1], and ..., numbers[99] to represent individual variables.

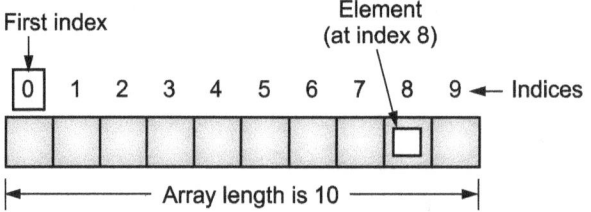

Fig. 3.12 : Array

Advantage of Java Array:

- **Random Access:** We can get any data located at any index position.

- **Code Optimization:** It makes the code optimized, we can retrieve or sort the data easily.

Disadvantage of Java Array:

Size Limit: We can store only fixed size of elements in the array. It doesn't grow its size at runtime. To solve this problem, collection framework is used in Java.

Declaring Array Variables:

- To use an array in a program, you must declare a variable to reference the array, and you must specify the type of array the variable can reference. Here is the syntax for declaring an array variable

Syntax:

```
dataType[] arrayRefVar;  // preferred way.
   or
dataType arrayRefVar[];  // works but not preferred way.
```

Note: The style **dataType[] arrayRefVar** is preferred. The style **dataType arrayRefVar[]** comes from the C/C++ language and was adopted in Java to accommodate C/C++ programmers.

Example:

- The following code snippets are examples of this syntax:

```
double[] myList;  // preferred way.
   or
double myList[];  // works but not preferred way.
```

Creating Arrays:

- You can create an array by using the new operator with the following syntax:

Syntax:

```
arrayRefVar = new dataType[arraySize];
```

The above statement does two things:

(i) It creates an array using new dataType[arraySize].

(ii) It assigns the reference of the newly created array to the variable arrayRefVar.

- Declaring an array variable, creating an array, and assigning the reference of the array to the variable can be combined in one statement, as shown below –

```
dataType[] arrayRefVar = new dataType[arraySize];
```

- Alternatively you can create arrays as follows:

```
dataType[] arrayRefVar = {value0, value1, ..., valuek};
```

- The array elements are accessed through the **index**. Array indices are 0-based; that is, they start from 0 to **arrayRefVar.length-1**.

Example:

- Following statement declares an array variable, myList, creates an array of 10 elements of double type and assigns its reference to myList –

```
double[] myList = new double[10];
```

- Following Fig. 3.13 represents array myList. Here, myList holds ten double values and the indices are from 0 to 9.

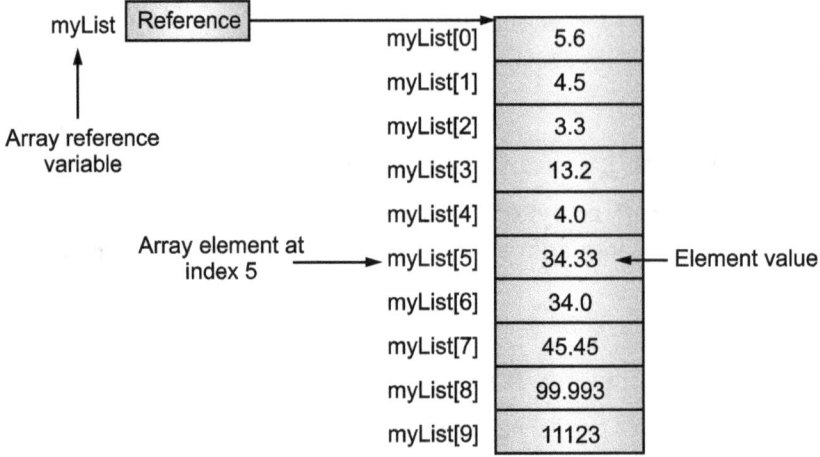

Fig. 3.13 : Array declaration

Types of Array in Java:

There are two types of array.

(i)   Single Dimensional Array

(ii) Multidimensional Array

3.16.1 Single Dimensional Array in Java

Syntax to Declare an Array in Java:

- dataType[] arr; (or)

- dataType []arr; (or)

- dataType arr[];

Instantiation of an Array in Java

    arrayRefVar=new datatype[size];

Example of Single Dimensional Java Array:

- Let's see the Program 3.2 of Java array, where we are going to declare, instantiate, initialize and traverse an array.

Program 3.2 :

```
class Testarray
{
    public static void main(String args[])
    {
        int a[]=new int[5];//declaration and instantiation
```

```
        a[0]=10;//initialization
        a[1]=20;
        a[2]=70;
        a[3]=40;
        a[4]=50;
        //printing array
        for(int i=0;i<a.length;i++)//length is the property of array
        System.out.println(a[i]);
    }
}
```

Output:

10

20

70

40

50

Declaration, Instantiation and Initialization of Java Array

- We can declare, instantiate and initialize the Java array together by:

  int a[]={33,3,4,5};//declaration, instantiation and initialization

- Let's see the simple example to print this array.

Program 3.3 : Simple Example to Print this Array

```
class Testarray1
{
    public static void main(String args[])
    {
        int a[]={33,3,4,5};//declaration, instantiation and initialization
        //printing array
        for(int i=0;i<a.length;i++)//length is the property of array
        System.out.println(a[i]);
    }
}
```

Output:

33

3

4

5

Passing Array to Method in Java:

- We can pass the Java array to method so that we can reuse the same logic on any array.
- Let's see the simple example to get minimum number of an array using method.

Program 3.4 : Simple Example to Get Minimum Number of an Array Using Method

```java
class Testarray2
{
    static void min(int arr[])
    {
        int min=arr[0];
        for(int i=1;i<arr.length;i++)
         if(min>arr[i])
          min=arr[i];
        System.out.println(min);
    }
    public static void main(String args[])
    {
            int a[]={33,3,4,5};
            min(a);//passing array to method
    }
}
```

Output:

3

3.16.2 Multidimensional Array in Java

- In such case, data is stored in row and column based index. It is also known as matrix form.

Syntax to Declare Multidimensional Array in Java

```java
    dataType[][] arrayRefVar; (or)
    dataType [][]arrayRefVar; (or)
    dataType arrayRefVar[][]; (or)
    dataType []arrayRefVar[];
```

Example to Instantiate Multidimensional Array in Java:

```
int[][] arr=new int[3][3];//3 row and 3 column
```

Example to Initialize Multidimensional Array in Java:

```
arr[0][0]=1;
arr[0][1]=2;
arr[0][2]=3;
arr[1][0]=4;
arr[1][1]=5;
arr[1][2]=6;
arr[2][0]=7;
arr[2][1]=8;
arr[2][2]=9;
```

Example of Multidimensional Java Array:

Program 3.5 : To Declare, Instantiate, Initialize and Print the Two Dimensional Array.

```java
class Testarray3
{
    public static void main(String args[])
    {
        //declaring and initializing 2D array
        int arr[][]={{1,2,3},{2,4,5},{4,4,5}};
        //printing 2D array
        for(int i=0;i<3;i++)
        {
            for(int j=0;j<3;j++)
            {
                System.out.print(arr[i][j]+" ");
            }
            System.out.println();
        }
    }
}
```

Output:

1 2 3

2 4 5

4 4 5

3.16.3 Alternative Array Declaration Syntax

- Here, the square brackets follow the type specifier, not the name of the array variable. For example, the following two declarations are equivalent:

```
int al[] = new int[3];
int[] a2 = new int[3];
```

- The following declarations are also equivalent:

```
char twod1[][] = new char[3][4];
char[][] twod2 = new char[3][4];
```

- This alternative declaration form offers convenience when declaring several arrays at the same time:

```
int[] nums, nums2, nums3; // create three arrays
```

3.17 SYMBOLIC CONSTANTS

- symbolic constants are named constants like :
  final double PI = 3.14 ;

- They are constants because of the 'final' keywords, so they cannot be reassigned a new value after being declared as final and they are symbolic, because they have a name. A non symbolic constant is like the value of '2' in expression
  int a = 2 * 3

3.18 TYPECASTING

- Assigning a value of one type to a variable of another type is known as Typecasting.

Example :

```
int x = 10;
byte y = (byte)x;
```

- The process of converting one data type to another is called casting. Casting is often necessary when a function returns a data of type in different form then we need to perform an operation.

- For example, the read() member function of the standard input stream (System.in) returns an int. If we want to store data of type int returned by read() into a variable of char type, we need to cast it :

```
char k = (char)System.in.read();
```

- The cast is performed by placing the desired type in parentheses to the left of the value to be converted. The System.in.read() function call returns an int value, which then is cast to a char value because of the (char) cast. The resulting char value is then stored in the char variable k.

```java
class IntToByteConversion
{
  public static void main(String arg[])
  {
    int a = 350;
    byte b;

    b = (byte) a;

    System.out.println("b = " + b );

  }
}
```

Output :

b = 94

- When a value of larger size in the 350 is casted into a byte whose range is -128 to 127, it is narrowed down to fit into that range. So, the value becomes 94 from 350.
  We need to be careful with this kind of conversion, since if the destination type range cannot store the source value it is shortened and possibly loses the data.

3.19 STANDARD DEFAULT VALUES

Standard default values in Java as follows :

Table 3.6 : Standard Default Value

Data Type	Default Value
byte	0
short	0
int	0
long	0L
float	0.0f
double	0.0d
char	'u0000'
String (or any object)	null
boolean	false

Example will illustrate Default Value Stored in Each Primitive Data Type Variable

Program 3.6 : Default Value Stored in each Primitive Data Type Variable

```java
public class DefaultValue
{
  static boolean bool;
  static byte by;
  static char ch;
  static double d;
  static float f;
  static int i;
  static long l;
  static short sh;
  static String str;

  public static void main(String[] args)
  {
    System.out.println("Bool :" + bool);
    System.out.println("Byte :" + by);
    System.out.println("Character:" + ch);
    System.out.println("Double :" + d);
    System.out.println("Float :" + f);
    System.out.println("Integer :" + i);
    System.out.println("Long :" + l);
    System.out.println("Short :" + sh);
    System.out.println("String :" + str);
  }
}
```

Output :

Bool   : false

Byte   : 0

Character:

Double : 0.0

Float   : 0.0

Integer : 0

Long   : 0

Short   : 0

String : null

3.20 OPERATORS

We can divide all the Java operators into the following groups:

1. Arithmetic Operators
2. Relational Operators
3. Bitwise Operators
4. Logical Operators
5. Assignment Operators
6. Miscellaneous Operators

1. Arithmetic Operators :

- Arithmetic operators are used in mathematical expressions in the same way that they are used in algebra.
- The following table 3.7 lists the arithmetic operators −Assume integer variable A holds 10 and variable B holds 20, then

Table 3.7 : Arithmetic Operators

Operator	Description	Example
+ (Addition)	Adds values on either side of the operator.	A + B will give 30
- (Subtraction)	Subtracts right-hand operand from left-hand operand.	A - B will give -10
* (Multiplication)	Multiplies values on either side of the operator.	A * B will give 200
/ (Division)	Divides left-hand operand by right-hand operand.	B / A will give 2
% (Modulus)	Divides left-hand operand by right-hand operand and returns remainder.	B % A will give 0
++ (Increment)	Increases the value of operand by 1.	B++ gives 21
-- (Decrement)	Decreases the value of operand by 1.	B-- gives 19

2. Relational Operators

- There are following relational operators supported by Java language.
- Assume variable A holds 10 and variable B holds 20, then

Table 3.8 : Relational Operators

Operator	Description	Example
== (equal to)	Checks if the values of two operands are equal or not, if yes then condition becomes true.	(A == B) is not true.
!= (not equal to)	Checks if the values of two operands are equal or not, if values are not equal then condition becomes true.	(A != B) is true.
> (greater than)	Checks if the value of left operand is greater than the value of right operand, if yes then condition becomes true.	(A > B) is not true.
< (less than)	Checks if the value of left operand is less than the value of right operand, if yes then condition becomes true.	(A < B) is true.
>= (greater than or equal to)	Checks if the value of left operand is greater than or equal to the value of right operand, if yes then condition becomes true.	(A >= B) is not true.
<= (less than or equal to)	Checks if the value of left operand is less than or equal to the value of right operand, if yes then condition becomes true.	(A <= B) is true.

3. **Bitwise Operators**

- Java defines several bitwise operators, which can be applied to the integer types, long, int, short, char, and byte.
- Bitwise operator works on bits and performs bit-by-bit operation.
- The following table 3.9 lists the bitwise operators. Assume integer variable A holds 60 and variable B holds 13 then

Table 3.9 : Bitwise Operators

Operator	Description	Example
& (bitwise and)	Binary AND Operator copies a bit to the result if it exists in both operands.	(A & B) will give 12 which is 0000 1100
| (bitwise or)	Binary OR Operator copies a bit if it exists in either operand.	(A | B) will give 61 which is 0011 1101
^ (bitwise XOR)	Binary XOR Operator copies the bit if it is set in one operand but not both.	(A ^ B) will give 49 which is 0011 0001
~ (bitwise compliment)	Binary Ones Complement Operator is unary and has the effect of 'flipping' bits.	(~A) will give -61 which is 1100 0011 in 2's complement form due to a signed binary number.
<< (left shift)	Binary Left Shift Operator. The left operands value is moved left by the number of bits specified by the right operand.	A << 2 will give 240 which is 1111 0000
>> (right shift)	Binary Right Shift Operator. The left operands value is moved right by the number of bits specified by the right operand.	A >> 2 will give 15 which is 1111
>>> (zero fill right shift)	Shift right zero fill operator. The left operands value is moved right by the number of bits specified by the right operand and shifted values are filled up with zeros.	A >>>2 will give 15 which is 0000 1111

4. Logical Operators

- The following table 3.10 lists the logical operators Assume Boolean variables A holds true and variable B holds false, then

Table 3.10 : Logical Operators

Operator	Description	Example
&& (logical and)	Called Logical AND operator. If both the operands are non-zero, then the condition becomes true.	(A && B) is false
|| (logical or)	Called Logical OR Operator. If any of the two operands are non-zero, then the condition becomes true.	(A || B) is true
! (logical not)	Called Logical NOT Operator. Use to reverses the logical state of its operand. If a condition is true then Logical NOT operator will make false.	!(A && B) is true

5. **Assignment Operators**

- Following table 3.11 are the assignment operators supported by Java language

Table 3.11 : Assignment Operators

Operator	Description	Example
=	Simple assignment operator. Assigns values from right side operands to left side operand.	C = A + B will assign value of A + B into C
+=	Add AND assignment operator. It adds right operand to the left operand and assign the result to left operand.	C += A is equivalent to C = C + A
-=	Subtract AND assignment operator. It subtracts right operand from the left operand and assign the result to left operand.	C -= A is equivalent to C = C – A
*=	Multiply AND assignment operator. It multiplies right operand with the left operand and assign the result to left operand.	C *= A is equivalent to C = C * A
/=	Divide AND assignment operator. It divides left operand with the right operand and assign the result to left operand.	C /= A is equivalent to C = C / A

...Conti.

%=	Modulus AND assignment operator.	C %= A is equivalent to C = C % A

	It takes modulus using two operands and assign the result to left operand.	
<<=	Left shift AND assignment operator.	C <<= 2 is same as C = C << 2
>>=	Bitwise AND assignment operator.	C >>= 2 is same as C = C >> 2
&=	Right shift AND assignment operator.	C &= 2 is same as C = C & 2
^=	bitwise exclusive OR and assignment operator.	C ^= 2 is same as C = C ^ 2
|=	bitwise inclusive OR and assignment operator.	C |= 2 is same as C = C | 2

6. Miscellaneous Operators

- There are few other operators supported by Java Language.

(a) Conditional Operator (? :)

- Conditional operator is also known as the ternary operator. This operator consists of three operands and is used to evaluate Boolean expressions.
- The goal of the operator is to decide, which value should be assigned to the variable. The operator is written as :

variable x = (expression) ? value if true : value if false

Following is an example :

```
public class Test
{

  public static void main(String args[])
    {

                int a, b;
                a = 10;
  b = (a == 1) ? 20: 30;
                System.out.println( "Value of b is : " + b );


                b = (a == 10) ? 20: 30;
```

```
                    System.out.println( "Value of b is : " + b );
    }
}
```

Output :

Value of b is : 30

Value of b is : 20

(b) instanceof Operator

- This operator is used only for object reference variables.

- The operator checks whether the object is of a particular type.

- instanceof operator is written as :

(Object reference variable) instanceof (class/interface type)

- If the object referred by the variable on the left side of the operator passes the IS-A check for the class/interface type on the right side, then the result will be true. Following is an example –

Program 3.7 :

```
public class Test
{

  public static void main(String args[])
  {

    String name = "abc";

    // following will return true since name is type of String
    boolean result = name instanceof String;
    System.out.println( result );
  }
}
```

Output :

true

- This operator will still return true, if the object being compared is the assignment compatible with the type on the right.

3.21 EXPRESSIONS

- Expression is a construct made up of variables, operators, and method invocations, which are constructed according to the syntax of the language, that evaluates to a single value.

- Expressions perform operations on data and move data around.

- The data type of the value returned by an expression depends on the elements used in the expression.

- The Java programming language allows you to construct compound expressions from various smaller expressions as long as the data type required by one part of the expression matches the data type of the other.

- Example of a compound expression :

      1 * 2 * 3

- In this particular example, the order in which the expression is evaluated is unimportant because the result of multiplication is independent of order, the outcome is always the same, no matter in which order you apply the multiplications.

- However, this is not true of all expressions. For example, the following expression gives different results, depending on whether you perform the addition or the division operation first:

  x + y / 100   // ambiguous

- You can specify exactly how an expression will be evaluated using balanced parenthesis: ( ).

- For example, to make the previous expression unambiguous, you could write the following:

  (x + y) / 100 // unambiguous, recommended

- If you don't explicitly indicate the order for the operations to be performed, the order is determined by the precedence assigned to the operators in use within the expression.

- Operators that have a higher precedence get evaluated first.

- For example, the division operator has a higher precedence than does the addition operator. Therefore, the following two statements are equivalent:

      x + y / 100

  x + (y / 100) // unambiguous, recommended

- When writing compound expressions, be explicit and indicate with parentheses which operators should be evaluated first. This practice makes code easier to read and to maintain.

3.22 TYPE CONVERSION IN EXPRESSIONS

- Operators work on the same data type. However, Java has wide variety of data types from which we can choose the suitable for a particular purpose.

- To perform the operation on variables from two different types of data we have to convert both types to the same.

- All expressions in the Java language have type. This type can be derived from structure of the expression and the types variables and literals used in the expression.

- It is possible to write an expression that is inappropriate for the type context. In some cases, this will lead to an error in compilation of the program, but in other context can accept type which is similar or related to the type of the expression. In this case, the program carry secret type conversion.

Converted to Java by Type into Two Categories:

1. Covert transformation.
2. Explicit conversion.

Implicitly Type Conversion

- Implicit type conversion is only possible when there is no possibility of data loss in the conversion that is when you convert type to a smaller range to type with greater. For example from int to long.

- To make implicit conversion is not need to use any operator, so called hidden.
  The conversion is done automatically by the compiler when mapping value of small-scale variable in a larger scope, or when expression types has a different scope. Then convert it to type with a greater range.

Example :

```
int VarInt = 5;
System.out.println(VarInt); // 5
long Varlong = VarInt;
System.out.println(Varlong); // 5
System.out.println(Varlong + VarInt); // 10
```

1. **Explicitly Type Conversion**

- Explicit type conversion is needed when it is probable loss of data. When you convert a floating-point type to an integer type, there is always loss of data coming from the float and must use explicit conversion (double to long).

- To make such conversion it is necessary to explicitly use operator for data conversion (cast operator): (type). Possibly there may be data loss also when converting from type larger range to type with less (double to float or long to int).

Example :

```
double VarDouble = 5.1d;
System.out.println(VarDouble); // 5.1
long Varlong = (long)VarDouble;
System.out.println(Varlong); // 5
VarDouble = 5e9d; // 5 * 10^9
System.out.println(VarDouble); // 5.0E9
int VarInt = (int) VarDouble;
System.out.println(VarInt); // 2147483647
System.out.println(Integer.MAX_VALUE); // 2147483647
```

- The first line of the example you assign a value to the variable 5.1 VarDouble. Once you convert it by the operator (long) long to type and print the console variable Varlong, we see that the variable is the value lost after float (for long to integer). Then on the seventh row Assign variable VarDouble 5 billion.

- Finally convert VarDouble to int by the operator (int) and print variable VarInt. Then same result as when print Integer MAX_VALUE, this is because VarDouble incorporates more value of the range of int.

3.23 OPERATOR PRECEDENCE AND ASSOCIATIVITY

- Java operators have two properties those are precedence, and associativity.

- Precedence is the priority order of an operator, if there are two or more operators in an expression then the operator of highest priority will be executed first then higher, and then high.

- For example, in expression 1 + 2 * 5, multiplication (*) operator will be processed first and then addition. It's because multiplication has higher priority or precedence than addition.

- What if all operators in an expression have same priority? In that case the second property associated with an operator comes into play, which is associativity.

- Associativity tells the direction of execution of operators that can be either left to right or right to left.

- For example, in expression a = b = c = 8 the assignment operator is executed from right to left that means c will be assigned by 8, then b will be assigned by c, and finally a will be assigned by b. You can parenthesize this expression as (a = (b = (c = 8))).

- Following table 3.12 presents all Java operators from highest to lowest precedence along with their associativity.

Table 3.12 : Java Operators

Java operators - precedence chart highest to lowest			
Precedence	**Operator**	**Description**	**Associativity**
1	[] () .	array index method call member access	Left -> Right
2	++ -- + - ~ !	pre or postfix increment pre or postfix decrement unary plus, minus bitwise NOT logical NOT	Right -> Left
3	(type cast) new	type cast object creation	Right -> Left
4	* / %	multiplication division modulus (remainder)	Left -> Right
5	+ - +	addition, subtraction string concatenation	Left -> Right
6	<< >> >>>	left shift signed right shift unsigned or zero-fill right shift	Left -> Right
7	< <= > >= instanceof	less than less than or equal to greater than greater than or equal to reference test	Left -> Right
8	== !=	equal to not equal to	Left -> Right
9	&	bitwise AND	Left -> Right
10	^	bitwise XOR	Left -> Right
11	|	bitwise OR	Left -> Right
12	&&	logical AND	Left -> Right
13	||	logical OR	Left -> Right
14	? :	conditional (ternary)	Right -> Left

...Conti.

15	=	assignment and short hand	Right -> Left

	+=	assignment operators	
	-=		
	*=		
	/=		
	%=		
	&=		
	^=		
	|=		
	<<=		
	>>=		
	>>>=		

3.24 MATHEMATICAL FUNCTIONS

- The Java.lang.Math class contains methods for performing basic numeric operations such as the elementary exponential, logarithm, square root, and trigonometric functions.

Following is the declaration for Java.lang.Math class:

Public final class Math extends Object

Following are the fields for Java.lang.Math class:

- **static double E** -This is the double value that is closer than any other to e, the base of the natural logarithms.

- **static double PI** -This is the double value that is closer than any other to pi, the ratio of the circumference of a circle to its diameter.

Class Methods

Sr. No.	Method	Description
1	static double abs(double a)	This method returns the absolute value of a double value.
2	static float abs(float a)	This method returns the absolute value of a float value.
3	static int abs(int a)	This method returns the absolute value of an int value.
4	static long abs(long a)	This method returns the absolute value of a long value.

...Conti.

| 5 | static double acos(double a) | This method returns the arc cosine of a |

		value; the returned angle is in the range 0.0 through pi.
6	static double asin(double a)	This method returns the arc sine of a value; the returned angle is in the range -pi/2 through pi/2.
7	static double atan(double a)	This method returns the arc tangent of a value; the returned angle is in the range -pi/2 through pi/2.
8	static double atan2(double y, double x)	This method returns the angle theta from the conversion of rectangular coordinates (x, y) to polar coordinates (r, theta).
9	static double cbrt(double a)	This method returns the cube root of a double value.
10	static double ceil(double a)	This method returns the smallest (closest to negative infinity) double value that is greater than or equal to the argument and is equal to a mathematical integer.
11	static double copySign(double magnitude, double sign)	This method returns the first floating-point argument with the sign of the second floating-point argument.
12	static float copySign(float magnitude, float sign)	This method returns the first floating-point argument with the sign of the second floating-point argument.
13	static double cos(double a)	This method returns the trigonometric cosine of an angle.
14	static double cosh(double x)	This method returns the hyperbolic cosine of a double value.
15	static double exp(double a)	This method returns Euler's number e raised to the power of a double value.
16	static double expm1(double x)	This method returns $e^x - 1$.

...Conti.

17	static double floor(double a)	This method returns the largest

		(closest to positive infinity) double value that is less than or equal to the argument and is equal to a mathematical integer.
18	static int getExponent(double d)	This method returns the unbiased exponent used in the representation of a double.
19	static int getExponent(float f)	This method returns the unbiased exponent used in the representation of a float.
20	static double hypot(double x, double y)	This method returns $sqrt(x^2 + y^2)$ without intermediate overflow or underflow.

3.25 CONTROL STATEMENT

- A program executes from top to bottom except when we use control statements, we can control the order of execution of the program, based on logic and values.

- In Java, control statements can be divided into the following three categories:

  (1) Selection Statements

  (2) Iteration Statements

  (3) Jump Statements

3.25.1 Selection Statements

Selection statements allow you to control the flow of program execution on the basis of the outcome of an expression or state of a variable known during runtime.

Selection statements can be divided into the following categories:

- The if and if-else statements

- The if-else statements

- The if-else-if statements

- The switch statements

- The Nested switch statements

The if Statements:

- The first contained statement that can be a block of an if statement only executes when the specified condition is true.

- If the condition is false and there is not else keyword, then the first contained statement will be skipped and execution continues with the rest of the program.
- The condition is an expression that returns a Boolean value.

Example:

```
import Java.util.Scanner;
public class IfDemo
{
    public static void main(String[] args)
    {
        int age;
        Scanner inputDevice = new Scanner(System.in);
        System.out.print("Please enter Age: ");
        age = inputDevice.nextInt();
        if(age > 18)
            System.out.println("above 18 ");
    }
}
```

Output:

Please enter Age: 19

above 18

The if-else Statements:

- In if-else statements, if the specified condition in the if statement is false, then the statement after the else keyword that can be a block will execute.

Example:

```
import Java.util.Scanner;
public class IfElseDemo
{
    public static void main( String[] args )
    {
        int age;
        Scanner inputDevice = new Scanner( System.in );
```

```
        System.out.print( "Please enter Age: " );
    age = inputDevice.nextInt();
        if ( age >= 18 )
            System.out.println( "above 18 " );
        else
            System.out.println( "below 18" );
    }
  }
```

Output:

Please enter Age: 11

below 18

The if-else-if Statements:

- if-else-if statements is also called as nested if else.
- This statement following the else keyword can be another if or if-else statement.

Syntax:

```
if(condition)
    statements;
else if (condition)
    statements;
else if(condition)
    statement;
else
    statements;
```

- Whenever the condition is true, the associated statement will be executed and the remaining conditions will be bypassed. If none of the conditions are true, then the else block will execute.

Example:

```
import Java.util.Scanner;
public class IfElseIfDemo
{
    public static void main( String[] args )
```

```
{
   int age;
   Scanner inputDevice = new Scanner( System.in );
   System.out.print( "Please enter Age: " );
   age = inputDevice.nextInt();
   if ( age >= 18 && age <=35 )
      System.out.println( "between 18-35 " );
   else if(age >35 && age <=60)
         System.out.println("between 36-60");
      else
         System.out.println( "not matched" );
   }
}
```

Output:

Please enter Age: 55

between 36-60

The Switch Statements:

- The switch statement is a multi-way branch statement.

- The switch statement of Java is another selection statement that defines multiple paths of execution of a program.

- It provides a better alternative than a large series of if-else-if statements.

Example:

```
import Java.util.Scanner;
public class SwitchDemo
{
   public static void main( String[] args )
   {
      int age;
      Scanner inputDevice = new Scanner( System.in );
      System.out.print( "Please enter Age: " );
      age = inputDevice.nextInt();
```

```
switch ( age )
{
    case 18:
        System.out.println( "age 18" );
        break;
    case 19:
            System.out.println( "age 19" );
            break;
        default:
            System.out.println( "not matched" );
            break;
    }
  }
}
```

Output :

Please enter Age: 19

age 19

- An expression must be of a type of byte, short, int or char. Each of the values specified in the case statement must be of a type compatible with the expression. Duplicate case values are not allowed.

- The break statement is used inside the switch to terminate a statement sequence. The break statement is optional in the switch statement.

The Nested Switch Statements :

- We can use a switch as part of the statement sequence of an outer switch. This is called a nested switch. Since a switch statement defines its own block, no conflicts arise between the case constants in the inner switch and those in the outer switch.

Example :

```
switch(count)
{
case 1:
switch(target)
{ // nested switch
```

```
    case 0:
        System.out.println("target is zero");
        break;
    case 1: // no conflicts with outer switch
        System.out.println("target is one");
        break;
}
break;
case 2: // ...
}
```

- Here, the case 1: statement in the inner switch does not conflict with the case 1: statement in the outer switch. The count variable is compared only with the list of cases at the outer level.

- If count is 1, then target is compared with the inner list cases.

- The switch looks only for a match between the value of the expression and one of its case constants.

- No two case constants in the same switch can have identical values. Of course, a switch statement and an enclosing outer switch can have case constants in common.

- A switch statement is usually more efficient than a set of nested if's. The last point is particularly interesting because it gives insight into how the Java compiler works.

- When it compiles a switch statement, the Java compiler will inspect each of the case constants and create a "jump table" that it will use for selecting the path of execution depending on the value of the expression.

- Therefore, if you need to select among a large group of values, a switch statement will run much faster than the equivalent logic coded using a sequence of if-elses. The compiler can do this because it knows that the case constants are all the same type and simply must be compared for equality with the switch expression.

3.25.2 Iteration Statements

Repeating the same code fragment several times until a specified condition is satisfied is called iteration statement. Iteration statements execute the same set of instructions until a termination condition is met. Java provides the following loop for iteration statements:

- The while loop

- The for loop

- The do-while loop

- The for each loop
- Declaring Loop Control Variables Inside the for Loop
- Using the Comma

The while Loop:

- It continually executes a statement that is usually be a block while a condition is true. The condition must return a Boolean value.

Example:

```java
public class WhileDemo
{
  public static void main( String[] args )
  {
    int i = 0;
    while ( i < 5 )
    {
      System.out.println( "Value :: " + i );
      i++;
    }
  }
}
```

Output:

Value :: 0

Value :: 1

Value :: 2

Value :: 3

Value :: 4

The do-While Loop:

- The do-while loop executes at least one time then it will check the expression prior to the next iteration.
- The only difference between a while and a do-while loop is that do-while evaluates its expression at the bottom of the loop instead of the top.

Example:

```java
public class DoWhileDemo
{
    public static void main( String[] args )
    {
        int i = 0;
        do
        {
            System.out.println( "value :: " + i );
            i++;
        }
        while ( i < 5);
    }
}
```

Output:

value ::0

value ::1

value ::2

value ::3

value ::4

The for Loop:

- A for loop executes a statement that is usually a block as long as the Boolean condition evaluates to true.
- A for loop is a combination of the three elements initialization statement, Boolean expression and increment or decrement statement.

Syntax:

```java
for(<initialization>;  <condition>;  <increment or decrement statement>)
    {
        <block of code>
    }
```

- The initialization block executes first before the loop starts. It is used to initialize the loop variable.
- The condition statement evaluates every time prior to when the statement that is usually a block executes, if the condition is true then only the statement that is usually a block will execute.
- The increment or decrement statement executes every time after the statement that is usually a block.

Example:

```java
public class WhileDemo
{
   public static void main( String[] args )
   {
      int i = 0;
      while ( i < 5 )
      {
         System.out.println( "Value :: " + i );
         i++;
      }
   }
}
```

Output:

value ::0

value ::1

value ::2

value ::3

value ::4

The for Each Loop:

- This was introduced in Java 5. This loop is basically used to traverse the array or collection elements.

Example:

```java
public class ForEachDemo
{
   public static void main( String[] args )
   {
      int[] i = { 1, 2, 3, 4, 5 };
      for ( int j : i )
      {
         System.out.println( "value :: " + j );
      }
   }
}
```

Output:

value ::1

value ::2

value ::3

value ::4

value ::5

Declaring Loop Control Variables Inside the for Loop

- Variable that controls a for loop is needed only for the purposes of the loop and is not used in another place. When this is the case, it is possible to declare the variable inside the initialization portion of the for.

- For example, here is the preceding program recoded so that the loop control variable n is declared as an int inside the for:

```java
// Declare a loop control variable inside the for.
class ForTick
{
    public static void main(String args[])
    {
        // here, n is declared inside of the for loop
        for(int n=10; n>0; n--)
            System.out.println("tick " + n);
    }
}
```

- When you declare a variable inside a for loop, there is one important point to remember: the scope of that variable ends when the for statement does.

- If you need to use the loop control variable elsewhere in your program, you will not be able to declare it inside the for loop. When the loop control variable will not be needed elsewhere, most Java programmers declare it inside the for.

- For example, here is a simple program that tests for prime numbers. Notice that the loop control variable i is declared inside the for since it is not needed elsewhere.

Program 3.8 : Test for Primes

```java
// Test for primes.
class FindPrime
{
public static void main(String args[])
{
    int num;
```

```
    boolean isPrime;
    num = 14;
    if(num < 2)
        isPrime = false;
    else
        isPrime = true;
    for(int i=2; i <= num/i; i++)
    {
        if((num % i) == 0)
        {
            isPrime = false;
            break;
        }
    }
    if(isPrime)
        System.out.println("Prime");
    else
        System.out.println("Not Prime");
  }
}
```

Using the Comma

- There will be times when you will want to include more than one statement in the initialization and iteration portions of the for loop.
- For example, consider the loop in the following program:

```
class Sample
{
    public static void main(String args[])
    {
        int x, y;
        y = 4;
        for(x=1; x<y; x++)
        {
            System.out.println("x = " + x);
            System.out.println("y = " + y);
            y--;
        }
    }
}
```

- The loop is controlled by the interaction of two variables. Since the loop is governed by two variables, it would be useful if both could be included in the for statement, itself, instead of y being handled manually.
- Java provides a way to accomplish this to allow two or more variables to control x for loop, Java permits you to include multiple statements in both the initialization and iteration portions of the for. Each statement is separated from the next by a comma.
- Using the comma, the preceding for loop can be more efficiently coded, as shown in following example:

```java
// Using the comma.
class Comma
{
    public static void main(String args[])
    {
        int a, b;
        for(a=1, b=4; a<b; a++, b--)
        {
            System.out.println("a = " + a);
            System.out.println("b = " + b);
        }
    }
}
```

- In this example, the initialization portion sets the values of both **a** and **b**. The two comma separated statements in the iteration portion are executed each time the loop repeats.

Output:

a = 1
b = 4
a = 2
b = 3

3.25.3 Jump Statements

Jump statements are used to unconditionally transfer the program control to another part of the program.

Java provides the following jump statements:

- Break statement
- Continue statement
- Return statement

Break Statement:

- The break statement immediately quits the current iteration and goes to the first statement following the loop. Another form of break is used in the switch statement.
- The break statement has the following two forms:
  1. Unlabeled Break Statement   2. Labeled Break Statement

1. Unlabeled Break Statement:

This is used to jump program control out of the specific loop on the specific condition.

Example:

```java
public class UnLabeledBreakDemo
{
   public static void main( String[] args )
   {
      for ( int var = 0; var < 5; var++ )
      {
         System.out.println( "Var is : " + var );
         if ( var == 3 )
            break;
      }
   }
}
```

Output:

value ::0
value ::1
value ::2
value ::3

2. Labeled Break Statement:

This is used for when we want to jump the program control out of nested loops or multiple loops.

Example:

```java
public class LabeledBreakDemo
{
   public static void main( String[] args )
   {
      Outer: for ( int var1 = 0; var1 < 5; var1++ )
      {
         for ( int var2 = 1; var2 < 5; var2++ )
         {
            System.out.println( "var1:" + var1 + ", var2:" + var2 );
            if ( var1 == 3 )
               break Outer;
         }
      }
   }
}
```

Output:

var1:0,var2:1

var1:0,var2:2

var1:0,var2:3

var1:0,var2:4

var1:1,var2:1

var1:1,var2:2

var1:1,var2:3

var1:1,var2:4

var1:2,var2:1

var1:2,var2:2

var1:2,var2:3

var1:2,var2:4

var1:3,var2:1

Continue Statement:

The continue statement is used when you want to continue running the loop with the next iteration and want to skip the rest of the statements of the body for the current iteration.

The continue statement has the following two forms:

    1. Unlabeled Continue Statement 2. Labeled Continue Statement

1. Unlabeled Continue Statement:

This statement skips the current iteration of the innermost for, while and do-while loop.

Example:

```
public class UnlabeledContinueDemo
{
  public static void main( String[] args )
  {
    for ( int var1 = 0; var1 < 4; var1++ )
    {
      for ( int var2 = 0; var2 < 4; var2++ )
      {
        if ( var2 == 2 )
          continue;
        System.out.println( "var1:" + var1 + ", var2:" + var2 );
      }
    }
  }
}
```

Example:
var1:0,var2:0
var1:0,var2:1
var1:0,var2:3
var1:1,var2:0
var1:1,var2:1
var1:1,var2:3
var1:2,var2:0
var1:2,var2:1
var1:2,var2:3
var1:3,var2:0
var1:3,var2:1
var1:3,var2:3

2. Labeled Continue Statement:

This statement skips the current iteration of the loop with the specified label.

Example:

```
public class LabeledContinueDemo
{
    public static void main( String[] args )
    {
        Outer: for ( int var1 = 0; var1 < 5; var1++ ) {
            for ( int var2 = 0; var2 < 5; var2++ ) {
                if ( var2 == 2 )
                    continue Outer;
                System.out.println( "var1:" + var1 + ", var2:" + var2 );
            }
        }
    }
}
```

Output:
var1:0,var2:0
var1:0,var2:1
var1:1,var2:0
var1:1,var2:1
var1:2,var2:0
var1:2,var2:1
var1:3,var2:0
var1:3,var2:1
var1:4,var2:0
var1:4,var2:1

Return Statement:

- The return statement is used to immediately quit the current method and return to the calling method.
- It is mandatory to use a return statement for non-void methods to return a value.

Example:

```
public class ReturnDemo
{
  public static void main( String[] args )
  {
    ReturnDemo returnDemo = new ReturnDemo();
    System.out.println( "No : " + returnDemo.returnCall() );
  }

  int returnCall()
  {
    return 5;
  }
}
```

Output:

No:5

EXERCISE

1. Explain the different features of JAVA.
2. What is JVM? Explain in brief.
3. Explain the different Data types in JAVA.
4. Differentiate between Primitive data types and User defined data types.
5. What is Array? Explain Single and Multi dimensional array.
6. Explain Selection Control Statements.
7. Explain Iterative Control Statements.
8. Explain Jump Control Statements.
9. Differentiate between Java and C++.
10. Write a short note on Java Tokens, Java Statements, Constants, variables.
11. What is Typecasting? Explain with example?
12. Explain Operator precedence and associativity in JAVA.

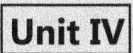

CLASSES, METHODS AND OBJECTS IN JAVA

4.1 CLASS FUNDAMENTALS

- A class is a template that defines the form of an object. It specifies both the data and the code that will operate on that data.
- A class is declared by using class keyword.
- General form of a class definition is shown here:

```
class classname
{
        datatype instance-variable1;
        datatype instance-variable2;
        // ...
        datatype instance-variableN;
    returntype methodname1(parameter-list)
    {
        // body of method
    }
    returntype methodname2(parameter-list)
    {
        // body of method
    }
    // ...
    returntype methodnameN(parameter-list)
    {
        // body of method
    }
}
```

- The data, or variables, defined within a class are called instance variables.
- The code is contained within methods.
- The methods and variables defined within a class are called members of the class.
- Everything in Java is defined in a class.

Example:

```
class Employee
{
    String name;
    int empid;
    String emailAddress;
    int yearOfBirth;
        void read()
    {
        //          ...
    }
    void disp()
    {
        //          ...
    }
}
```

- The order of data fields and methods in a class is not significant.
- If you recall, each class must be saved in a file that matches its name, for example: Employee.Java

4.2 DECLARING OBJECTS

- An object is an instance of a particular class.
- To create an object of a particular class, use the new operator, followed by an invocation of a constructor for that class, such as:

  new MyClass()

  ➤ The constructor method initializes the state of the new object.
  ➤ The new operator returns a *reference* to the newly created object.
- As with primitives, the variable type must be compatible with the value type when using object references as follows:

  Employee e = new Employee();
- To access member data or methods of an object, use the dot (.) notation: variable.method()

• Consider this simple example of creating and using instances of the Employee class:

Program 4.1 : Example of Creation of Instance of Employee Class

```java
public class EmployeeDemo
{
    public static void main(String[] args)
    {

        Employee e1 = new Employee();
        e1.name = "John";
        e1.empid = "555";
        e1.emailAddress = "john@company.com";
        Employee e2 = new Employee();
        e2.name = "Tom";
        e2.empid = "456";
        e2.yearOfBirth = 1974;
        System.out.println("Name: " + e1.name);
        System.out.println("Empid: " + e1.empid);
        System.out.println("Email Address: " +  e1.emailAddress);
        System.out.println("Year Of Birth: " + e1.yearOfBirth);
        System.out.println("Name: " + e2.name);
        System.out.println("Empid: " + e2.empid);
        System.out.println("Email Address: " + e2.emailAddress);
        System.out.println("Year Of Birth: " + e2.yearOfBirth);
    }
}
```

Output:

Name: John

SSN: 555

Email Address: john@company.com

Year Of Birth: 0

Name: Tom

SSN: 456

Email Address: null

Year Of Birth: 1974

4.3 CLASS VS OBJECT

- A *class* is a template for how to build an object.
  - ➤ A class is a prototype that defines state placeholders and behaviour common to all objects of its kind.
  - ➤ Each object is a member of a single class — there is no multiple inheritance in Java.
- An *object* is an instance of a particular class.
  - ➤ There are typically many object instances for any one given class.
  - ➤ Each object of a given class has the same built-in behaviour but possibly a different data.
  - ➤ Objects are *instantiated*.
- For example, each car starts of with a design that defines its features and properties.
- It is the design that is used to build a car of a particular type or class.
- When the physical cars roll off the assembly line, those cars are *instances* of that class.
- Many people can have an BMW, but there is typically only one design for that particular class of cars.

4.4 ASSIGNING OBJECT REFERENCE VARIABLES

- Object reference variables act differently than do variables of a primitive type, such as int.
- When you assign one primitive-type variable to another, the situation is straightforward. The variable on the left receives a *copy* of the *value* of the variable on the right.
- When you assign one object reference variable to another, the situation is a bit more complicated because you are changing the object that the reference variable refers to.
- The effect of this difference can cause some results. For example, consider the following example:

        Vehicle car1=new Vehicle();

        Vehicle car2=car1;

- car2 is being assigned a reference to a copy of the object referred to by car1. That is, you might think that car1 and car2 refer to separate and distinct objects. However, this would be wrong. Instead, after this fragment executes, car1 and car2 will both refer to the same object.
- The assignment of car1 to car2 did not allocate any memory or copy any part of the original object. It simply makes car2 refer to the same object as does car1. Thus, any changes made to the object through car2 will affect the object to which car1 is referring, since they are the same object.

4.5 METHODS

- Methods are subroutines that manipulate the data defined by the class and, in many cases, provide access to that data.

- General form of a method is as follows:

```
return_type name(parameter-list)
{
    // body of method
}
```

- Here, return_type specifies the type of data returned by the method. This can be any valid type, including class types that you create. If the method does not return a value, its return type must be void.

- The name of the method is specified by name. This can be any identifier other than those already used by other items within the current scope.

- The parameter-list is a sequence of type and identifier pairs separated by commas. Parameters are essentially variables that receive the value of the arguments passed to the method when it is called. If the method has no parameters, then the parameter list will be empty.

- Methods that have a return type other than void return a value to the calling routine using the following form of the return statement:

    return value;

    Here, value is the value returned.

- Let's begin by adding a method to the Box class as shown following:

Program 4.2 : Example of Adding Method to Box Class

```
class Box
{
    double width;
    double height;
    double depth;
    void volume() //Method definition
    {
        System.out.print("Volume is ");
        System.out.println(width * height * depth);
    }
}
```

```
class BoxDemo
{
    public static void main(String args[])
    {
        Box mybox1 = new Box();
        mybox1.width = 10;
        mybox1.height = 10;
        mybox1.depth = 10;
        mybox1.volume();//Method invoking
    }
}
```

Output:

Volume is 1000.0

4.6 CONSTRUCTORS

- Constructor in Java is a special type of method that is used to initialize the object.
- Java constructor is invoked at the time of object creation. It constructs the values that is provides data for the object that is why it is known as Constructor.

4.6.1 Rules for Creating Constructor

- Constructor name must be same as its class name
- Constructor must have no explicit return type
- Every class has a constructor whether it's normal one or a abstract class.
- Constructor are not methods and they don't have any return type.
- Constructor can use any access specifier, they can be declared as private also. Private constructors are possible in Java but their scope is within the class only.
- If you don't define any constructor within the class, compiler will do it for you and it will create a constructor for you.
- this() and super() should be the first statement in the constructor code. If you don't mention them, compiler does it for you accordingly.
- Constructor overloading is possible but overriding is not possible. Which means we can have overloaded constructor in our class but we can't override a constructor.
- Constructors can not be inherited.
- Interfaces do not have constructors.

- Abstract can have constructors and these will get invoked when a class, which implements interface, gets instantiated i.e. object creation of concrete class.
- A constructor can also invoke another constructor of the same class – By using this().

4.6.2 Types of Java Constructors

There are three types of constructors:

1. Default constructor
2. Parameterized constructor
3. Copy constructor

1. Default Constructor

- A constructor that have no parameter is known as default constructor.

Syntax :

```
<class_name>()
{

}
```

Example :

In this example, we are creating the no-argument constructor in the Bike class. It will be invoked at the time of object creation.

```
class Bike1
{
    Bike1()
    {
        System.out.println("Bike is created");
    }
    public static void main(String args[])
    {
        Bike1 b=new Bike1();
    }
}
```

Output:

Bike is created

Rule: If there is no constructor in a class, compiler automatically creates a default constructor.

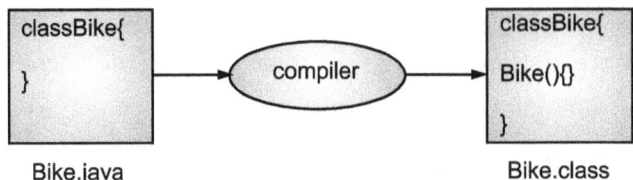

Bike.java   Bike.class

Fig. 4.1: Example of default constructor

Program 4.3 : Default Constructor that Displays the Default Values

```
class Student
     {
          int id;
          String name;
          void display()
          {
          System.out.println(id+" "+name);
          }
          public static void main(String args[])
          {
               Student s1=new Student();
               Student s2=new Student();
               s1.display();
               s2.display();
          }
     }
```

Output:

0 null

0 null

- **Explanation:** In the above class, you are not creating any constructor so compiler provides you a default constructor. Here 0 and null values are provided by default constructor.

2. **Parameterized Constructor**
   - A constructor that have parameters Is known as parameterIzed constructor
   - Parameterized constructor is used to provide different values to the distinct objects.
   - Example of parameterized constructor

Here, we have created the constructor of Student class that have two parameters. We can have any number of parameters in the constructor.

Program 4.4 : Example of Parameterized Constructor

```java
class Student
{
    int id;
    String name;
    Student(int i, String n)
    {
        id = i;
        name = n;
    }
    void display()
    {
        System.out.println(id+" "+name);
    }
    public static void main(String args[])
    {
        Student s1 = new Student4(111,"abc");
        Student s2 = new Student4(222,"pqr");
        s1.display();
        s2.display();
    }
}
```

Output:

111 abc

222 pqr

3. Copy Constructor

- There is no copy constructor in Java. But, we can copy the values of one object to another like copy constructor in C++.
- There are many ways to copy the values of one object into another in Java. They are:
  - ➢ By constructor
  - ➢ By assigning the values of one object into another
  - ➢ By clone() method of Object class

Example: In this example, we are going to copy the values of one object into another using Java constructor.

Program 4.5 : Example of Copy Constructor

```java
class Student
{
        int id;
        String name;
        Student(int i,String n)
        {
                id = i;
            name = n;
        }
        Student(Student  s)
        {
                id = s.id;
            name =s.name;
        }
        void display()
        {
        System.out.println(id+" "+name);
        }
        public static void main(String args[])
        {
        Student s1 = new Student(111,"abc");
        Student s2 = new Student(s1);
            s1.display();
            s2.display();
        }
}
```

Output:

111 abc

111 abc

4.6.3 Difference between Constructor and Method in Java

Sr. No.	Java Constructor	Java Method
1.	Constructor is used to initialize the state of an object.	Method is used to expose behaviour of an object.
2.	Constructor must not have return type.	Method must have return type.
3.	Constructor is invoked implicitly.	Method is invoked explicitly.
4.	The Java compiler provides a default constructor if you don't have any constructor.	Method is not provided by compiler in any case.
5.	Constructor name must be same as the class name.	Method name may or may not be same as class name.

4.7 this KEYWORD

- There can be a lot of usage of Java this keyword. In Java, this is a reference variable that refers to the current object.

- Here are given the 6 usages of Java this keyword.

   ➢ This keyword can be used to refer current class instance variable.

   ➢ This can be used to invoke current class constructor.

   ➢ This keyword can be used to invoke current class method.

   ➢ This can be passed as an argument in the method call.

   ➢ This can be passed as argument in the constructor call.

   ➢ This keyword can also be used to return the current class instance.

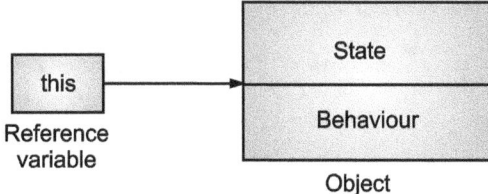

Fig. 4.2: This keyword

The 'this' Keyword can be Used to Refer Current Class Instance Variable.

- If there is ambiguity between the instance variable and parameter, this keyword resolves the problem of ambiguity

- Let's understand the problem if we don't use this keyword by the example given below:

Program 4.6 : Without this Keyword

```java
class Student
{
    int id;
    String name;
    Student10(int id,String name)
    {
        id = id;
        name = name;
    }
    void display()
    {
        System.out.println(id+" "+name);
    }
    public static void main(String args[])
    {
      Student10 s1 = new Student10(111,"abc");
      Student10 s2 = new Student10(321,"pqr");
      s1.display();
      s2.display();
    }
}
```

Output:

0 null

0 null

- In the above example, parameter formal arguments and instance variables are same that is why we are using this keyword to distinguish between local variable and instance variable

Solution of the Above Problem by this Keyword

Program 4.7 : Using this Keyword

```java
class Student
{
    int id;
    String name;
    Student(int id,String name)
    {
    this.id = id;
    this.name = name;
    }
    void display()
    {
        System.out.println(id+" "+name);
    }
    public static void main(String args[])
    {
    Student s1 = new Student (111,"Karan");
    Student s2 = new Student(222,"Aryan");
    s1.display();
    s2.display();
    }
}
```

Output:

```
111 Karan
222 Aryan
```

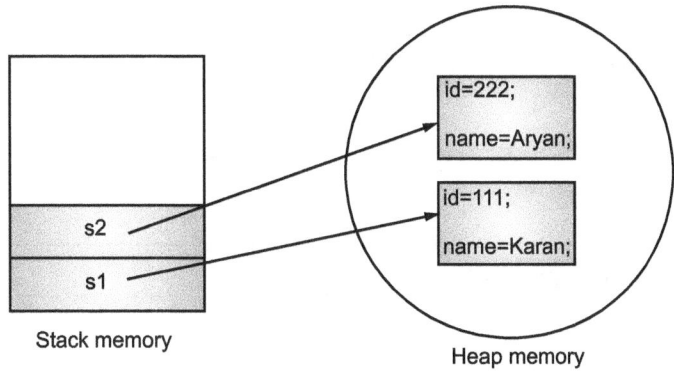

Fig. 4.3: Example of this keyword

Program where this Keyword is Not Required

- If local variables(formal arguments) and instance variables are different, there is no need to use this keyword like in the following program:

Program 4.8 : Example Where this Keyword is not Required

```java
class Student
{
    int id;
    String name;
    Student(int i,String n)
    {
        id = i;
        name = n;
    }
    void display()
    {
        System.out.println(id+" "+name);
    }
    public static void main(String args[])
    {
        Student e1 = new Student(111,"abc");
        Student e2 = new Student(222,"pqr");
        e1.display();
        e2.display();
    }
}
```

Output:

111 abc

222 pqr

4.8 GARBAGE COLLECTION

- In Java, garbage means unreferenced objects.
- Garbage Collection is process of reclaiming the runtime unused memory automatically. In other words, it is a way to destroy the unused objects.

- In C language, we were using free() function and in C++ language we were using delete() function But, in Java it is performed automatically. So, Java provides better memory management.

Advantage of Garbage Collection

- It makes Java memory efficient because garbage collector removes the unreferenced objects from heap memory.

- It is automatically done by the garbage collector so we don't need to make extra efforts.

There are many ways of object unreferenced:

1. By nulling the reference
2. By assigning a reference to another
3. By annonymous object etc.

1. **By Nulling a Reference:**

   - Employee e=new Employee();
   - e=null;

2. **By Assigning a Reference to Another:**

   - Employee e1=new Employee();
   - Employee e2=new Employee();
   - e1=e2;//now the first object referred by e1 is available for garbage collection

3. **By Annonymous Object:**

   - new Employee();

4.9 FINALIZE() METHOD

- The finalize() method is invoked each time before the object is garbage collected.

- The finalize() method can be used to perform cleanup processing. This method is defined in Object class as follows:

```
protected void finalize()

{

}
```

- The Garbage collector of JVM collects only those objects that are created by new keyword. So, if you have created any object without new, you can use finalize method to perform cleanup processing that is destroying remaining objects.

- The gc() method is used to invoke the garbage collector to perform cleanup processing. The gc() is found in System and Runtime classes.

```
public static void gc()
{

}
```

- Garbage collection is performed by a daemon thread called Garbage Collector(GC). This thread calls the finalize() method before object is garbage collected.
- Simple Example of garbage collection and finalize() in Java

Program 4.9 : Garbage Collection

```
public class TestGarbage
{
    public void finalize()
    {
        System.out.println("object is garbage collected");
    }
    public static void main(String args[])
    {
        TestGarbage s1=new TestGarbage();
        TestGarbage s2=new TestGarbage();
        s1=null;
        s2=null;
        System.gc();
    }
}
```

Output:

object is garbage collected

object is garbage collected

4.10 OVERLOADING METHODS

- If a class have multiple methods by same name but different parameters, it is known as **Method Overloading**.
- If we have to perform only one operation, having same name of the methods increases the readability of the program.

- Suppose you have to perform addition of the given numbers but there can be any number of arguments, if you write the method such as a(int,int) for two parameters, and b(int,int,int) for three parameters then it may be difficult for you as well as other programmers to understand the behavior of the method because its name differs. So, we perform method overloading to figure out the program quickly.

Advantage of Method Overloading

- Method overloading increases the readability of the program.

Different Ways to Overload the Method

- There are two ways to overload the method in Java
    1. By changing number of arguments
    2. By changing the data type

1. Example of Method Overloading by Changing the No. of Arguments

- In this example, we have created two overloaded methods, first sum method performs addition of two numbers and second sum method performs addition of three numbers.

Program 4.10 : Example of Method Overloading

```
class Calculation
{
    void sum(int a,int b)
    {
    System.out.println(a+b);
    }
    void sum(int a,int b,int c)
    {
    System.out.println(a+b+c);
    }
    public static void main(String args[])
    {
        Calculation obj=new Calculation();
        obj.sum(10,10,10);
        obj.sum(20,20);
    }
}
```

Output:

30

40

2. Example of Method Overloading by Changing Data Type of Argument

In this example, we have created two overloaded methods that differs in data type. The first sum method receives two integer arguments and second sum method receives two double arguments.

Program 4.11 :

```java
class Calculation
{
    void sum(int a,int b)
    {
        System.out.println(a+b);
    }
    void sum(double a,double b)
    {
        System.out.println(a+b);
    }
    public static void main(String args[])
    {
        Calculation obj=new Calculation();
        obj.sum(10.5,10.5);
        obj.sum(20,20);
    }
}
```

Output:

21.0

40

4.11 USING OBJECTS AS PARAMETERS

- We can pass Object as a parameter to methods.

Program 4.12 : Using Objects as a Parameter.

```java
// Objects may be passed to methods.
class Test
{
    int a, b;
    Test(int i, int j)
```

```java
        {
            a = i;
            b = j;
        }
        // return true if o is equal to the invoking object
        boolean equalTo(Test obj)
        {
            if(obj.a == a && obj.b == b)
                return true;
            else
                return false;
        }
    }
class PassOb
{
    public static void main(String args[])
    {
        Test ob1 = new Test(100, 22);
        Test ob2 = new Test(100, 22);
        Test ob3 = new Test(50, 60);
        System.out.println("ob1 == ob2: " + ob1.equalTo(ob2));
        System.out.println("ob1 == ob3: " + ob1.equalTo(ob3));
    }
}
```

Output:

ob1 == ob2: true

ob1 == ob3: false

- In above program, The equalTo( ) method inside Test compares two objects for equality and returns the result. That is, it compares the invoking object with the one that it is passed.

- If they contain the same values, then the method returns true. Otherwise, it returns false.

4.12 ARGUMENT PASSING

There are two ways that a computer language can pass an argument to a subroutine.

1. Call-by-Value

- This approach copies the *value* of an argument into the formal parameter of the subroutine. Therefore, changes made to the parameter of the subroutine have no effect on the argument.

- When you pass a primitive type to a method, it is passed by value. Thus, a copy of the argument is made and what occurs to the parameter that receives the argument has no effect outside the method.

- For example, consider the following program:

Program 4.13 : Call by Value

```java
class Test
    {
        void fun(int i, int j)
            {
            i *= 2;
                j /= 2;
            }
    }
    class CallByValue
        {
            public static void main(String args[])
            {
                Test ob = new Test();
                int a = 15, b = 20;
                System.out.println("a and b before call: " +a + " " + b);
                ob.fun(a, b);
                System.out.println("a and b after call: " +a + " " + b);
            }
        }
```

Output:

　　a and b before call: 15 20

　　a and b after call: 15 20

- As you can see, the operations that occur inside **fun( )** have no effect on the values of **a** and **b** used in the call , their values here did not change to 30 and 10.

2. Call-by-Reference

- In this approach, a reference to an argument not the value of the argument is passed to the parameter. Inside the subroutine, this reference is used to access the actual argument specified in the call. This means that changes made to the parameter will affect the argument used to call the subroutine.

- When you create a variable of a class type, you are only creating a reference to an object. Thus, when you pass this reference to a method, the parameter that receives it will refer to the same object as that referred to by the argument. This effectively means that objects act as if they are passed to methods by use of call-by-reference.

- Changes to the object inside the method *do* affect the object used as an argument.

- For example, consider the following program:

Program 4.14 : Call by Reference

```
class Test
{
    int a, b;
    Test(int i, int j)
    {
        a = i;
        b = j;
    }
    // pass an object
    void fun(Test obj)
    {
        obj.a *= 2;
        obj.b /= 2;
    }
}
class PassObjRef
{
    public static void main(String args[])
    {
        Test ob = new Test(15, 20);
```

```
            System.out.println("ob.a and ob.b before call: " +ob.a + " " + ob.b);
            ob.fun(ob);
            System.out.println("ob.a and ob.b after call: " +ob.a + " " + ob.b);
        }
    }
```

Output:

ob.a and ob.b before call: 15 20

ob.a and ob.b after call: 30 10

4.13 RETURNING OBJECTS

- A method can return any type of data, including class types that you create.
- For example, in the following program, the **fun( )** method returns an object in which the value of **a** is ten greater than it is in the invoking object.

Program 4.15 : Example of Returning an Object

```
    // Returning an object.
    class Test
    {
        int a;
        Test(int i)
        {
            a = i;
        }
        Test fun()
        {
            Test temp = new Test(a+10);
            return temp;
        }
    }
    class Demo
    {
        public static void main(String args[])
        {
            Test ob1 = new Test(2);
            Test ob2;
            ob2 = ob1.fun();
```

```
            System.out.println("ob1.a: " + ob1.a);
            System.out.println("ob2.a: " + ob2.a);
            ob2 = ob2.fun();
            System.out.println("ob2.a after second increase: "+ ob2.a);
        }
    }
```

Output:

    ob1.a: 2

    ob2.a: 12

    ob2.a after second increase: 22

- As you can see, each time **fun( )** is invoked, a new object is created, and a reference to it is returned to the calling routine.

4.14 RECURSION

- Recursion is the process of defining something in terms of itself. A method that calls itself is called as recursive.
- Recursion is the attribute that allows a method to call itself.
- Example of recursion is computation of the factorial of a number.
- The factorial of a number N is the product of all the whole numbers between 1 and N. For example, 3 factorial is $1 \times 2 \times 3 \times$, or 6. Here is how a factorial can be computed by use of a recursive method:

Program 4.16 : Recursion

```
class Factorial
{

    int fact(int n) //recursive method
    {
        int result;
        if(n==1) return 1;
        result = fact(n-1) * n;
        return result;

    }
}
class Recursion
{
```

```
public static void main(String args[])
{
    Factorial f = new Factorial();
    System.out.println("Factorial of 3 is " + f.fact(3));
    System.out.println("Factorial of 4 is " + f.fact(4));
    System.out.println("Factorial of 5 is " + f.fact(5));
}
}
```

Output:

Factorial of 3 is 6

Factorial of 4 is 24

Factorial of 5 is 120

- Recursive versions of many routines execute slowly than the iterative equivalent because of the added overhead of the additional method calls.
- The main advantage to recursive methods is that they can be used to create clearer and simpler versions of several algorithms than can their iterative relatives.
- Here is one more example of recursion. The recursive method printArray( ) prints the first i elements in the array values.

Program 4.17 : Recursion

```
class Demo
{
    int values[];
    Demo(int i)
    {
        values = new int[i];
    }
    void printArray(int i)
    {
        if(i==0)
            return;
        else
```

```
            printArray(i-1);
        System.out.println("[" + (i-1) + "] " + values[i-1]);
    }
}
class Recursion2
{
    public static void main(String args[])
    {
        Demo ob = new Demo(5);
        int i;
        for(i=0; i<5; i++)
        ob.values[i] = i;
        ob.printArray(5);
    }
}
```

Output:

[0] 0

[1] 1

[2] 2

[3] 3

[4] 4

4.15 ACCESS CONTROL

- Java supplies a rich set of access modifiers.
- Java's access modifiers are public, private, and protected. Java also defines a default access level. Protected applies only when inheritance is involved.
- When a member of a class is modified by public, then that member can be accessed by any other code.
- When a member of a class is specified as private, then that member can only be accessed by other members of its class.
- Now you can understand why main( ) has always been preceded by the public modifier. It is called by code that is outside the program that is, by the Java run-time system.
- When no access modifier is used, then by default the member of a class is public within its own package, but cannot be accessed outside of its package.
- To understand the effects of public and private access, consider the following program:

Program 4.18 : Effects of Public and Private Access

```java
class Test
{
        int a; // default access
        public int b; // public access
        private int c; // private access
        // methods to access c
        void setc(int i)
            {
                c = i;
            }
        int getc()
            {
                return c;
            }
}
class AccessTest
{
    public static void main(String args[])
    {
        Test ob = new Test();
        // These are OK, a and b may be accessed directly
        ob.a = 10;
        ob.b = 20;
        // This is not OK and will cause an error
        // ob.c = 100; // Error!
        // You must access c through its methods
        ob.setc(100); // OK
        System.out.println("a, b, and c: " + ob.a + " " +ob.b + " " + ob.getc());
    }
}
```

- As you can see, inside the Test class, a uses default access, which for this example is the same as specifying public. b is explicitly specified as public. Member c is given private access. This means that it cannot be accessed by code outside of its class. So, inside the AccessTest class, c cannot be used directly.

- It must be accessed through its public methods: setc( ) and getc( ). If you were to remove the comment symbol from the beginning of the following line, // ob.c = 100; // Error! then you would not be able to compile this program because of the access violation.

4.16 STATIC

- In JAVA, It is possible to create a member that can be used by itself, without reference to a specific instance. To create such a member, follow its declaration with the keyword static.

- When a member is declared static, it can be accessed before any objects of its class are created, and without reference to any object.

- You can declare methods and variables to be static.

- The most common example of a static member is main( ).

- main( ) is declared as static because it must be called before any objects exist.

- Instance variables declared as static are basically global variables. When objects of its class are declared, no copy of a static variable is made. Instead, all instances of the class share the same static variable.

- Methods declared as static have several limitations:
  - ➢ They can only directly call other static methods.
  - ➢ They can only directly access static data.
  - ➢ They cannot refer to this or super keywords.

- If you need to do computation in order to initialize your static variables, you can declare a static block that gets executed exactly once, when the class is first loaded.

- The following example shows a class that has a static method, some static variables, and a static initialization block:

Program 4.19 : Example of Static Keyword

```java
class UseStaticEg
{
    static int a = 3;
    static int b;
    static void fun(int x)
    {
        System.out.println("x = " + x);
        System.out.println("a = " + a);
```

```
        System.out.println("b = " + b);
    }
    static
    {
        System.out.println("Static block initialized.");
        b = a * 4;
    }
    public static void main(String args[])
    {
        fun(42);
    }
}
```

- In above program UseStaticEg class is loaded, all of the static statements are run. First, a is set to 3, then the static block executes, which prints a message and then initializes b to a*4 or 12. Then main( ) is called, which calls fun( ), passing 42 to x. The three println( ) statements refer to the two static variables a and b, as well as to the local variable x.

Output :

Static block initialized.

    x = 42

    a = 3

    b = 12

4.17 FINAL

- A field can be declared as final. Its contents from being modified, making it, essentially, a constant. This means that you must initialize a final field when it is declared.

- You can do this in one of two ways:

  ➢ You can give it a value when it is declared.

  ➢ You can assign it a value within a constructor.

Example:

        final int FILE_NEW = 1;

        final int FILE_OPEN = 2;

        final int FILE_SAVE = 3;

        final int FILE_QUIT = 4;

- Subsequent parts of your program can now use FILE_OPEN as if they were constants, without apprehension that a value has been changed. It is a common coding convention to choose all uppercase identifiers for final fields, as this example shows.

- In addition to fields, both method parameters and local variables can be declared final.

- Declaring a parameter final prevents it from being changed within the method. Declaring a local variable final prevents it from being assigned a value more than once.

- The keyword final can also be applied to methods, but its meaning is substantially different than when it is applied to variables.

4.18 ARRAY

- Array is a collection of similar type of elements that have contiguous memory location.

- Java array is an object the contains elements of similar data type. It is a data structure where we store similar elements. We can store only fixed set of elements in a Java array.

- Array in Java is index based, first element of the array is stored at 0 index.

- Instead of declaring individual variables, such as number0, number1, ..., and number99, you declare one array variable such as numbers and use numbers[0], numbers[1], and ..., numbers[99] to represent individual variables.

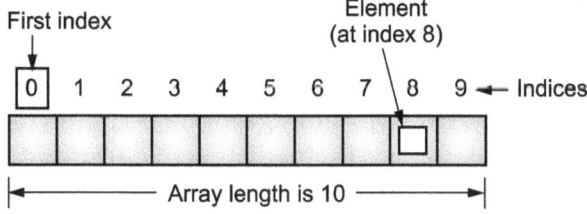

Fig. 4.4 ARRAY

Advantage of Java Array:

- **Random access:** We can get any data located at any index position.

- **Code Optimization:** It makes the code optimized, we can retrieve or sort the data easily.

Disadvantage of Java Array:

- **Size Limit:** We can store only fixed size of elements in the array. It doesn't grow its size at runtime. To solve this problem, collection framework is used in Java.

Declaring Array Variables

- To use an array in a program, you must declare a variable to reference the array, and you must specify the type of array the variable can reference. Here is the syntax for declaring an array variable

Syntax:

```
dataType[] arrayRefVar;  // preferred way.
    or
dataType arrayRefVar[]; // works but not preferred way.
```

Note: The style dataType[] arrayRefVar is preferred. The style dataType arrayRefVar[] comes from the C/C++ language and was adopted in Java to accommodate C/C++ programmers.

Example:

- The following code snippets are examples of this syntax:

```
double[] myList;  // preferred way.

  or

double myList[];  // works but not preferred way.
```

Creating Arrays

- You can create an array by using the new operator with the following syntax:

Syntax:

```
arrayRefVar = new dataType[arraySize];
```

The above statement does two things:

- It creates an array using new dataType[arraySize].

- It assigns the reference of the newly created array to the variable arrayRefVar.

- Declaring an array variable, creating an array, and assigning the reference of the array to the variable can be combined in one statement, as shown below –

```
dataType[] arrayRefVar = new dataType[arraySize];
```

- Alternatively you can create arrays as follows:

```
dataType[] arrayRefVar = {value0, value1, ..., valuek};
```

- The array elements are accessed through the index. Array indices are 0-based; that is, they start from 0 to arrayRefVar.length-1.

Example:

- Following statement declares an array variable, myList, creates an array of 10 elements of double type and assigns its reference to myList –

```
double[] myList = new double[10];
```

- Following Fig. 4.5 represents array myList. Here, myList holds ten double values and the indices are from 0 to 9.

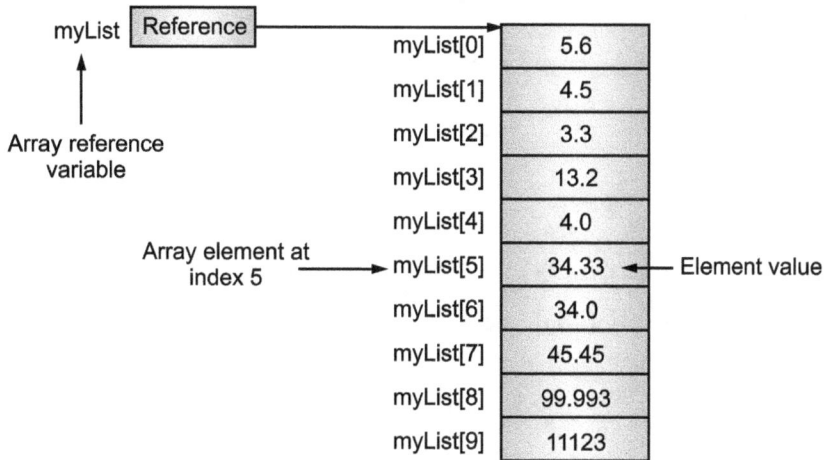

Fig. 4.5 : Creating an array

Types of Array in Java:

There are two types of array.

- Single Dimensional Array
- Multidimensional Array

4.18.1 Single Dimensional Array in Java

Syntax to Declare an Array in Java:

- dataType[] arr; (or)
- dataType []arr; (or)
- dataType arr[];

Instantiation of an Array in Java

arrayRefVar=new datatype[size];

Example of Single Dimensional Java Array:

- Let's see the simple example of Java array, where we are going to declare, instantiate, initialize and traverse an array.

```
class Testarray
    {
        public static void main(String args[])
        {
            int a[]=new int[5];//declaration and instantiation
            a[0]=10;//initialization
```

```
        a[1]=20;
        a[2]=70;
        a[3]=40;
        a[4]=50;
        //printing array
        for(int i=0;i<a.length;i++)//length is the property of array
        System.out.println(a[i]);
    }
}
```

Output:

10

20

70

40

50

Declaration, Instantiation and Initialization of Java Array

• We can declare, instantiate and initialize the Java array together by:

```
    int a[]={33,3,4,5};//declaration, instantiation and initialization
```

• Let's see the simple example to print this array.

Program 4.20 : To Print the Array.

```
class Testarray1
{
    public static void main(String args[])
    {
        int a[]={33,3,4,5};//declaration, instantiation and initialization
        //printing array
        for(int i=0;i<a.length;i++)//length is the property of array
        System.out.println(a[i]);
    }
}
```

Output:

33

3

4

5

Passing Array to Method in Java:

- We can pass the Java array to method so that we can reuse the same logic on any array.
- Let's see the simple example to get minimum number of an array using method.

Program 4.21 : Passing Array to Method in Java.

```java
class Testarray2
{
    static void min(int arr[])
    {
        int min=arr[0];
        for(int i=1;i<arr.length;i++)
         if(min>arr[i])
          min=arr[i];
        System.out.println(min);
    }
    public static void main(String args[])
        {
            int a[]={33,3,4,5};
            min(a);//passing array to method
        }
}
```

Output:

3

4.18.2 Multidimensional Array in Java

- In such case, data is stored in row and column based index. It is also known as matrix form.

Syntax to Declare Multidimensional Array in Java

```java
dataType[][] arrayRefVar; (or)
```

dataType [][]arrayRefVar; (or)

dataType arrayRefVar[][]; (or)

dataType []arrayRefVar[];

Example to Instantiate Multidimensional Array in Java:

int[][] arr=new int[3][3];//3 row and 3 column

Example to Initialize Multidimensional Array in Java:

arr[0][0]=1;

arr[0][1]=2;

arr[0][2]=3;

arr[1][0]=4;

arr[1][1]=5;

arr[1][2]=6;

arr[2][0]=7;

arr[2][1]=8;

arr[2][2]=9;

Example of Multidimensional Java Array:

- Let's see the simple example to declare, instantiate, initialize and print the 2 Dimensional array.

```java
class Testarray3
{
    public static void main(String args[])
    {
        //declaring and initializing 2D array
        int arr[][]={{1,2,3},{2,4,5},{4,4,5}};
        //printing 2D array
        for(int i=0;i<3;i++)
        {
            for(int j=0;j<3;j++)
            {
                System.out.print(arr[i][j]+" ");
            }
```

```
                System.out.println();
        }
     }
  }
```

Output:

1 2 3

2 4 5

4 4 5

4.18.3 Alternative Array Declaration Syntax

- Here, the square brackets follow the type specifier, not the name of the array variable. For example, the following two declarations are equivalent:

  int al[] = **new int**[3];

  int[] a2 = **new int**[3];

- The following declarations are also equivalent:

  char twod1[][] = new char[3][4];

  char[][] twod2 = new char[3][4];

- This alternative declaration form offers convenience when declaring several arrays at the same time:

  int[] nums, nums2, nums3; // create three arrays

4.19 STRING HANDLING: STRING CLASS

- Strings are a sequence of characters. In Java programming language, strings are treated as objects.

- The Java.lang.String class provides a lot of methods to work on string. By the help of these methods, we can perform operations on string such as trimming, concatenating, converting, comparing, replacing strings etc.

- Java String is a powerful concept because everything is treated as a string if you submit any form in window based, web based or mobile application.

- The Java platform provides the String class to create and manipulate strings.

Creating Strings

- Creation of string is as follows:

  String greeting = "Hello world!";

Example:

public class StringDemo

```
{
  public static void main(String args[])
  {
        char[] helloArray = { 'h', 'e', 'l', 'l', 'o', '.' };
        String helloString = new String(helloArray);
        System.out.println( helloString );
  }
}
```

Output:

hello

4.19.1 String Methods

List of methods supported by String class is as follows:

Sr. No.	Method	Description
1.	char charAt(int index)	Returns the character at the specified index.
2.	int compareTo(Object o)	Compares this String to another Object.
3.	int compareTo(String anotherString)	Compares two strings lexicographically.
4.	int compareToIgnoreCase(String str)	Compares two strings lexicographically, ignoring case differences.
5.	String concat(String str)	Concatenates the specified string to the end of this string.
6.	boolean contentEquals(StringBuffer sb)	Returns true if and only if this String represents the same sequence of characters as the specified StringBuffer.
7.	static String copyValueOf(char[] data)	Returns a String that represents the character sequence in the array specIfled.
8.	static String copyValueOf(char[] data, int offset, int count)	Returns a String that represents the character sequence in the array specified.

...Conti.

9.	boolean endsWith(String suffix)	Tests if this string ends with the specified suffix.
10.	boolean equals(Object anObject)	Compares this string to the specified object.
11.	boolean equalsIgnoreCase(String anotherString)	Compares this String to another String, ignoring case considerations.
12.	byte getBytes()	Encodes this String into a sequence of bytes using the platform's default charset, storing the result into a new byte array.
13.	byte[] getBytes(String charsetName)	Encodes this String into a sequence of bytes using the named charset, storing the result into a new byte array.
14.	void getChars(int srcBegin, int srcEnd, char[] dst, int dstBegin)	Copies characters from this string into the destination character array.
15.	int hashCode()	Returns a hash code for this string.
16.	int indexOf(int ch)	Returns the index within this string of the first occurrence of the specified character.
17.	int indexOf(int ch, int fromIndex)	Returns the index within this string of the first occurrence of the specified character, starting the search at the specified index.
18.	int indexOf(String str)	Returns the index within this string of the first occurrence of the specified substring.
19.	int indexOf(String str, int fromIndex)	Returns the index within this string of the first occurrence of the specified substring, starting at the specified index.
20.	String intern()	Returns a canonical representation for the string object.
21.	int lastIndexOf(int ch)	Returns the index within this string of the last occurrence of the specified character.
22.	int lastIndexOf(int ch, int fromIndex)	Returns the index within this string of the last occurrence of the specified character, searching backward starting at the specified index.

...Conti.

23.	int lastIndexOf(String str)	Returns the index within this string of the rightmost occurrence of the specified substring.
24.	int lastIndexOf(String str, int fromIndex)	Returns the index within this string of the last occurrence of the specified substring, searching backward starting at the specified index.
25.	int length()	Returns the length of this string.
26.	boolean matches(String regex)	Tells whether or not this string matches the given regular expression.
27.	boolean regionMatches(boolean ignoreCase, int toffset, String other, int ooffset, int len)	Tests if two string regions are equal.
28.	boolean regionMatches(int toffset, String other, int ooffset, int len)	Tests if two string regions are equal.
29.	String replace(char oldChar, char newChar)	Returns a new string resulting from replacing all occurrences of oldChar in this string with newChar.
30.	String replaceAll(String regex, String replacement	Replaces each substring of this string that matches the given regular expression with the given replacement.
31.	String replaceFirst(String regex, String replacement)	Replaces the first substring of this string that matches the given regular expression with the given replacement.
32.	String[] split(String regex)	Splits this string around matches of the given regular expression.
33.	String[] split(String regex, int limit)	Splits this string around matches of the given regular expression.
34.	boolean startsWith(String prefix)	Tests if this string starts with the specified prefix.
35.	boolean startsWith(String prefix, int toffset)	Tests if this string starts with the specified prefix beginning a specified index.
36.	CharSequence subSequence(int beginIndex, int endIndex)	Returns a new character sequence that is a subsequence of this sequence.

...Conti.

37.	String substring(int beginIndex)	Returns a new string that is a substring of this string.
38.	String substring(int beginIndex, int endIndex)	Returns a new string that is a substring of this string.
39.	char[] toCharArray()	Converts this string to a new character array.
40.	String toLowerCase()	Converts all of the characters in this String to lower case using the rules of the default locale.
41.	String toLowerCase(Locale locale)	Converts all of the characters in this String to lower case using the rules of the given Locale.
42.	String toString()	This object (which is already a string!) is itself returned.
43.	String toUpperCase()	Converts all of the characters in this String to upper case using the rules of the default locale.
44.	String toUpperCase(Locale locale)	Converts all of the characters in this String to upper case using the rules of the given Locale.
45.	String trim()	Returns a copy of the string, with leading and trailing whitespace omitted.

4.20 COMMAND-LINE ARGUMENTS

- We can pass information into a program at the time of execution of program. This is accomplished by passing command-line arguments to main( ).

- A command-line argument is the information that directly follows the program's name on the command line when it is executed.

- To access the command-line arguments inside a Java program is quite easy, they are stored as strings in a String array passed to the args parameter of main( ).

- The first command-line argument is stored at args[0], the second at args[1], and so on.

- For example, the following program displays all of the command-line arguments that it is called with:

```
// Display all command-line arguments.
class CommandLine
```

```
    {
        public static void main(String args[])
        {
            for(int i=0; i<args.length; i++)
            System.out.println("args[" + i + "]: " +args[i]);
        }
    }
```

- To execute above program use following statement

    Javac CommandLine.Java

    Java CommandLine this is Java program 100 200

- When you do, you will see the following output:

    args[0]: this

    args[1]: is

    args[2]: Java

    args[3]: program

    args[4]: 100

    args[5]: 200

EXERCISE

1. Explain Class and Object fundamentals.
2. What is Constructor? Explain its Types.
3. Explain 'this' keyword.
4. Write a short note on Garbage collection.
5. Explain Finalize() methods.
6. Explain the term 'Method overloading'.
7. Explain Command line argument with example.
8. Write a short note on Recursion.
9. Explain following keywords 'static' and 'final'.
10. Explain Arrays in detail.

INHERITANCE, PACKAGES AND INTERFACES

5.1 INHERITANCE BASICS

- Inheritance is one of the features of Object-Oriented Programming.
- Inheritance allows a class to use the properties and methods of another class. In other words, the derived class inherits the states and behaviors from the base class.
- The class which inherits the properties of other is known as subclass (derived class, child class) and the class whose properties are inherited is known as superclass (base class, parent class).
- The derived class is also called subclass and the base class is also known as super-class.
- The derived class can add its own additional variables and methods. These additional variable and methods differentiates the derived class from the base class.
- Inheritance is a compile-time mechanism. A super-class can have any number of subclasses. But a subclass can have only one superclass.
- The superclass and subclass have "is-a" relationship between them.
- Inheritance can be defined as the process where one class acquires the properties (methods and fields) of another. With the use of inheritance, the information is made manageable in a hierarchical order.

5.1.1 extends Keyword

- **extends** is the keyword used to inherit the properties of a class. Following is the syntax of extends keyword.

Syntax :

```
class Super
{
    .....
    .....
}
class Sub extends Super
{
```

```
            .....
            .....
    }
```

Example :

```
class Calculation
{
  int z;
  public void addition(int x, int y)
    {
            z = x + y;
            System.out.println("The sum of the given numbers:"+z);
    }
  public void Subtraction(int x, int y)
    {
    z = x - y;
    System.out.println("The difference between the given numbers:"+z);
    }
}
public class My_Calculation extends Calculation
{
  public void multiplication(int x, int y)
    {
        z = x * y;
        System.out.println("The product of the given numbers:"+z);
    }
  public static void main(String args[])
    {
            int a = 20, b = 10;
            My_Calculation demo = new My_Calculation();
            demo.addition(a, b);
```

```
        demo.Subtraction(a, b);

        demo.multiplication(a, b);

    }

}
```

Output :

The sum of the given numbers:30

The difference between the given numbers:10

The product of the given numbers:200

- In the given program, when an object to **My_Calculation** class is created, a copy of the contents of the superclass is made within it. That is why, using the object of the subclass you can access the members of a superclass.

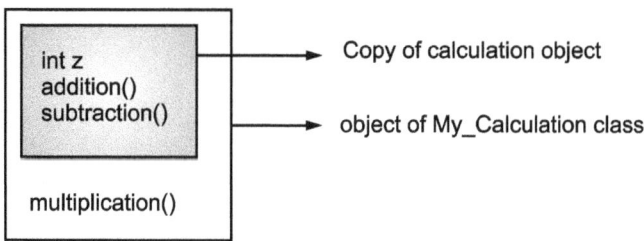

Fig. 5.1: Example of extend keyword

- The superclass reference variable can hold the subclass object, but using that variable you can access only the members of the superclass, so to access the members of both classes it is recommended to always create reference variable to the subclass.

5.1.2 Types of Inheritance

There are various types of inheritance

1. Single Inheritance

2. Multilevel Inheritance

3. Hierarchical Inheritance

4. Multiple Inheritance

5. Hybrid Inheritance

Explanation is as follows:

1. Single Inheritance

- Single inheritance is a type of inheritance in which single derived class is inheriting the properties from single base class.

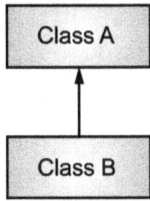

Fig. 5.2: Single inheritance

Syntax:

```
public class A
{
    ..............
}
public class B extends  A
{
    ................
}
```

Example:

```
class Vehicle
{
  String color;
  int speed;
  int size;
  void attributes()
    {
        System.out.println("Color : " + color);
        System.out.println("Speed : " + speed);
        System.out.println("Size : " + size);
    }
}
// A subclass which extends for vehicle
class Car extends Vehicle
{
```

```java
int CC;
int gears;
void attributescar()
  {
    // The subclass refers to the members of the superclass
        System.out.println("Color of Car : " + color);
        System.out.println("Speed of Car : " + speed);
      System.out.println("Size of Car : " + size);
      System.out.println("CC of Car : " + CC);
      System.out.println("No of gears of Car : " + gears);
  }
}
public class Test
{
  public static void main(String args[])
    {
        Car b1 = new Car();
        b1.color = "Blue";
        b1.speed = 200 ;
        b1.size = 22;
        b1.CC = 1000;
      b1.gears = 5;
        b1.attributescar();
    }
}
```

Output :

Color of Car : Blue

Speed of Car : 200

Size of Car : 22

CC of Car : 1000

No of gears of Car : 5

- The derived class inherits all the members and methods that are declared as public or protected.

- If declared as private it can not be inherited by the derived classes. The private members can be accessed only in its own class.

- The derived class cannot inherit a member of the base class if the derived class declares another member with the same name.

2. Multilevel Inheritance

- Class C inherits class B and class B inherits class A which means B is a parent class of C and A is a parent class of B. So, in this case class C is implicitly inheriting the properties and method of class A along with B that's what is called multilevel inheritance.

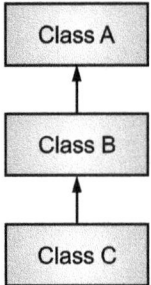

Fig. 5.3: Multilevel inheritance

Syntax :

```
public class A
{

          ............

}
public class B extends  A
{

        ...............

}
public class C extends B
{

         ..........

}
```

Example:

In this example, we have three classes – Car, Maruti and Maruti800. We have done a setup – class Maruti extends Car and class Maurit800 extends Maurti. With the help of this Multilevel hierarchy setup our Maurti800 class is able to use the methods of both the classes Car and Maruti.

```java
class Car
{
    public Car()
    {
        System.out.println("Class Car");
    }
    public void vehicleType()
    {
        System.out.println("Vehicle Type: Car");
    }
}
class Maruti extends Car
{
    public Maruti()
    {
        System.out.println("Class Maruti");
    }
    public void brand()
    {
        System.out.println("Brand: Maruti");
    }
    public void speed()
    {
        System.out.println("Max: 90Kmph");
    }
}
public class Maruti800 extends Maruti
{
    public Maruti800()
    {
```

```
        System.out.println("Maruti Model: 800");
    }
    public void speed()
    {
        System.out.println("Max: 80Kmph");
    }
    public static void main(String args[])
    {
        Maruti800 obj=new Maruti800();
        obj.vehicleType();
        obj.brand();
        obj.speed();
    }
}
```

Output :

Class Car

Class Maruti

Maruti Model: 800

Vehicle Type: Car

Brand: Maruti

Max: 80Kmph

3. Hierarchical Inheritance

When a class has more than one child classes (sub classes) or in other words more than one child classes have the same parent class then such kind of inheritance is known as Hierarchical Inheritance.

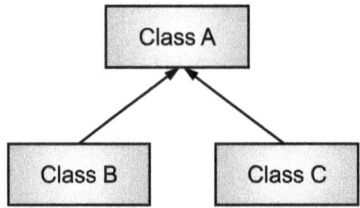

Fig. 5.4: Hierarchical inheritance

Example:

```
Class A
{
  public void methodA()
  {
     System.out.println("method of Class A");
  }
}
Class B extends A
{
  public void methodB()
  {
     System.out.println("method of Class B");
  }
}
Class C extends A
{
 public void methodC()
 {
     System.out.println("method of Class C");
 }
}
Class D extends A
{
  public void methodD()
  {
     System.out.println("method of Class D");
  }
}
Class MyClass
```

```
{
  public void methodB()
  {
    System.out.println("method of Class B");
  }
  public static void main(String args[])
  {
    B obj1 = new B();
    C obj2 = new C();
    D obj3 = new D();
    obj1.methodA();
    obj2.methodA();
    obj3.methodA();
  }
}
```

Output :

method of Class A

method of Class A

method of Class A

4. Multiple Inheritance

C++ , Common lisp and few other languages supports multiple inheritance while Java doesn't support it. It is just to remove ambiguity, because multiple inheritance can cause ambiguity in few scenarios. One of the most common scenario is Diamond problem.

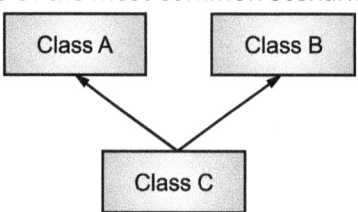

Fig. 5.5: Multiple inheritance

- What is diamond problem?

  Consider the below diagram which shows multiple inheritance as Class D extends both Class B and C. Now let's assume we have a method in class A and class B and C overrides that method in their own way. Because D is extending both B and C so if D wants to use the same method which method would be called (the overridden method of B or the overridden method of C). Ambiguity. That's the main reason why Java doesn't support multiple inheritance.

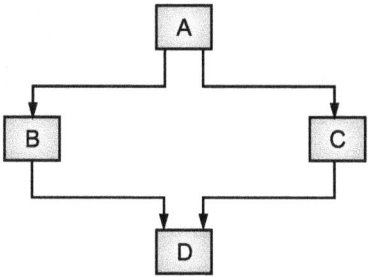

Fig. 5.6: Hybrid inheritance

Program 5.1 : How to Achieve Multiple Inheritance in Java using Interfaces?

```
interface X
{
  public void myMethod();
}
interface Y
{
  public void myMethod();
}
class Demo implements X, Y
{
  public void myMethod()
  {
    System.out.println(" Multiple inheritance using interfaces");
  }
}
```

- As you can see that the class implemented two interfaces. A class can implement any number of interfaces. In this case, there is no ambiguity even though both the interfaces are having same method. Because methods in an interface are always abstract by default, which doesn't let them to give their implementation (or method definition) in interface itself.

5. Hybrid Inheritance

- If you are using only classes to implement hybrid inheritance then this is not allowed in Java, however using interfaces it's possible to have hybrid inheritance in Java.

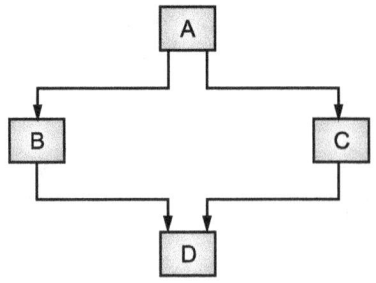

Fig. 5.7: Hybrid inheritance

- Java doesn't support multiple inheritance, the hybrid inheritance is also not possible.

Case 1: Using classes: If in above figure B and C are classes then this inheritance is not allowed as a single class cannot extend more than one class (Class D is extending both B and C).

Case 2: Using Interfaces: If B and C are interfaces then the above hybrid   inheritance is allowed as a single class can implement any number of interfaces in Java.

- Let's understand the above concept with the help of examples:

Program 5.2 : Using Classes to Form Hybrid

```
public class A
{
   public void methodA()
   {
       System.out.println("Class A methodA");
   }
}
public class B extends A
{
  public void methodA()
  {
  System.out.println("Childclass B is overriding inherited method A");
  }
   public void methodB()
   {
       System.out.println("Class B methodB");
   }
```

```
}
public class C extends A
{
    public void methodA()
    {
      System.out.println("Child class C is overriding the methodA");
    }
    public void methodC()
    {
        System.out.println("Class C methodC");
    }
}
public class D extends B, C
{
    public void methodD()
    {
        System.out.println("Class D methodD");
    }
    public static void main(String args[])
    {
        D obj1= new D();
        obj1.methodD();
        obj1.methodA();
    }
}
```

Output :

Error!!

- Above code shows an error, because Multiple inheritance is not allowed in Java so class D cannot extend two classes (B and C).

- In the above program class B and C both are extending class A and they both have overridden the methodA(), which they can do as they have extended the class A. But since both have different version of methodA(), compiler is confused which one to call when there has been a call made to methodA() in child class D (child of both B and C, it's object is allowed to call their methods), this is a ambiguous situation and to avoid it, such kind of scenarios are not allowed in Java.

Program 5.3 : Using Interfaces to form Hybrid

```
interface A
{
    public void methodA();
}
interface B extends A
{
    public void methodB();
}
interface C extends A
{
    public void methodC();
}
class D implements B, C
{
    public void methodA()
    {
        System.out.println("MethodA");
    }
    public void methodB()
    {
        System.out.println("MethodB");
    }
    public void methodC()
    {
        System.out.println("MethodC");
```

```
    }
    public static void main(String args[])
    {
        D obj1= new D();
        obj1.methodA();
        obj1.methodB();
        obj1.methodC();
    }
}
```

Output :

MethodA

MethodB

MethodC

- Even though class D didn't implement interface "A" still we have to define the methodA() in it. It is because interface B and C extends the interface A.

- The above code would work without any issues and that's how we implemented hybrid inheritance in Java using interfaces.

5.2 MEMBER ACCESS AND INHERITANCE

- A subclass cannot access the private members of the superclass.

- For example, consider the following simple class hierarchy: If you try to compile the following program, you will get the error message.

```
class A
{
    private int j; // private to A
}
class B extends A
{
    int total;
    void sum()
    {
```

```
        total = j; // ERROR, j is not accessible here
    }
}
```

Output:

The field A.j is not visible

- Java's access specifiers are public, private, protected and a default access level.A public class member can be accessed by any other code. A private class member can only be accessed within its class.

5.2.1 Default (without an Access Modifier)

- A class's fields, methods and the class itself may be default.
- A class's default features are accessible to any class in the same package.
- A default method may be overridden by any subclass that is in the same package as the superclass.

5.2.2 Protected

- Protected features are more accessible than default features.
- Only variables and methods may be declared protected.
- A protected feature of a class is available to all classes in the same package(like a default).
- Moreover, a protected feature of a class can be available to its subclasses.
- Example: Here is an example for a public member variable

    public int i;

- The following code defines a private member variable and a private member method:

Program 5.4 : Private Data Member and Method Example

```
private double j;
private int myMethod(int a, char b)
{ // ...}
        class Test
        {
    int a;      // default access
    public int b; // public access
    private int c; // private access
```

```java
        // methods to access c
        void setc(int i)
        {
            c = i;
        }
        int getc()
        {
            return c;
        }
    }
public class Main
{
    public static void main(String args[])
    {
        Test ob = new Test();
        ob.a = 1;
        ob.b = 2;
        // This is not OK and will cause an error
        // ob.c = 100; // Error!
        // You must access c through its methods
        ob.setc(100); // OK
        System.out.println("a, b, and c: " + ob.a + " " + ob.b + " " +          ob.getc());
    }
}
```

Output:

a, b, and c: 1 2 100

5.3 SUPER CLASS REFERENCE

- A reference variable of a superclass can be assigned a reference to any subclass derived from that superclass.

Example :

```java
class RefDemo
{
```

```
    public static void main(String args[])
    {
        BoxWeight weightbox = new BoxWeight(3, 5, 7, 8.37);
        Box plainbox = new Box();
        double vol;
        vol = weightbox.volume();
        System.out.println("Volume of weightbox is " + vol);
        System.out.println("Weight of weightbox is " +weightbox.weight);
        System.out.println();
        // assign BoxWeight reference to Box reference
        plainbox = weightbox;
        vol = plainbox.volume(); // OK, volume() defined in Box
        System.out.println("Volume of plainbox is " + vol);
    }
}
```

- Here, weightbox is a reference to BoxWeight objects, and plainbox is a reference to Box objects. Since BoxWeight is a subclass of Box, it is permissible to assign plainbox a reference to the weightbox object.

- It is important to understand that it is the type of the reference variable not the type of the object that it refers to that determines what members can be accessed. That is, when a reference to a subclass object is assigned to a superclass reference variable, you will have access only to those parts of the object defined by the superclass. This is why plainbox can't access weight even when it refers to a BoxWeight object.

5.4 USING SUPER

- Whenever a subclass needs to refer to its immediate superclass, it can do so by use of the keyword super.

- Super has two general forms. The first calls the superclass' constructor. The second is used to access a member of the superclass that has been hidden by a member of a subclass.

(a) Using super to Call Superclass Constructors

- A subclass can call a constructor defined by its superclass by use of the following form of super:

        super(arg-list);

- Here, arg-list specifies any arguments needed by the constructor in the superclass. Super( ) must always be the first statement executed inside a subclass' constructor.

- If a class is inheriting the properties of another class, the subclass automatically acquires the default constructor of the superclass. But if you want to call a parameterized constructor of the superclass, you need to use the super keyword as shown below.

  super(values);

- Example demonstrates how to use the super keyword to invoke the parametrized constructor of the superclass. This program contains a superclass and a subclass, where the superclass contains a parameterized constructor which accepts a string value, and we used the super keyword to invoke the parameterized constructor of the superclass.

Program 5.5 : Using Super to call Superclass Constructor.

```
class Superclass
{
  int age;
  Superclass(int age)
  {
    this.age = age;
  }
  public void getAge()
  {
    System.out.println("The value of the variable named age in super class is: " +age);
  }
}
public class Subclass extends Superclass
{
  Subclass(int age)
   {
     super(age);
   }
  public static void main(String argd[])
  {
    Subclass s = new Subclass(24);
```

```
    s.getAge();
  }
}
```

Compile and execute the above code using the following syntax.

Javac Subclass

Java Subclass

Output

The value of the variable named age in super class is: 24

(b) Using Super to Access a Member of the Superclass that has been Hidden by a Member of a Subclass

- The second form of super acts somewhat like this, except that it always refers to the superclass of the subclass in which it is used. This usage has the following general form:

        super.member

    Here, member can be either a method or an instance variable.

- This second form of super is most applicable to situations in which member names of a subclass hide members by the same name in the superclass.

- Consider this simple class hierarchy:

Program 5.6 : Using Super to Overcome Hiding

```
// Using super to overcome name hiding.
class A
  {
      int i;
  }
// Create a subclass by extending class A.
class B extends A
  {
      int i; // this i hides the i in A
      B(int a, int b)
      {
          super.i = a; // i in A
          i = b; // i in B
      }
```

```
        void show
        {
            System.out.println("i in superclass: " + super.i);
            System.out.println("i in subclass: " + i);
        }
    }
class UseSuper
    {
        public static void main(String args[])
        {
            B subOb = new B(1, 2);
            subOb.show();
        }
    }
```

Output:

i in superclass: 1

i in subclass: 2

- Although the instance variable i in B hides the i in A, super allows access to the i defined in the superclass. As you will see, super can also be used to call methods that are hidden by a subclass.

5.5 CONSTRUCTORS IN DERIVED CLASS

- When a class hierarchy is created, in what order are the constructors for the classes that make up the hierarchy executed?

- For example, given a subclass called B and a superclass called A, is A's constructor executed before B's, or vice versa? The answer is that in a class hierarchy, constructors complete their execution in order of derivation, from superclass to subclass. Further, since super( ) must be the first statement executed in a subclass' constructor, this order is the same whether or not super( ) is used.

- If super( ) is not used, then the default or parameter less constructor of each superclass will be executed.

- The following program illustrates when constructors are executed:

Program 5.7 : Constructors in Derived Class

```java
class A
{
    A()
    {
        System.out.println("Inside A's constructor.");
    }
}
// Create a subclass by extending class A.
class B extends A
{
    B()
    {
        System.out.println("Inside B's constructor.");
    }
}
// Create another subclass by extending B.
class C extends B
{
    C()
    {
        System.out.println("Inside C's constructor.");
    }
}
class CallingCons
{
    public static void main(String args[])
    {
        C c = new C();
    }
}
```

Output:

Inside A's constructor

Inside B's constructor

Inside C's constructor

- As you can see, the constructors are executed in order of derivation.
- If you think about it, it makes sense that constructors complete their execution in order of derivation. Because a superclass has no knowledge of any subclass, any initialization it needs to perform is separate from and possibly prerequisite to any initialization performed by the subclass. Therefore, it must complete its execution first.

5.6 METHOD OVERRIDING

- Method overriding means to override the functionality of an existing method.
- If a class inherits a method from its superclass, then there is a chance to override the method provided that it is not marked final.
- The benefit of overriding is: ability to define a behavior that's specific to the subclass type, which means a subclass can implement a parent class method based on its requirement.

Rules for Method Overriding

- The argument list should be exactly the same as that of the overridden method.
- The return type should be the same or a subtype of the return type declared in the original overridden method in the superclass.
- The access level cannot be more restrictive than the overridden method's access level. For example: If the superclass method is declared public then the overridding method in the sub class cannot be either private or protected.
- Instance methods can be overridden only if they are inherited by the subclass.
- A method declared final cannot be overridden.
- A method declared static cannot be overridden but can be re-declared.
- If a method cannot be inherited, then it cannot be overridden.
- A subclass within the same package as the instance's superclass can override any superclass method that is not declared private or final.
- A subclass in a different package can only override the non-final methods declared public or protected.
- An overriding method can throw any uncheck exceptions, regardless of whether the overridden method throws exceptions or not. However, the overriding method should not throw checked exceptions that are new or broader than the ones declared by the overridden method. The overriding method can throw narrower or fewer exceptions than the overridden method.
- Constructors cannot be overridden.

Program 5.8 : Method Overriding

```java
class Animal
{
    public void move()
    {
        System.out.println("Animals can move");
    }
}
class Dog extends Animal
{
    public void move()
    {
        System.out.println("Dogs can walk and run");
    }
}
public class TestDog
{
  public static void main(String args[])
    {
        Animal a = new Animal();   // Animal reference and object
        Animal b = new Dog();   // Animal reference but Dog object
        a.move();   // runs the method in Animal class
        b.move();   // runs the method in Dog class
    }
}
```

Output:

Animals can move

Dogs can walk and run

- In the above example, you can see that even though **b** is a type of Animal it runs the move method in the Dog class. The reason for this is: In compile time, the check is made on the reference type.

- However, in the runtime, JVM figures out the object type and would run the method that belongs to that particular object.

- Therefore, in the above example, the program will compile properly since Animal class has the method move. Then, at the runtime, it runs the method specific for that object.
- Consider the following example:

Program 5.9 : Method Overriding

```java
class Animal
{
  public void move()
    {
            System.out.println("Animals can move");
    }
}
class Dog extends Animal
{
  public void move()
    {
     System.out.println("Dogs can walk and run");
    }
  public void bark()
    {
            System.out.println("Dogs can bark");
    }
}
public class TestDog
{
  public static void main(String args[])
    {
     Animal a = new Animal();   // Animal reference and object
     Animal b = new Dog();   // Animal reference but Dog object
      a.move();   // runs the method in Animal class
         b.move();   // runs the method in Dog class
      b.bark();
    }
}
```

Output :

TestDog.Java:26: error: cannot find symbol

    b.bark();

    ∧

 symbol: method bark()

 location: variable b of type Animal

1 error

- This program will throw a compile time error since b's reference type Animal doesn't have a method by the name of bark.

5.7 DYNAMIC METHOD DISPATCH

- Dynamic method dispatch is the mechanism by which a call to an overridden method is resolved at run time, rather than compile time.

- Dynamic Method Dispatch is related to a principle that states that a super class reference can store the reference of subclass object. However, it can't call any of the newly added methods by the subclass but a call to an overridden method results in calling a method of that object whose reference is stored in the super class reference.

- It simply means that which method would be executed, simply depends on the object reference stored in super class object.

When parent class reference variable refers to child class object, it is called **upcasting**.

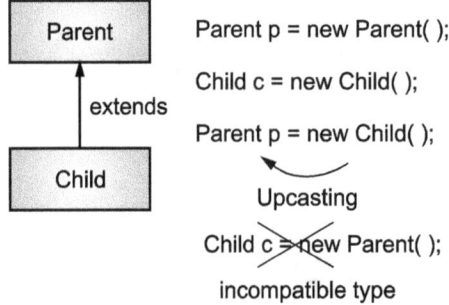

Fig. 5.8: Dynamic method dispatch

Program 5.10 : Example for Dynamic Method Dispatch

```
class A
{
        void callme()
        {
            System.out.println("Inside A's callme method");
```

```java
        }
}
class B extends A
{
    void callme()  // override callme()
    {
        System.out.println("Inside B's callme method");
    }
}
class C extends A
{
     void callme() // override callme()
    {
        System.out.println("Inside C's callme method");
    }
}
public class Dynamic_disp
{
    public static void main(String args[])
    {
        A a = new A(); // object of type A
        B b = new B(); // object of type B
        C c = new C(); // object of type C
        A r; // obtain a reference of type A
        r = a; // r refers to an A object
        r.callme(); // calls A's version of callme
        r = b; // r refers to a B object
        r.callme(); // calls B's version of callme
        r = c; // r refers to a C object
        r.callme(); // calls C's version of callme
    }
}
```

Output:

Inside A's callme method

Inside B's callme method

Inside C's callme method

- Here reference of type A, called r, is declared. The program then assigns a reference to each type of object to r and uses that reference to invoke callme( ).

- As the output shows, the version of callme( ) executed is determined by the type of object being referred to at the time of the call.

5.8 ABSTRACT CLASS

- A class that is declared with abstract keyword, is known as abstract class in Java. It can have abstract and non-abstract methods (method with body).

- Abstraction is a process of hiding the implementation details and showing only functionality to the user.

- Another way, it shows only important things to the user and hides the internal details for example sending sms, you just type the text and send the message. You don't know the internal processing about the message delivery.

- One of the way to achieve Abstraction is Abstract class

- A class that is declared as abstract is known as abstract class. It needs to be extended and its method implemented. It cannot be instantiated.

Syntax:

```
abstract class A
{
}
```

Program 5.11 : Example of Abstract Class

```
abstract class Shape
{
    abstract void draw();
}
//In real scenario, implementation is provided by others i.e. unknown by end user
class Rectangle extends Shape
{
    void draw()
```

```
    {
        System.out.println("drawing rectangle");
    }
}
    class Circle1 extends Shape
    {
        void draw()
        {
            System.out.println("drawing circle");
        }
    }
    //In real scenario, method is called by programmer or user
        class TestAbstraction1
        {
            public static void main(String args[])
            {
                    Shape s=new Circle1();

    //In real scenario, object is provided through method e.g. getShape() method
                    s.draw();
            }
        }
```

Output:

drawing circle

5.9 USING FINAL WITH INHERITANCE

Final keyword used for two purposes

1. Using final to Prevent Overriding
2. Using final to Prevent Inheritance

Explanation is as follows:

5.9.1 Using Final to Prevent Overriding

Method overriding is one of Java's most powerful features, there will be times when you will want to prevent it from occurring.

To disallow a method from being overridden, specify final as a modifier at the start of its declaration.

Methods declared as final cannot be overridden.

Example:

```
class A
{
    final void Fun()
    {
        System.out.println("This is a final method.");
    }
}
class B extends A
{
    void Fun()
    {
        System.out.println("Illegal!");
    }
}
```

Because Fun( ) is declared as final, it cannot be overridden in B. If you attempt to do so, a compile-time error will result.

5.9.2 Using Final to Prevent Inheritance

To prevent a class from being inherited, precede the class declaration with final.

Declaring a class as final implicitly declares all of its methods as final, as you might expect, it is illegal to declare a class as both abstract and final since an abstract class is incomplete by itself and its subclasses to provide complete implementations.

Example of a final class:

```
    final class A
    {
        //...
    }
    // The following class is illegal.
```

```
class B extends A
{
    //...
}
```

It is illegal for B to inherit A since A is declared as final.

5.10 THE OBJECT CLASS

- There is one special class Object, defined by Java.

- All other classes are subclasses of Object. That is, Object is a superclass of all other classes.

- Reference variable of type Object can refer to an object of any other class. Also, since arrays are implemented as classes, a variable of type Object can also refer to any array.

- Object defines the following methods, which means that they are available in every object.

Sr. No.	Method	Purpose
1.	Object clone( )	Creates a new object that is the same as the object being cloned.
2.	boolean equals(Object *object*)	Determines whether one object is equal to another.
3.	void finalize( )	Called before an unused object is recycled.
4.	Class<?> getClass( )	Obtains the class of an object at run time.
5.	int hashCode( )	Returns the hash code associated with the invoking object.
6.	void notify( )	Resumes execution of a thread waiting on the invoking object.
7.	void notifyAll( )	Resumes execution of all threads waiting on the invoking object.
8.	String toString( ).	Returns a string that describes the object

5.11 PACKAGES

- Packages are used in Java in order to prevent naming conflicts, to control access, to make searching/locating and usage of classes, interfaces, enumerations and annotations easier, etc.

- A Package can be defined as a grouping of related types classes, interfaces, enumerations and annotations providing access protection and namespace management.

- Some of the existing packages in Java are:

  (a) Java.lang – bundles the fundamental classes

  (b) Java.io – classes for input , output functions are bundled in this package

- Package in Java can be categorized in two form, built-in package and user-defined package.

Built-in Package: Existing Java package for example Java.lang, Java.util etc.

User-defined-package: Java package created by user to categorized classes and interface

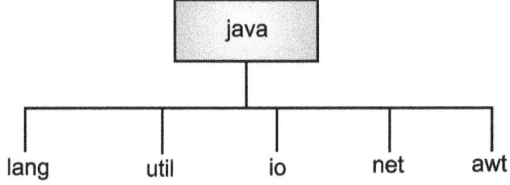

Fig. 5.9: Packages

5.11.1 Advantage of Java Package

- Java package is used to categorize the classes and interfaces so that they can be easily maintained.

- Java package provides access protection.

- Java package removes naming collision.

5.11.2 Defining a Package

- In Java any classes declared within that file will belong to the specified package.

- The package statement defines a name space in which classes are stored. If you skip the package statement, the class names are put into the default package, which has no name.

- Most of the time, you will define a package for your code.

- This is the general form of the package statement:

        package *pkg*;

    Here, *pkg* is the name of the package.

- For example, the following statement creates a package called **MyPackage**:

    package MyPackage;

- Java uses file system directories to store packages. For example, the .class files for any classes you declare to be part of MyPackage must be stored in a directory called MyPackage.

- Remember that case is significant, and the directory name must match the package name exactly.

- The **package** statement simply specifies to which package the classes defined in a file belong. It does not exclude other classes in other files from being part of that same package.

- Most real-world packages are spread across many files. You can create a hierarchy of packages. To do so, simply separate each package name from the one above it by use of a period.

- The general form of a multileveled package statement is shown here:

    package *pkg1*[.*pkg2*[.*pkg3*]];

- A package hierarchy must be reflected in the file system of your Java development system.

- Example, a package declared as package Java.awt.image; needs to be stored in **Java\awt\image** in a Windows environment. Be sure to choose your package names carefully. You cannot rename a package without renaming the directory in which the classes are stored.

5.11.3 Finding Packages and CLASSPATH

- Packages are mirrored by directories.

- Java run-time system uses the current working directory as its starting point. Thus, if your package is in a subdirectory of the current directory, it will be found.

- You can specify a directory path or paths by setting the CLASSPATH environmental variable.

- You can use the -classpath option with Java and Javac to specify the path to your classes.

- For example, consider the following package specification:

    package MyPack

- In order for a program to find MyPack, one of three things must be true. Either the program can be executed from a directory immediately above MyPack, or the CLASSPATH must be set to include the path to MyPack, or the -classpath option must specify the path to MyPack when the program is run via Java.

- When the second two options are used, the class path must not include MyPack, itself. It must simply specify the path to MyPack.

- For example, in a Windows environment, if the path to MyPack is

    C:\MyPrograms\Java\MyPack

    then the class path to MyPack is

    C:\MyPrograms\Java

5.11.4 Access Protection

- Java provides many levels of protection to allow fine-grained control over the visibility of variables and methods within classes, subclasses, and packages.

- Classes and packages are both means of encapsulating and containing the name space and scope of variables and methods.

- Packages act as containers for classes and other subordinate packages. Classes act as containers for data and code.

- The class is Java's smallest unit of abstraction because of the interplay between classes and packages.

- Java addresses four categories of visibility for class members:
    ➢ Subclasses in the same package
    ➢ Non-subclasses in the same package
    ➢ Subclasses in different packages
    ➢ Classes that are neither in the same package nor subclasses

- The three access modifiers, private, public, and protected, provide a variety of ways to produce the many levels of access required by these categories.

- Anything declared public can be accessed from anywhere. Anything declared private cannot be seen outside of its class. When a member does not have an explicit access specification, it is visible to subclasses as well as to other classes in the same package. This is the default access.

- If you want to allow an element to be seen outside your current package, but only to classes that subclass your class directly, then declare that element protected.

- Following Table 5.1 applies only to members of classes. A non-nested class has only two possible access levels: default and public.

- When a class is declared as public, it is accessible by any other code. If a class has default access, then it can only be accessed by other code within its same package.

- When a class is public, it must be the only public class declared in the file, and the file must have the same name as the class.

Table 5.1 : Access Specifier

	Private	No Modifier	Protected	Public
Same class	Yes	Yes	Yes	Yes
Same package subclass	No	Yes	Yes	Yes
Same package non-subclass	No	Yes	Yes	Yes
Different package subclass	No	No	Yes	Yes
Different package non-subclass	No	No	No	Yes

5.11.5 Importing Packages

- **import** keyword is used to import built-in and user-defined packages into your Java source file so that your class can refer to a class that is in another package by directly using its name.
- There are 3 different ways to refer to class that is present in different package

1. **Using Fully Qualified Name**

   Example :

   ```
   class MyDate extends Java.util.Date
   {
   //statement;
   }
   ```

2. **Import the Only Class you Want to Use.**

   Example :

   ```
   import Java.util.Date;
   class MyDate extends Date
   {
   //statement.
   }
   ```

3. **Import all the Classes from the Particular Package**

   Example :

   ```
   import Java.util.*;
   class MyDate extends Date
   {
   //statement;
   }
   ```

5.12 INTERFACES

- An interface is a reference type in Java. It is similar to a class. It is a collection of abstract methods.

- A class implements an interface, thereby inheriting the abstract methods of the interface.

- Along with abstract methods, an interface may also contain constants, default methods, static methods, and nested types. Method bodies exist only for default methods and static methods.

- Writing an interface is similar to writing a class. But a class describes the attributes and behaviors of an object. And an interface contains behaviors that a class implements.

Interfaces have the following properties:

- An interface is implicitly abstract. You do not need to use the **abstract** keyword while declaring an interface.

- Each method in an interface is also implicitly abstract, so the abstract keyword is not needed.

- Methods in an interface are implicitly public.

An interface is similar to a class in the following ways –

- An interface can contain any number of methods.

- An interface is written in a file with a **.Java** extension, with the name of the interface matching the name of the file.

- The byte code of an interface appears in a **.class** file.

- Interfaces appear in packages, and their corresponding bytecode file must be in a directory structure that matches the package name.

An interface is different from a class in several ways, including –

- You cannot instantiate an interface.

- An interface does not contain any constructors.

- All of the methods in an interface are abstract.

- An interface cannot contain instance fields. The only fields that can appear in an interface must be declared both static and final.

- An interface is not extended by a class; it is implemented by a class.

- An interface can extend multiple interfaces.

5.12.1 Defining an Interface

- An interface is defined much like a class. This is a simplified general form of an interface:

access interface name

{

    return-type method-name1(parameter-list);

```
    return-type method-name2(parameter-list);
    type final-varname1 = value;
    type final-varname2 = value;
    //...
    return-type method-nameN(parameter-list);
    type final-varnameN = value;
}
```

- The interface keyword is used to declare an interface. Here is a simple example to declare an interface –

```
import Java.lang.*;
// Any number of import statements
public interface NameOfInterface
{
  // Any number of final, static fields
  // Any number of abstract method declarations\
}
```

5.12.2 Implementing Interfaces

- Once an interface has been defined, one or more classes can implement that interface.

- To implement an interface, include the implements clause in a class definition, and then create the methods required by the interface.

- The general form of a class that includes the implements clause looks like this:

```
    class classname [extends superclass] [implements interface [,interface...]]
    {
        // class-body
    }
```

- If a class implements more than one interface, the interfaces are separated with a comma.

- If a class implements two interfaces that declare the same method, then the same method will be used by clients of either interface.

- The methods that implement an interface must be declared public. Also, the type signature of the implementing method must match exactly the type signature specified in the interface definition.

- Here is a small example class that implements the Callback interface shown earlier:

```
class Client implements Callback
{
// Implement Callback's interface
    public void callback(int p)
    {
        System.out.println("callback called with " + p);
    }
}
```

- Here, callback( ) is declared using the public access modifier.
- When you implement an interface method, it must be declared as public. It is both permissible and common for classes that implement interfaces to define additional members of their own.
- For example, the following version of Client implements callback( ) and adds the method nonIfaceMeth( ):

```
class Client implements Callback
{
    // Implement Callback's interface
    public void callback(int p)
    {
        System.out.println("callback called with " + p);
    }
    void nonIfaceMeth()
    {
        System.out.println("Classes that implement interfaces " + "may also
define other members, too.");
    }
}
```

5.12.3 Nested Interfaces

- An interface can be declared a member of a class or another interface. Such an interface is called a member interface or a nested interface.
- A nested interface can be declared as public, private, or protected. This differs from a top-level interface, which must either be declared as public or use the default access level, as previously described.

- When a nested interface is used outside of its enclosing scope, it must be qualified by the name of the class or interface of which it is a member. Thus, outside of the class or interface in which a nested interface is declared, its name must be fully qualified.

- Here is an example that demonstrates a nested interface:

Program 5.12 : Nested Interface

```
// A nested interface example.
// This class contains a member interface.
class A
{
    // this is a nested interface
    public interface NestedIF
    {
        boolean isNotNegative(int x);
    }
}
// B implements the nested interface.
class B implements A.NestedIF
{
    public boolean isNotNegative(int x)
    {
        return x < 0 ? false: true;
    }
}
class NestedIFDemo
{
    public static void main(String args[])
    {
        // use a nested interface reference
        A.NestedIF nif = new B();
        if(nif.isNotNegative(10))
        System.out.println("10 is not negative");
```

```
        if(nif.isNotNegative(-12))
        System.out.println("this won't be displayed");
    }
}
```

- Notice that A defines a member interface called NestedIF and that it is declared public. Next, B implements the nested interface by specifying implements A.NestedIF Notice that the name is fully qualified by the enclosing class' name. Inside the main( ) method, an A.NestedIF reference called nif is created, and it is assigned a reference to a B object. Because B implements A.NestedIF, this is legal.

5.12.4 Extending Interfaces

- One interface can inherit another by use of the keyword extends.

- An interface can extend another interface in the same way that a class can extend another class.

- The extends keyword is used to extend an interface, and the child interface inherits the methods of the parent interface.

- The syntax is the same as for inheriting classes. When a class implements an interface that inherits another interface, it must provide implementations for all methods required by the interface inheritance chain.

Program 5.13 : Extending Interfaces

```
// One interface can extend another.
interface A
{
    void fun1();
    void fun2();
}
// B now includes fun1() and fun2() -- it adds fun3().
interface B extends A
{
    void fun3();
}
// This class must implement all of A and B
class MyClass implements B
```

```
{
    public void fun1()
    {
        System.out.println("Implement fun1().");
    }
    public void fun2()
    {
        System.out.println("Implement fun2().");
    }
    public void fun3()
    {
        System.out.println("Implement fun3().");
    }
}
class IFExtend
{
    public static void main(String arg[])
        {
            MyClass ob = new MyClass();
            ob. fun1();
            ob. fun2();
            ob. fun3();
        }
}
```

- As an experiment, you might want to try removing the implementation for fun1( ) in MyClass. This will cause a compile-time error.
- Any class that implements an interface must implement all methods required by that interface, including any that are inherited from other interfaces.

5.12.5 Variables in Interfaces

- You can use interfaces to import shared constants into multiple classes by simply declaring an interface that contains variables that are initialized to the desired values.
- When you include that interface in a class that is, when you "implement" the interface, all those variable names will be in scope as constants.

- If an interface contains no methods, then any class that includes such an interface doesn't actually implement anything.

- It is as if that class were importing the constant fields into the class name space as final variables.

5.13 DEFAULT INTERFACE METHODS

- The methods specified by an interface were abstract which doesn't content body. This is the traditional form of an interface.

- The release of JDK 8 has changed this by adding a new capability to interface called the default method.

- A default method defines a default implementation for an interface method. In other words, by use of a default method, it is now possible for an interface method to provide a body rather than being abstract.

- During its development, the default method was also referred to as an extension method.

- A primary motivation for the default method was to provide a means by which interfaces could be expanded without breaking existing code.

- If a new method were added to a popular, widely used interface, then the addition of that method would break existing code because no implementation would be found for that new method.

- The default method solves this problem by supplying an implementation that will be used if no other implementation is explicitly provided. Thus, the addition of a default method will not cause preexisting code to break.

- Another motivation for the default method was the desire to specify methods in an interface that are, essentially, optional, depending on how the interface is used.

- For example, an interface might define a group of methods that act on a sequence of elements. One of these methods might be called remove(), and its purpose is to remove an element from the sequence.

- However, if the interface is intended to support both modifiable and nonmodifiable sequences, then remove() is essentially optional because it won't be used by nonmodifiable sequences.

- It is important to point out that the addition of default methods does not change a key aspect of interface: its inability to maintain state information. An interface still cannot have instance variables.

- It is still not possible to create an instance of an interface by itself.

- It must be implemented by a class. Therefore, even though, beginning with JDK 8, an interface can define default methods, the interface must still be implemented by a class if an instance is to be created.

Example:

```
public interface Demo
{
    int getNumber();
    default String getString()
    {
        return "Default String";
    }
}
```

- Demo declares two methods. The first, getNumber( ), is a standard interface method declaration. It defines no implementation. The second method is getString( ), and it does include a default implementation.

- In this case, it simply returns the string "Default String". Pay special attention to the way getString( ) is declared. Its declaration is preceded by the default modifier. This syntax can be generalized.

- To define a default method, precede its declaration with default. Because getString( ) includes a default implementation, it is not necessary for an implementing class to override it.

- In other words, if an implementing class does not provide its own implementation, the default is used.

Example :

```
class MyIFImp implements Demo
{
    public int getNumber()
    {
        return 100;
    }
}
```

- The following code creates an instance of MyIFImp and uses it to call both getNumber( ) and getString( ).

```
// Use the default method.
class DefaultMethodDemo
{
    public static void main(String args[])
    {
        MyIFImp obj = new MyIFImp();
        System.out.println(obj.getNumber());
        System.out.println(obj.getString());
    }
}
```

The output is shown here:

100

Default String

- The default implementation of getString( ) was automatically used. It was not necessary for MyIFImp to define it. Thus, for getString( ), implementation by a class is optional.

- It is both possible and common for an implementing class to define its own implementation of a default method.

- For example, MyIFImp2 overrides getString( ):

```
class MyIFImp2 implements Demo
{
    public int getNumber()
    {
        return 100;
    }
    public String getString()
    {
        return "This is a different string.";
    }
}
```

Now, when getString( ) is called, a different string is returned.

5.14 USE STATIC METHOD IN INTERFACE

- A static method defined by an interface can be called independently of any object. Thus, no implementation of the interface is necessary and no instance of the interface is required in order to call a static method.

- A static method is called by specifying the interface name, followed by the method name.

- General form is as follows:

    InterfaceName.staticMethodName

- This is similar to the way that a static method in a class is called.

- Example shows an static method in an interface by adding one to Demo interface, The static method is getDefaultNumber( ) and It returns zero.

```
public interface Demo
{
    int getNumber();
    default String getString()
    {
        return "Default String";
    }
    // static interface method.
    static int getDefaultNumber()
    {
        return 0;
    }
}
```

The getDefaultNumber( ) method can be called, as shown here:

    int defNum = MyIF.getDefaultNumber();

static interface methods are not inherited by either an implementing class or a sub interface.

No implementation or instance of Demo is required to call getDefaultNumber( ) because it is static.

EXERCISE

1. Explain Inheritance in detail.

2. Explain the term Method overriding.

3. Differentiate between Method overloading and Method Overriding.

4. Explain Dynamic method dispatch.

5. What are Abstract Classes? Explain with example.

6. Explain the term Packages.

7. Explain the term Interfaces.

8. How to use final with inheritance?

9. What is Object class?

10. Explain Default interface methods.

11. How to use static method in interface?

MULTITHREADING, EXCEPTION HANDLING AND APPLETS

6.1 INTRODUCTION TO MULTITHREADING

- Thread is a lightweight process.
- A program can be divided into a number of small processes. Each process can be addressed as a single thread (a lightweight process).
- Multithreaded programs contain two or more threads that can run concurrently. This means that a single program can perform two or more tasks simultaneously.
- For example, one thread is writing content on a file at the same time another thread is performing spelling check.
- An instance of Thread class is an object, like any other object in Java. But a thread of execution means an individual "lightweight" process that has its own call stack.
- In Java, each thread has its own call stack.

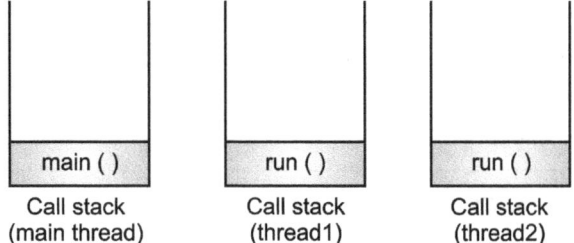

Fig. 6.1: Thread

6.1.1 The Main Thread

- In Multithreading, if you don't create any thread in your program, a thread called main thread is still created.
- Main thread is automatically created, you can control it by obtaining a reference to it by calling currentThread() method.

Two important things to know about main thread are,

1. It is the thread from which other threads will be produced.
2. Main thread must be always the last thread to finish execution.

Example:

```
class MainThread
    {
    public static void main(String[] args)
```

```
    {
    Thread t=Thread.currentThread();
    t.setName("MainThread");
     System.out.println("Name of thread is "+t);
     }
 }
```

Output :

Name of thread is Thread[MainThread,5,main]

- Java is a multi-threaded programming language which means we can develop multi-threaded program using Java.
- A multi-threaded program contains two or more parts that can run concurrently and each part can handle a different task at the same time making optimal use of the available resources specially when your computer has multiple CPUs.
- Multitasking is when multiple processes share common processing resources such as a CPU.
- Multi-threading extends the idea of multitasking into applications where you can subdivide specific operations within a single application into individual threads. Each of the threads can run in parallel.
- The OS divides processing time not only among different applications, but also among each thread within an application.
- Multi-threading enables you to write in a way where multiple activities can proceed concurrently in the same program.

6.1.2 Life Cycle of a Thread

- A Thread has various stages in its life cycle.
- For example, a thread is born, started, runs, and then dies.
- The following diagram shows the complete life cycle of a thread.

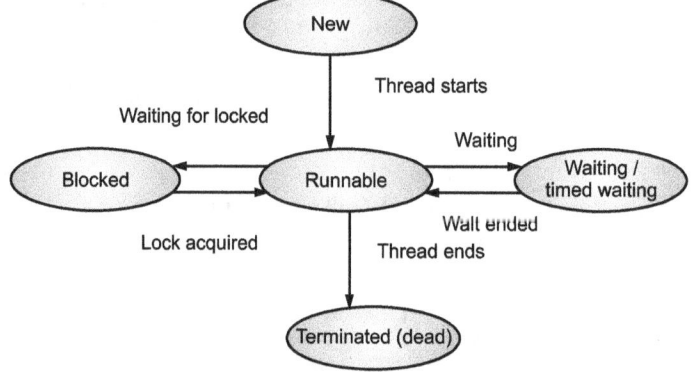

Fig. 6.2: Life cycle of a thread

Following are the Stages of the Life Cycle:

- **New :** A new thread begins its life cycle in the new state. It remains in this state until the program starts the thread. It is also referred to as a born thread.

- **Runnable :** After a newly born thread is started, the thread becomes runnable. A thread in this state is considered to be executing its task.

- **Blocked:** A thread that has suspended execution because it is waiting to acquire a lock.

- **Waiting :** Sometimes, a thread transitions to the waiting state while the thread waits for another thread to perform a task. A thread transitions back to the runnable state only when another thread signals the waiting thread to continue executing.

- **Timed Waiting:** A runnable thread can enter the timed waiting state for a specified interval of time. A thread in this state transitions back to the runnable state when that time interval expires or when the event it is waiting for occurs.

- **Terminated (Dead):** A runnable thread enters the terminated state when it completes its task or otherwise terminates.

6.1.3 Thread Priorities

- Every Java thread has a priority that helps the operating system determine the order in which threads are scheduled.

- Java thread priorities are in the range between MIN_PRIORITY (a constant of 1) and MAX_PRIORITY (a constant of 10).

- By default, every thread is given priority NORM_PRIORITY (a constant of 5).

- Threads with higher priority are more important to a program and should be allocated processor time before lower-priority threads.

- Thread priorities cannot guarantee the order in which threads execute and are very much platform dependent.

6.1.4 Create a Thread by Implementing a Runnable Interface

If your class is intended to be executed as a thread, then you can achieve this by implementing a Runnable interface.

You will need to follow three basic steps –

Step 1

- Implement a run() method provided by a Runnable interface. This method provides an entry point for the thread and you will put your complete business logic inside this method.

Syntax of the run() method –

```
public void run( )
{

}
```

Step 2

- Instantiate a Thread object using the following constructor –

  Thread(Runnable threadObj, String threadName);

Here, threadObj is an instance of a class that implements the Runnable interface and threadName is the name given to the new thread.

Step 3

Once a Thread object is created, you can start it by calling start() method, which executes a call to run( ) method.

Syntax of start() method

```
void start()
{

}
```

Program 6.1 : To Create a New Thread and Starts Running it.

```
class RunnableDemo implements Runnable
{
  private Thread t;
  private String threadName;

  RunnableDemo( String name)
  {
    threadName = name;
        System.out.println("Creating " + threadName );
  }

  public void run()
  {
      System.out.println("Running " + threadName );
        try
      {
          for(int i = 4; i > 0; i--)
        {
```

```java
                System.out.println("Thread: " + threadName + ", " + i);
                // Let the thread sleep for a while.
                Thread.sleep(50);
            }
        }
        catch (InterruptedException e)
        {
            System.out.println("Thread " + threadName + " interrupted.");
        }
        System.out.println("Thread " + threadName + " exiting.");
    }

    public void start ()
    {
        System.out.println("Starting " + threadName );
        if (t == null)
        {
            t = new Thread (this, threadName);
            t.start ();
        }
    }
}

public class TestThread
{

    public static void main(String args[])
    {
        RunnableDemo R1 = new RunnableDemo( "Thread-1");
        R1.start();
```

```
    RunnableDemo R2 = new RunnableDemo( "Thread-2");
    R2.start();
  }
}
```

Output:

Creating Thread-1

Starting Thread-1

Creating Thread-2

Starting Thread-2

Running Thread-1

Thread: Thread-1, 4

Running Thread-2

Thread: Thread-2, 4

Thread: Thread-1, 3

Thread: Thread-2, 3

Thread: Thread-1, 2

Thread: Thread-2, 2

Thread: Thread-1, 1

Thread: Thread-2, 1

Thread Thread-1 exiting.
Thread Thread-2 exiting.

6.1.5 Create a Thread by Extending a Thread Class

- The second way to create a thread is to create a new class that extends Thread class using the following two simple steps.
- This approach provides more flexibility in handling multiple threads created using available methods in Thread class.

Step 1

- You will need to override run( ) method available in Thread class. This method provides an entry point for the thread and you will put your complete business logic inside this method.

Syntax of run() method –

```
    public void run( )
    {

    }
```

Step 2

- Once Thread object is created, you can start it by calling start() method, which executes a call to run( ) method.

Syntax of start() method –

```
void start( )
{
}
```

Program 6.2 : To Create a Thread by Extending a Thread Class.

```
class ThreadDemo extends Thread
{
  private Thread t;
  private String threadName;

  ThreadDemo( String name)
  {
    threadName = name;
    System.out.println("Creating " + threadName );
  }

  public void run()
  {
    System.out.println("Running " + threadName );
    try
    {
      for(int i = 4; i > 0; i--)
      {
        System.out.println("Thread: " + threadName + ", " + i);
        // Let the thread sleep for a while.
        Thread.sleep(50);
      }
    }
  }
```

```java
     catch (InterruptedException e)
     {
        System.out.println("Thread " + threadName + " interrupted.");
     }
     System.out.println("Thread " + threadName + " exiting.");
  }

  public void start ()
  {
     System.out.println("Starting " + threadName );
     if (t == null)
     {
        t = new Thread (this, threadName);
        t.start ();
     }
  }
}

public class TestThread
{
  public static void main(String args[])
  {
     ThreadDemo T1 = new ThreadDemo( "Thread-1");
     T1.start();
     ThreadDemo T2 = new ThreadDemo( "Thread-2");
     T2.start();
  }
}
```

Output :

Creating Thread-1

Starting Thread-1

Creating Thread-2

Starting Thread-2

Running Thread-1

Thread: Thread-1, 4

Running Thread-2

Thread: Thread-2, 4

Thread: Thread-1, 3

Thread: Thread-2, 3

Thread: Thread-1, 2

Thread: Thread-2, 2

Thread: Thread-1, 1

Thread: Thread-2, 1

Thread Thread-1 exiting.

Thread Thread-2 exiting.

6.1.6 Thread Methods

Sr. No.	Method	Description
1	public void start()	Starts the thread in a separate path of execution, then invokes the run() method on this Thread object.
2	public void run()	If this Thread object was instantiated using a separate Runnable target, the run() method is invoked on that Runnable object.
3	public final void setName(String name)	Changes the name of the Thread object. There is also a getName() method for retrieving the name.
4	public final void setPriority(int priority)	Sets the priority of this Thread object. The possible values are between 1 and 10.
5	public final void setDaemon(boolean on)	A parameter of true denotes this Thread as a daemon thread.
6	public final void join(long millisec)	The current thread invokes this method on a second thread, causing the current thread to block until the second thread terminates or the specified number of milliseconds passes.

...Conti.

7	public void interrupt()	Interrupts this thread, causing it to continue execution if it was blocked for any reason.
8	public final boolean isAlive()	Returns true if the thread is alive, which is any time after the thread has been started but before it runs to completion.

6.2 CONCEPT OF EXCEPTION HANDLING

- Exception is an abnormal condition. In Java, exception is an event that disrupts the normal flow of the program. It is an object which is thrown at runtime.

- An exception is a problem that arises during the execution of a program. When an exception occurs the normal flow of the program is disrupted and the program /application terminates abnormally.

- An exception can occur for many different reasons. Following are some scenarios where an exception occurs.

  ➤ A user has entered an invalid data.

  ➤ A file that needs to be opened cannot be found.

  ➤ A network connection has been lost in the middle of communications or the JVM has run out of memory.

- The exception handling in Java is one of the powerful mechanism to handle the runtime errors so that normal flow of the application can be maintained.

- Exception Handling is a mechanism to handle runtime errors such as ClassNotFound, IO, SQL, Remote etc.

- There are five keywords used in Java exception handling.

  ➤ try

  ➤ catch

  ➤ finally

  ➤ throw

  ➤ throws

6.2.1 Advantage of Exception Handling

- The core advantage of exception handling is to maintain the normal flow of the application.

- Exception normally disrupts the normal flow of the application that is why we use exception handling. Let's take a scenario:

- ➤ statement 1;
- ➤ statement 2;
- ➤ statement 3;
- ➤ statement 4;
- ➤ statement 5; //exception occurs
- ➤ statement 6;
- ➤ statement 7;
- ➤ statement 8;
- ➤ statement 9;
- ➤ statement 10;
- Suppose there is 10 statements in your program and exception occurs at statement 5, rest of the code will not be executed i.e. statement 6 to 10 will not run. If we perform exception handling, rest of the statement will be executed. That is why we use exception handling in Java.

6.2.2 Hierarchy of Java Exception Classes

- All exception classes are subtypes of the Java.lang.Exception class. The exception class is a subclass of the Throwable class.
- Other than the exception class there is another subclass called Error which is derived from the Throwable class.
- Errors are abnormal conditions that happen in case of severe failures, these are not handled by the Java programs.
- Errors are generated to indicate errors generated by the runtime environment. Example: JVM is out of memory. Normally, programs cannot recover from errors.
- The Exception class has two main subclasses: IOException Class and RuntimeException Class.

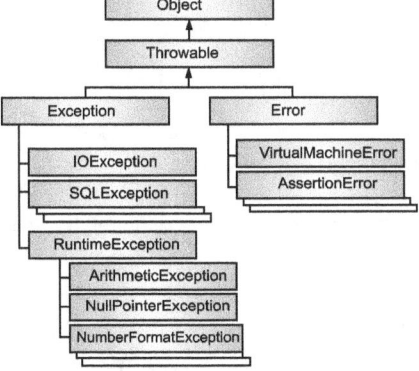

Fig. 6.3: Hierarchy of Java exception classes

6.3 TYPES OF EXCEPTION

- There are mainly two types of exceptions: checked and unchecked where error is considered as unchecked exception.

- The Sun micro-system says there are three types of exceptions:

  1. Checked Exception
  2. Unchecked Exception
  3. Error

1. Checked Exception

- A checked exception is an exception that occurs at the compile time, these are also called as compile time exceptions. These exceptions cannot simply be ignored at the time of compilation, the programmer should take care of these exceptions.

- The classes that extend Throwable class except RuntimeException and Error are known as checked exceptions e.g.IOException, SQLException etc. Checked exceptions are checked at compile-time.

- For example, if you use FileReader class in your program to read data from a file, if the file specified in its constructor doesn't exist, then a *FileNotFoundException* occurs and the compiler prompts the programmer to handle the exception.

Example:

```
import Java.io.File;
import Java.io.FileReader;
public class FilenotFound_Demo
{
    public static void main(String args[])
      {
          File file = new File("E://file.txt");
          FileReader fr = new FileReader(file);
      }
}
```

- If you try to compile the above program, you will get the following exceptions.

Output:

C:\>Javac FilenotFound_Demo.Java

FilenotFound_Demo.Java:8: error: unreported exception FileNotFoundException; must be caught or declared to be thrown

FileReader fr = new FileReader(file);

      ^

1 error

- The methods read() and close() of FileReader class throws IOException, you can observe that the compiler notifies to handle IOException, along with FileNotFoundException.

2. Unchecked Exception

- An unchecked exception is an exception that occurs at the time of execution. These are also called as Runtime Exceptions. These include programming bugs, such as logic errors or improper use of an API.

- Runtime exceptions are ignored at the time of compilation.

- The classes that extend RuntimeException are known as unchecked exceptions e.g. ArithmeticException, NullPointerException, ArrayIndexOutOfBoundsException etc.

- Unchecked exceptions are not checked at compile-time rather they are checked at runtime.

- For example, if you have declared an array of size 5 in your program, and trying to call the 6th element of the array then an *ArrayIndexOutOfBoundsExceptionexception* occurs.

Example:

```
public class Unchecked_Demo
{
    public static void main(String args[])
    {
        int num[] = {1, 2, 3, 4};
            System.out.println(num[5]);
    }
}
```

- If you compile and execute the above program, you will get the following exception.

Output:

Exception in thread "main" Java.lang.ArrayIndexOutOfBoundsException: 5

at Exceptions.Unchecked_Demo.main(Unchecked_Demo.Java:8)

- **There are given some scenarios where unchecked exceptions can occur. They are as follows:**

  ➢ Scenario where ArithmeticException occurs

  If we divide any number by zero, there occurs an ArithmeticException.

  int a=50/0;//ArithmeticException

➢ Scenario where NullPointerException occurs

If we have null value in any variable, performing any operation by the variable occurs an NullPointerException.

String s=null;

System.out.println(s.length());//NullPointerException

➢ Scenario where NumberFormatException occurs

The wrong formatting of any value, may occur

NumberFormat Exception.

Suppose I have a string variable that have characters, converting this variable into digit will occu

NumberFormatException.

```
String s="abc";

int i=Integer.parseInt(s);//NumberFormatException
```

➢ Scenario where ArrayIndexOutOfBoundsException occurs

If you are inserting any value in the wrong index, it would result

ArrayIndexOutOfBoundsException as shown below:

int a[]=new int[5];

a[10]=50; //ArrayIndexOutOfBoundsException

3. Error:

• Error is irrecoverable e.g. OutOfMemoryError, VirtualMachineError, AssertionError etc.

• Errors are not exceptions at all, but problems that arise beyond the control of the user or the programmer.

• Errors are typically ignored in your code because you can rarely do anything about an error.

• For example, if a stack overflow occurs, an error will arise. They are also ignored at the time of compilation.

6.4 UNCAUGHT EXCEPTIONS

• In following program includes an expression that intentionally causes a divide-by-zero error:

```
class Exc
{
    public static void main(String args[])
```

```
        {
            int d = 0;
            int a = 42 / d;
        }
    }
```

- When the Java run-time system detects the attempt to divide by zero, it constructs a new exception object and then throws this exception. This causes the execution of Exc to stop, because once an exception has been thrown, it must be caught by an exception handler and deal with immediately.

- In this example, we haven't supplied any exception handlers of our own, so the exception is caught by the default handler provided by the Java run-time system.

- Any exception that is not caught by your program will ultimately be processed by the default handler. The default handler displays a string describing the exception, prints a stack trace from the point at which the exception occurred, and terminates the program.

- Here is the exception generated when this example is executed:

  Java.lang.ArithmeticException: / by zero

  at Exc0.main(Exc0.Java:4)

- Java supplies several built-in exception types that match the various sorts of run-time errors that can be generated.

- The stack trace will always show the sequence of method invocations that led up to the error. For example, here is another version of the preceding program that introduces the same error but in a method separate from main( ):

```
class Exc1
{
    static void subroutine()
    {
        int d = 0;
        int a = 10 / d;
    }
    public static void main(String args[])
    {
        Exc1.subroutine();
    }
}
```

- The resulting stack trace from the default exception handler shows how the entire call stack is displayed:

  Java.lang.ArithmeticException: / by zero

  at Exc1.subroutine(Exc1.Java:4)

  at Exc1.main(Exc1.Java:7)

6.5 TRY BLOCK

- Try block is used to enclose the code that might throw an exception. It must be used within the method.

- Try block must be followed by either catch or finally block.

Syntax of Try-Catch Block:

```
try
{
    //code that may throw exception
}
catch(Exception_class_Name ref)
{
}
```

Syntax of Try-Finally Block:

```
try
{
//code that may throw exception
}
finally
{
}
```

6.6 CATCH BLOCK

- Catch block is used to handle the Exception. It must be used after the try block only.

- You can use multiple catch block with a single try.

- A method catches an exception using a combination of the try and catch keywords.

- A try catch block is placed around the code that might generate an exception. Code within a try catch block is referred to as protected code, and the syntax for using try catch looks like the following:

Syntax:

```
try
{
   // Protected code
}
catch(ExceptionName e1)
{
   // Catch block
}
```

- The code which is prone to exceptions is placed in the try block. When an exception occurs, that exception occurred is handled by catch block associated with it.

- Every try block should be immediately followed either by a catch block or finally block.

- A catch statement involves declaring the type of exception you are trying to catch. If an exception occurs in protected code, the catch block (or blocks) that follows the try is checked.

- If the type of exception that occurred is listed in a catch block, the exception is passed to the catch block much as an argument is passed into a method parameter.

Example:

The following is an array declared with 2 elements. Then the code tries to access the 3rd element of the array which throws an exception.

```
import Java.io.*;
public class ExcepTest
{
   public static void main(String args[])
   {
      try
      {
         int a[] = new int[2];
         System.out.println("Access element three :" + a[3]);
      }
      catch(ArrayIndexOutOfBoundsException e)
```

```
    {
        System.out.println("Exception thrown  :" + e);
    }
    System.out.println("Out of the block");
  }
}
```

This will produce the following result

Output:

Exception thrown :Java.lang.ArrayIndexOutOfBoundsException: 3

Out of the block

Internal Working of Try-Catch Block

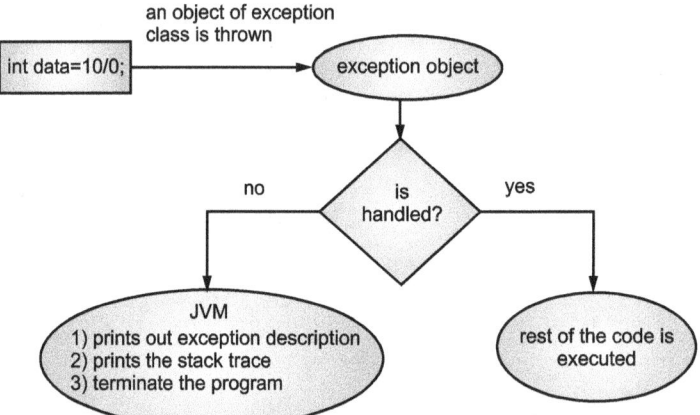

Fig. 6.4: Internal working of Try-catch block

- The JVM firstly checks whether the exception is handled or not. If exception is not handled, JVM provides a default exception handler that performs the following tasks:
  - ➢ Prints out exception description.
  - ➢ Prints the stack trace (Hierarchy of methods where the exception occurred).
  - ➢ Causes the program to terminate.
- But if exception is handled by the application programmer, normal flow of the application is maintained i.e. rest of the code is executed.

6.7 THROW KEYWORD

- The Java throw keyword is used to explicitly throw an exception.
- You can throw an exception, either a newly instantiated one or an exception that you just caught, by using the throw keyword.

- We can throw either checked or unchecked exception in Java by throw keyword. The throw keyword is mainly used to throw custom exception.

- The syntax of Java throw keyword is given below.

  throw exception;

- Example of throw IOException.

  throw new IOException("sorry device error);

- In the following example, we have created the validate method that takes integer value as a parameter. If the age is less than 18, we are throwing the ArithmeticException otherwise print a message welcome to vote.

Program 6.3 : Using Throw Keyword.

```
public class TestThrow
{
  static void validate(int age)
    {
      if(age<18)
          throw new ArithmeticException("not valid");
      else
          System.out.println("welcome to vote");
    }
    public static void main(String args[])
    {
          validate(13);
          System.out.println("Rest of the code...");
    }
}
```

Output:

Exception in thread main Java.lang.ArithmeticException: not valid

6.8 THROWS KEYWORD

- The Java throws keyword is used to declare an exception. It gives an information to the programmer that there may occur an exception so it is better for the programmer to provide the exception handling code so that normal flow can be maintained.

- Exception Handling is mainly used to handle the checked exceptions. If there occurs any unchecked exception such as NullPointerException, it is programmers fault that he is not performing check up before the code being used.

- If a method does not handle a checked exception, the method must declare it using the throws keyword. The throws keyword appears at the end of a method's signature.

Syntax of Throws:

```
return_type method_name() throws exception_class_name
{
//method code
}
```

Example:

```
import Java.io.IOException;
class Testthrows
{
    void m() throws IOException
        {
            throw new IOException("device error"); //checked exception
        }
    void n() throws IOException
        {
            m();
        }
    void p()
        {
            try
            {
                n();
            }
            catch(Exception e)
            {
                System.out.println("exception handled");
            }
        }
public static void main(String args[])
```

```
    {
        Testthrows obj=new Testthrows();
        obj.p();
        System.out.println("normal flow...");
    }
}
```

Output:

exception handled

normal flow...

Difference between Throw and Throws in Java:

There are many differences between throw and throws keywords

Sr. No.	Throw	Throws
1.	Java throw keyword is used to explicitly throw an exception.	Java throws keyword is used to declare an exception.
2.	Checked exception cannot be propagated using throw only.	Checked exception can be propagated with throws.
3.	Throw is followed by an instance.	Throws is followed by class.
4.	Throw is used within the method.	Throws is used with the method signature.
5.	You cannot throw multiple exceptions.	You can declare multiple exceptions e.g. public void method() throws IOException,SQLException.

6.9 THE FINALLY BLOCK

- The finally block follows a try block or a catch block. A finally block of code always executes, irrespective of occurrence of an Exception.
- Using a finally block allows you to run any cleanup-type statements that you want to execute, no matter what happens in the protected code.
- A finally block appears at the end of the catch blocks and has the following Syntax:

```
try
{
    // Protected code
}
```

```
catch(ExceptionType1 e1)
{
    // Catch block
}
catch(ExceptionType2 e2)
{
    // Catch block
}
catch(ExceptionType3 e3)
{
    // Catch block
}
finally
{
    // The finally block always executes.
}
```

Example:

```
public class ExcepTest
{
  public static void main(String args[])
    {
        int a[] = new int[2];
        try
        {
            System.out.println("Access element three :" + a[3]);
        }
        catch(ArrayIndexOutOfBoundsException e)
        {
            System.out.println("Exception thrown :" + e);
        }
```

```
    finally
    {
            a[0] = 6;
            System.out.println("First element value: " + a[0]);
            System.out.println("The finally statement is executed");
    }
  }
}
```

Output:

Exception thrown :Java.lang.ArrayIndexOutOfBoundsException: 3

First element value: 6

The finally statement is executed

Note:

- A catch clause cannot exist without a try statement.
- It is not compulsory to have finally clauses whenever a try/catch block is present.
- The try block cannot be present without either catch clause or finally clause.
- If you don't handle exception, before terminating the program, JVM executes finally block (if any).
- Finally block in Java can be used to put "cleanup" code such as closing a file, closing connection etc.

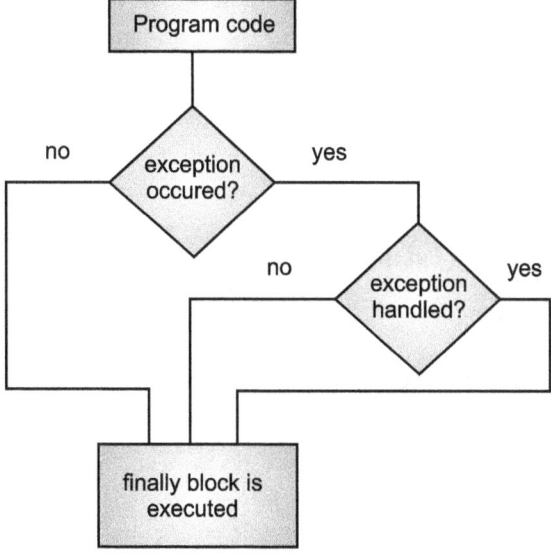

Fig. 6.5: Finally block

Let's see the different cases where finally block can be used.

Case 1

Program 6.4 : The Java Finally Example where Exception doesn't Occur.

```java
class TestFinallyBlock
{
  public static void main(String args[])
    {
        try
          {
              int data=25/5;
              System.out.println(data);
          }
        catch(NullPointerException e)
          {
              System.out.println(e);
          }
        finally
          {
              System.out.println("finally block is always executed");
          }
              System.out.println("rest of the code...");
    }
}
```

Output:

5

finally block is always executed

rest of the code...

Case 2

Program 6.5 : The Java Finally Example where Exception Occurs and not Handled.

```java
class TestFinallyBlock1
{
  public static void main(String args[])
    {
    try
      {
            int data=25/0;
            System.out.println(data);
```

```
        }
    catch(NullPointerException e)
        {
            System.out.println(e);
        }
     finally
        {
            System.out.println("finally block is always executed");
        }
    System.out.println("rest of the code...");
        }
}
```

Output:

Finally block is always executed

Exception in thread main Java.lang.ArithmeticException:/ by zero

Case 3

Program 6.6 : The Java Finally Example where Exception Occurs and Handled.

```
public class TestFinallyBlock2
{
  public static void main(String args[])
    {
    try
        {
            int data=25/0;
            System.out.println(data);
        }
    catch(ArithmeticException e)
        {
            System.out.println(e);
        }
    finally
        {
            System.out.println("finally block is always executed");
        }
    System.out.println("rest of the code...");
    }
}
```

Output:

Exception in thread main Java.lang.ArithmeticException:/ by zero

finally block is always executed

rest of the code...

Difference Between Final, Finally and Finalize:

Sr. No.	Final	Finally	Finalize
1.	Final is used to apply restrictions on class, method and variable. Final class can't be inherited, final method can't be overridden and final variable value can't be changed.	Finally is used to place important code, it will be executed whether exception is handled or not.	Finalize is used to perform clean up processing just before object is garbage collected.
2.	Final is a keyword.	Finally is a block.	Finalize is a method.

3.	class FinalExample
	
	{
	
	public static void main(String[] args)
	
	{
	
	final int x=100;
	
	x=200;//Compile Time Error
	
	}
	
	}
		class FinallyExample
		
		{
		
		public static void main(String[] args)
		
		{
		
		Try
		
		{
		
		int x=300;
		
		}
		
		catch(Exception e)
		
		{
		
		System.out.println(e);
		
		}
		
		Finally
		
		{
		
		System.out.println("finally block is executed");
		
		}
		
		}
		
		}
			class FinalizeExample
			
			{
			
			public void finalize()
			
			{
			
			System.out.println("finalize called");
			
			}
			
			public static void main(String[] args)
			
			{
			
			FinalizeExample f1=new FinalizeExample();
			
			FinalizeExample f2=new FinalizeExample();
			
			f1=null;
			
			f2=null;
			
			System.gc();
			
			}
			
			}

6.10 MULTIPLE CATCH BLOCKS

- A try block can be followed by multiple catch blocks.

Syntax :

```
try
{
    // Protected code
}
catch(ExceptionType1 e1)
{
    // Catch block
}
catch(ExceptionType2 e2)
{
    // Catch block
}
catch(ExceptionType3 e3)
{
    // Catch block
}
```

- The previous syntax demonstrate three catch blocks, but you can have any number of them after a single try.

- If an exception occurs in the protected code, the exception is thrown to the first catch block in the list.

- If the data type of the exception thrown matches ExceptionType1, it gets caught there. If not, the exception passes down to the second catch statement. This continues until the exception either is caught or falls through all catches, in which case the current method stops execution and the exception is thrown down to the previous method on the call stack.

Example:

```
try
{
file = new FileInputStream(fileName);
```

```
   x = (byte) file.read();
        }
      catch(IOException i)
      {
          i.printStackTrace();
   return -1;
      }
      catch(FileNotFoundException f) // Not valid!
      {
        f.printStackTrace();
        return -1;
      }
```

- If you have to perform different tasks at the occurrence of different Exceptions, use Java multi catch block.
- Let's see a simple example of Multi-catch block.

Program 6.7 : Multi-Catch Block

```
public class TestMultipleCatchBlock
{
 public static void main(String args[])
 {
  try
  {
   int a[]=new int[5];
   a[5]=30/0;
  }
  catch(ArithmeticException e)
   {
      System.out.println("task1 is completed");
   }
  catch(ArrayIndexOutOfBoundsException e)
   {
      System.out.println("task 2 completed");
   }
  catch(Exception e)
```

```
  {
    System.out.println("common task completed");
  }
    System.out.println("rest of the code...");
}
```

Output:

> task1 completed
>
> rest of the code...

- At a time only one Exception is occurred and at a time only one catch block is executed.
- All catch blocks must be ordered from most specific to most general i.e. catch for ArithmeticException must come before catch for Exception .

Example:

```
class TestMultipleCatchBlock1
{
 public static void main(String args[])
  {
  try
  {
   int a[]=new int[5];
   a[5]=30/0;
  }
  catch(Exception e)
  {
      System.out.println("common task completed");
  }
  catch(ArithmeticException e)
  {
      System.out.println("task1 is completed");
  }
  catch(ArrayIndexOutOfBoundsException e)
  {
      System.out.println("task 2 completed");
```

```
}
  System.out.println("rest of the code...");
 }
}
```

Output:

Compile-time error

6.11 NESTED TRY STATEMENTS

- The try block within a try block is known as nested try block in Java.
- Sometimes a situation may arise where a part of a block may cause one error and the entire block itself may cause another error. In such cases, exception handlers must be nested.

Syntax:

```
try
{
  statement 1;
  statement 2;
  try
  {
    statement 1;
    statement 2;
  }
  catch(Exception e)
  {
  }
}
catch(Exception e)
{
}
```

Program 6.8 : Java Nested Try Block.

```
class Excep
{
    public static void main(String args[])
    {
```

```
    try
      {
      try
        {
            System.out.println("going to divide");
            int b =39/0;
        }
      catch(ArithmeticException e)
        {
            System.out.println(e);
        }
      try
        {
            int a[]=new int[5];
            a[5]=4;
        }
      catch(ArrayIndexOutOfBoundsException e)
        {
            System.out.println(e);
        }
        System.out.println("other statement);
    }catch(Exception e)
      {
            System.out.println("handeled");
      }
  System.out.println("normal flow..");
}
}
```

6.12 BUILT-IN EXCEPTIONS

- Java defines several exception classes inside the standard package Java.lang.
- The most general of these exceptions are subclasses of the standard type RuntimeException. Since Java.lang is implicitly imported into all Java programs, most exceptions derived from RuntimeException are automatically available.
- Java defines several other types of exceptions that relate to its various class libraries.

- Following is the list of Java Unchecked RuntimeException.

Sr. No.	Exception	Description
1.	ArithmeticException	Arithmetic error, such as divide-by-zero.
2.	ArrayIndexOutOfBoundsException	Array index is out-of-bounds.
3.	ArrayStoreException	Assignment to an array element of an incompatible type.
4.	ClassCastException	Invalid cast.
5.	IllegalArgumentException	Illegal argument used to invoke a method.
6.	IllegalMonitorStateException	Illegal monitor operation, such as waiting on an unlocked thread.
7.	IllegalStateException	Environment or application is in incorrect state.
8.	IllegalThreadStateException	Requested operation not compatible with the current thread state.
9.	IndexOutOfBoundsException	Some type of index is out-of-bounds.
10.	NegativeArraySizeException	Array created with a negative size.
11.	NullPointerException	Invalid use of a null reference.
12.	NumberFormatException	Invalid conversion of a string to a numeric format.
13.	SecurityException	Attempt to violate security.
14.	StringIndexOutOfBounds	Attempt to index outside the bounds of a string.
15.	UnsupportedOperationException	An unsupported operation was encountered.

- Following is the list of Java Checked Exceptions Defined in Java.lang.

Sr. No.	Exception	Description
1.	ClassNotFoundException	Class not found.
2.	CloneNotSupportedException	Attempt to clone an object that does not implement the Cloneable interface.
3.	IllegalAccessException	Access to a class is denied.
4.	InstantiationException	Attempt to create an object of an abstract class or interface.

...Conti.

5.	InterruptedException	One thread has been interrupted by another thread.
6.	NoSuchFieldException	A requested field does not exist.
7.	NoSuchMethodException	A requested method does not exist.

6.13 CUSTOM EXCEPTION

- If you are creating your own Exception that is known as custom exception or user-defined exception.

- Java custom exceptions are used to customize the exception according to user need.

- By the help of custom exception, you can have your own exception and message.

- You can create your own exceptions in Java. Keep the following points in mind when writing your own exception classes

  ➢ All exceptions must be a child of Throwable.

  ➢ If you want to write a checked exception that is automatically enforced by the Handle or Declare Rule, you need to extend the Exception class.

  ➢ If you want to write a runtime exception, you need to extend the RuntimeException class.

- We can define our own Exception class as below:

```
class MyException extends Exception
{

}
```

Program 6.9 : Java Custom Exception.

```
class InvalidAgeException extends Exception
{
 InvalidAgeException(String s)
   {
   super(s);
   }
}
class TestCustomException1
{
  static void validate(int age)throws InvalidAgeException
   {
```

```
    if(age<18)
        throw new InvalidAgeException("not valid");
    else
        System.out.println("welcome to vote");
}

public static void main(String args[])
{
    try
    {
        validate(13);
    }
    catch(Exception m)
    {
        System.out.println("Exception occured: "+m);
    }
    System.out.println("rest of the code...");
}
}
```

Output:

Exception occured: InvalidAgeException: not valid

rest of the code..

6.14 I/O BASICS: STREAM

- A stream can be defined as a sequence of data.
- There are two kinds of Streams –

1. **InputStream**
   - The InputStream is used to read data from a source.
   - This stream is used for reading data from the files. Objects can be created using the keyword **new** and there are several types of constructors available.
   - Following constructor takes a file name as a string to create an input stream object to read the file

   ```
   InputStream f = new FileInputStream("C:/Java/hello");
   ```

- Following constructor takes a file object to create an input stream object to read the file. First we create a file object using File() method as follows:

```
File f = new File("C:/Java/hello");

InputStream f = new FileInputStream(f);
```

- Once you have InputStream object in hand, then there is a list of helper methods which can be used to read to stream or to do other operations on the stream.

Sr. No.	Method	Description
1.	public void close() throws IOException{}	This method closes the file output stream. Releases any system resources associated with the file. Throws an IOException.
2.	protected void finalize()throws IOException {}	This method cleans up the connection to the file. Ensures that the close method of this file output stream is called when there are no more references to this stream. Throws an IOException.
3.	public int read(int r)throws IOException{}	This method reads the specified byte of data from the InputStream. Returns an int. Returns the next byte of data and -1 will be returned if it's the end of the file.
4.	public int read(byte[] r) throws IOException{}	This method reads r.length bytes from the input stream into an array. Returns the total number of bytes read. If it is the end of the file, -1 will be returned.
5.	public int available() throws IOException{}	Gives the number of bytes that can be read from this file input stream. Returns an int.

2. OutputStream:

- The OutputStream is used for writing data to a destination.
- FileOutputStream is used to create a file and write data into it. The stream would create a file, if it doesn't already exist, before opening it for output.
- Here are two constructors which can be used to create a FileOutputStream object.
- Following constructor takes a file name as a string to create an input stream object to write the file –

```
OutputStream f = new FileOutputStream("C:/Java/hello")
```

- Following constructor takes a file object to create an output stream object to write the file. First, we create a file object using File() method as follows:

File f = new File("C:/Java/hello");

OutputStream f = new FileOutputStream(f);

- Once you have *OutputStream* object in hand, then there is a list of helper methods, which can be used to write to stream or to do other operations on the stream.

Sr. No.	Method	Description
1.	public void close() throws IOException{}	This method closes the file output stream. Releases any system resources associated with the file. Throws an IOException.
2.	protected void finalize()throws IOException {}	This method cleans up the connection to the file. Ensures that the close method of this file output stream is called when there are no more references to this stream. Throws an IOException.
3.	public void write(int w)throws IOException{}	This method writes the specified byte to the output stream.
4.	public void write(byte[] w)	Writes w.length bytes from the mentioned byte array to the OutputStream.

Example:

Following is the example to demonstrate InputStream and OutputStream:

```
import Java.io.*;
public class fileStreamTest
{
  public static void main(String args[])
  {
   try
   {
     byte bWrite [] = {11,21,3,40,5};
     OutputStream os = new FileOutputStream("test.txt");
     for(int x = 0; x < bWrite.length ; x++)
```

```
      {
        os.write( bWrite[x] );   // writes the bytes
      }
    os.close();


    InputStream is = new FileInputStream("test.txt");
    int size = is.available();
    for(int i = 0; i < size; i++)
    {
      System.out.print((char)is.read() + " ");
    }
    is.close();
  }catch(IOException e)
  {
    System.out.print("Exception");
  }
  }
}
```

The above code would create file test.txt and would write given numbers in binary format. Same would be the output on the stdout screen.

6.15 BYTE STREAMS

- Java byte streams are used to perform input and output of 8-bit bytes.

- There are many classes related to byte streams but the most frequently used classes are, **FileInputStream** and **FileOutputStream**.

- Following is an example which makes use of these two classes to copy an input file into an output file:

Program 6.10 : Copy an Input file into an Output File

```
import Java.io.*;
public class CopyFile
{
  public static void main(String args[]) throws IOException
```

```java
{
    FileInputStream in = null;
    FileOutputStream out = null;
    try
    {
        in = new FileInputStream("input.txt");
        out = new FileOutputStream("output.txt");

        int c;
        while ((c = in.read()) != -1)
        {
                out.write(c);
        }
    }
    finally
    {
        if (in != null)
        {
            in.close();
        }
        if (out != null)
        {
            out.close();
        }
    }
}
}
```

- Now let's have a file **input.txt** with the following content

    This is test for copy file.

- As a next step, compile the above program and execute it, which will result in creating output.txt file with the same content as we have in input.txt. So let's put the above code in CopyFile.Java file and do the following:

$Javac CopyFile.Java

$Java CopyFile

6.16 CHARACTER STREAMS

- Java **Character** streams are used to perform input and output for 16-bit unicode.

- There are many classes related to character streams but the most frequently used classes are, **FileReader** and **FileWriter**.

- Internally FileReader uses FileInputStream and FileWriter uses FileOutputStream but here the major difference is that FileReader reads two bytes at a time and FileWriter writes two bytes at a time.

- We can re-write the above example, which makes the use of these two classes to copy an input file (having unicode characters) into an output file:

Program 6.11 : Copy an Input File having Unicode Character into an Output File

```java
import Java.io.*;
public class CopyFile
{
  public static void main(String args[]) throws IOException
  {
    FileReader in = null;
    FileWriter out = null;
    try
    {
      in = new FileReader("input.txt");
      out = new FileWriter("output.txt");
      int c;
      while ((c = in.read()) != -1)
      {
        out.write(c);
      }
    }finally
    {
      if (in != null)
```

```
      {
        in.close();
      }
      if (out != null)
      {
        out.close();
      }
    }
  }
}
```

- Now let's have a file **input.txt** with the following content:

  This is test for copy file.

- As a next step, compile the above program and execute it, which will result in creating output.txt file with the same content as we have in input.txt. So let's put the above code in CopyFile.Java file and do the following:

  $Javac CopyFile.Java

  $Java CopyFile

6.17 PREDEFINED STREAMS

- All Java programs automatically import the Java.lang package, which defines a class called system, which encapsulates several aspects of the runtime environment.

- System also contains three predefined stream variables: in, out, err. These are declared as public and static within the system.

- System.out refers to the standard OutputStream by default,this is console.

- System.in refers to the standard InputStream which is the keyboard by default.

- System.in is an object of type InputStream, and System.out, and System.err are objects of type OutputStream. These are byte streams and if desired ,you can wrap these within character based streams.

6.18 READING CONSOLE INPUT

- The preferred method of reading console input for Java is to use a character-oriented stream, which makes your program easier to internationalize and maintain.

- In Java, input is accomplished by reading from System.in and for that you wrap System.in in a BufferedReader object, to create a character stream.

6.19 WRITING CONSOLE OUTPUT

- Console output is most easily accomplished with print() and println() which are declared inside PrintStream class which is the type of the object referenced by System.out.

(A) write()

- PrintStream is an outputStream derived from OutputStream, it also implements the low-level method write(). Thus write() can be used to write to the console.

Syntax:

void write(int bytevalue)

here, bytevalue is in integer, only the low-order 8 bits are written.

Example:

```
import Java.io.*;
public class Main
{
    public static void main(String[] args) throws IOException
    {
        BufferedReader br=new BufferedReader(new InputStreamReader(System.in));
        System.out.println("Enter the number");
        int a=Integer.parseInt(br.readLine());
        System.out.println("The number is "+a);
    }
}
```

Output:

Enter the number

10

The number is 10

(B) Reading Characters

To read a character from BufferedReader use read().

Syntax:

int read() throws IOException

Each time that read() is called, it reads a character from the InputStream and returns it as an integer value. It returns -1 when the end of the stream is encountered.

Example:

```
import Java.io.*;
public class Main
{
    public static void main(String[] args) throws IOException
    {
        BufferedReader br=new BufferedReader(new InputStreamReader(System.in));
        System.out.println("Enter the character");
        char a;
        for(int i=0;i<5;i++)
        {
            a=(char) br.read();
            System.out.println(a);
        }
    }
}
```

Output:

Enter the character

hello

h

e

l

l

o

(C) Reading Strings

- To read a string from the keyboard, use the version of readLine() that is a member of BufferedReader class.

Syntax:

String readLine throws IOException

It returns a String object.

Example:

```
import Java.io.*;
public class Main
```

```
{
public static void main(String[] args) throws IOException
{
BufferedReader br=new BufferedReader(new InputStreamReader(System.in));
System.out.println("Enter the string");
String a=br.readLine();
System.out.println("The character is "+a);
}
}
```

Output:

Enter the string

Hello Streams!

The character is Hello Streams!

6.20 APPLET FUNDAMENTALS

- A Applet is a Java program that runs in a Web browser.

- An applet can be a fully functional Java application because it has the entire Java API at its disposal.

- Applets are small applications that are accessed on an Internet server, transported over the Internet, automatically installed, and run as part of a web document. After an applet arrives on the client, it has limited access to resources so that it can produce a graphical user interface and run various computations without introducing the risk of viruses or breaching data integrity.

6.20.1 The Applet Class

- Every applet is an extension of the *Java.applet*.

- The base Applet class provides methods that a derived Applet class may call to obtain information and services from the browser context.

- These include methods that do the following:
  - ➢ Get applet parameters
  - ➢ Get the network location of the HTML file that contains the applet
  - ➢ Get the network location of the applet class directory
  - ➢ Print a status message in the browser
  - ➢ Fetch an image

> Fetch an audio clip

> Play an audio clip

> Resize the applet

- The Applet class provides an interface by which the viewer or browser obtains information about the applet and controls the applet's execution.

- The Applet class provides default implementations of each of these methods. Those implementations may be overridden as necessary.

- The "Hello World" applet is complete as it stands. The only method overridden is the paint method.

- Example of simple applet named HelloWorldApplet.Java as follows:

```java
import Java.applet.*;
import Java.awt.*;
public class HelloWorldApplet extends Applet
{
    public void paint (Graphics g)
    {
      g.drawString ("Hello World", 25, 50);
    }
}
```

These import statements bring the classes into the scope of our applet class:

- Java.applet.Applet

- Java.awt.Graphics

Without those import statements, the Java compiler would not recognize the classes Applet and Graphics, which the applet class refers to.

6.20.2 Invoking an Applet

- An applet may be invoked by embedding directives in an HTML file and viewing the file through an applet viewer or Java-enabled browser.

- The <applet> tag is the basis for embedding an applet in an HTML file.

- Following is an example that invokes the "Hello World" applet –

```html
<html>
<title>The Hello, World Applet</title>
<hr>
```

```
<applet code = "HelloWorldApplet.class" width = "320" height="120">
    If your browser was Java-enabled, a "Hello, World"
    message would appear here.
</applet>
<hr>
</html>
```

- The code attribute of the <applet> tag is required. It specifies the Applet class to run.
- Width and height are also required to specify the initial size of the panel in which an applet runs.
- The applet directive must be closed with an </applet> tag.
- If an applet takes parameters, values may be passed for the parameters by adding <param> tags between <applet> and </applet>.
- The browser ignores text and other tags between the applet tags.
- Non-Java-enabled browsers do not process <applet> and </applet>. Therefore, anything that appears between the tags, not related to the applet, is visible in non-Java-enabled browsers.

6.21 DIFFERENCE BETWEEN APPLET AND APPLICATION PROGRAM

Sr. No.	Applet	Application Program
1.	Applet is Small Program	Application is Large Program
2.	It is used to run a program on client Browser	It can be executed on stand alone computer system
3.	Applet is portable and can be executed by any JAVA supported browser.	It need JDK, JRE, JVM installed on client machine.
4.	Applet applications are executed in a Restricted Environment	Application can access all the resources of the computer
5.	Applets are created by extending the Java.applet.Applet	Applications are created by writing public static void main(String[] s) method.
6.	Applet application has 5 methods which will be automatically invoked on occurrence of specific event	Application has a single start point which is main method
7.	Main() is not Present	Main() is Present

...Conti.

8.	It requires some third party tool help like a browser to execute.	It is called as stand-alone application as application can be executed from command prompt
9.	It cannot access any thing on the system except browser's services.	It can access any data or software available on the system.
10.	It requires highest security for the system as they are untrusted.	It does not require any security

11.	Example:
	import Java.awt.*;
	import Java.applet.*;
	public class Myclass extends Applet
	{
	   public void init() { }
	   public void start() { }
	   public void stop() {}
	   public void destroy() {}
	   public void paint(Graphics g) {}
	}
		Example:
		public class MyClass
		{
		public static void main(String args[])
		   {
		   }
		}

6.22 LIFE CYCLE OF APPLET

- When Applet is created it under goes series of changes in its state. The applet state includes
  - ➢ Born or initialize state
  - ➢ Running state
  - ➢ Idle state
  - ➢ Dead or destroyed state

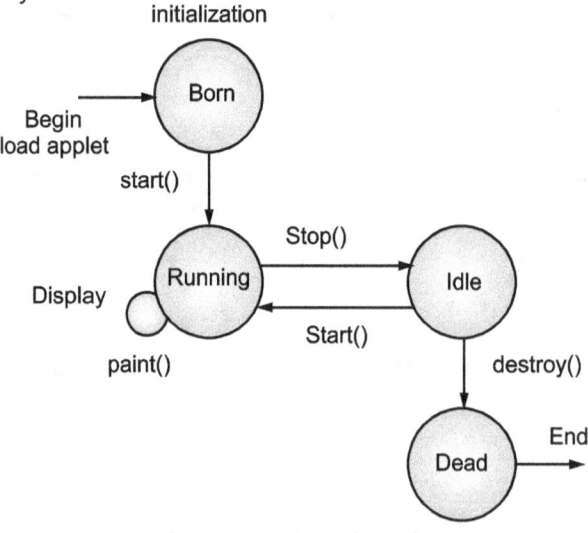

Fig. 6.6: Applet Life cycle

Explanation about above is as follows:

1. Initialization state or init()

- Applet enters the initialization state when it is first loaded. This is achieved by overriding init() method.

- This method is intended for whatever initialization is needed for your applet. It is called after the param tags inside the applet tag have been processed.

Syntax:

```
public void init()
{

}
```

- The **init( )** method is the first method to be called.

- This is where you should initialize variables.

- This method is called only once during the run time of applet.

- With init() method following task may do.

  ➤ Create objects needed by applet

  ➤ Set up initial values.

  ➤ Load images or fonts.

  ➤ Set up colors.

2. Running state or start()

- An applet enters in running state when system calls the start().This is achieved by overriding start() method.

- This method is automatically called after the browser calls the init method. It is also called whenever the user returns to the page containing the applet after having gone off to other pages.

Syntax:

```
public void start()
{

}
```

- The **start( )** method is called after **init( )**.

- It is also called to restart an applet after it has been stopped. Whereas **init( )** is called once—the first time an applet is loaded

- **start( )** is called each time an applet's HTML document is displayed onscreen. So, if a user leaves a web page and comes back, the applet resumes execution at **start( )**.

3. Idle or Stopped State or stop()

- An applet become idle when it is stopped from running. This is achieved by overriding stop() method.

- This method is automatically called when the user moves off the page on which the applet sits. It can, therefore, be called repeatedly in the same applet.

Syntax:

```
public void stop()
{

}
```

- The **stop( )** method is called when a web browser leaves the HTML document containing the applet—when it goes to another page.

- For example. When **stop( )** is called, the applet is probably running. **stop( )** method is also used to suspend threads that don't need to run.

- When the applet is not visible. It can be restarted when **start( )** is called if the user returns to the page.

4. Dead State or destroy()

- An applet is said to be dead when it is removed from memory. This is achieved by overriding destroy() method.

- This method is only called when the browser shuts down normally. Because applets are meant to live on an HTML page, you should not normally leave resources behind after a user leaves the page that contains the applet.

Syntax:

```
public void destroy()
{

}
```

- The **destroy( )** method is called when the environment determines that applet needs to be removed completely from memory. this point, you should free up any resources the applet may be using stop( ) method is always called before **destroy( )**.

- Like initialization, destroying stage occurs only once in the applet's life cycle.

5. Display state or paint()

- Applet moves to the display state whenever it must perform some output operations on the screen.

- This happens immediately after the applet enters into the running state. The paint method is called to accomplish this task. This is achieved by overriding destroy() method.

- Invoked immediately after the start() method, and also any time the applet needs to repaint itself in the browser. The paint() method is actually inherited from the Java.awt.

Syntax:

```
public void paint(Graphics g)
{
}
```

Example:

```
import Java.applet.*;
import Java.awt.*;
/*
 <applet code="AppletLifecycle" width=300 height=300>
 </applet>
*/
public class AppletLifecycle extends Applet
{
  String str = "";
  public void init()
  {
     str += "init; ";
  }
  public void start()
  {
     str += "start; ";
  }
  public void stop()
  {
    // stop
  }
  public void destroy()
  {
    //destroy
```

```
}
public void paint(Graphics g)
 {

    str += "Paint; ";

    g.drawString(str, 10, 25);

 }
}
```

6.23 CREATING A SIMPLE APPLET

- When an applet begins, the AWT calls the following methods, in this sequence:
    1. **init( )**
    2. **start( )**
    3. **paint( )**
- When an applet is terminated, the following sequence of method calls takes place:
    4. **stop( )**
    5. **destroy( )**

Explanation is as follows

1. init( )

- The init() method is called exactly once in an applet's life, when the applet is first loaded.
- It's normally used to read parameter tags, start downloading any other images or media files you need, and set up the user interface.

2. start( )

The start() method is called at least once in an applet's life, when the applet is started or restarted.

In some cases, it may be called more than once. Many applets you write will not have explicit **start()**methods and will merely inherit one from their super class.

A start() method is often used to start any threads the applet will need while it runs.

3. Paint()

The paint() method is called each time your applet's output must be redrawn. This situation can occur for several reasons.

For example, in which the applet is running may be overwritten by another window and the uncovered or the applet window may be minimized and then restored.

paint() is also called when the applet begins execution . Whatever the cause, whenever the applet must redraw its output, paint () is called .

The paint() method has one parameter of type Graphics. This parameter will contain the graphics context which describes the graphics environment in which the applet is running.

4. stop( )

The stop() method is called at least once in an applet's life, when the browser leaves the page in which the applet is embedded.

The applet's start() method will be called if at some later point the browser returns to the page containing the applet.

In some cases the **stop()** method may be called multiple times in an applet's life.

Many applets you write will not have explicit stop() methods and will merely inherit one from their superclass.

Your applet should use the **stop()** method to pause any running threads. When your applet is stopped, it should not use any CPU cycles.

5. destroy( )

The destroy() method is called exactly once in an applet's life, just before the browser unloads the applet. This method is generally used to perform any final clean-up.

For example, an applet that stores state on the server might send some data back to the server before it's terminated. many applets will not have explicit destroy() methods and just inherit one from their superclass.

Example:

```
import Java.awt.*;
import Java.applet.*;
/*
<applet code="AppletSkel" width=300 height=100>
</applet>
*/
public class AppletSkel extends Applet
{
        // Called first.
    public void init()
    {
        // initialization
    }
/* Called second, after init(). Also called whenever the applet is restarted. */
```

```
    public void start()
    {
        // start or resume execution
    }
```

// Called when the applet is stopped.

```
    public void stop()
    {
        // suspends execution
    }
```

/* Called when applet is terminated. This is the last method executed. */

```
    public void destroy()
    {
        // perform shutdown activities
    }
```

// Called when an applet's window must be restored.

```
    public void paint(Graphics g)
    {
        // redisplay contents of window
    }
}
```

6.24 REQUESTING REPAINTING

- An applet writes to its window only when its update() or paint() methods are called by the AWT.

- For example, if an applet is displaying a moving banner, what mechanism does the applet use to update the window each time this banner scrolls? Remember, you cannot create a loop inside paint due the fundamental constraints imposed on an applet - An applet must quickly return control to the AWT run time system.

- Providentially the people who designed Java foresaw this predicament and included the repaint() method. Whenever your applet needs to update the information displayed in its window, it simply calls repaint().

- The repaint() method is defined by the AWT. It causes the AWT run time system to call to your applet's update() method, which in its default implementation, calls paint().

- Again for example if a part of your applet needs to output a string, it can store this string in a variable and then call repaint(). Inside paint(), you can output the string using drawstring().
- The repaint method has four forms.

1. void repaint()

This causes the entire window to be repainted

2. void repaint(int left, int top, int width, int height)

- This specifies a region that will be repainted. the integers left, top, width and height are in pixels. You save time by specifying a region to repaint instead of the whole window.

3. void repaint(long maxDelay)
4. void repaint(long maxDelay, int x, int y, int width, int height)

- Calling repaint() is essentially a request that your applet be repainted sometime soon. However, if your system is slow or busy, update() might not be called immediately. This gives rise to a problem of update() being called sporadically.
- If your task requires consistent update time, like in animation, then use the above two forms of repaint().
- Here, the maxDelay() is the maximum number of milliseconds that can elapse before update() is called.

6.25 STATUS WINDOW

- In addition to displaying information in its window, an applet can also output a message to the status window of the browser or applet viewer on which it is running.
- To do so, call **showStatus( )**, which is defined by **Applet**, with the string that you want displayed.
- The general form of **showStatus( )** is shown here:

  void showStatus(String *msg*)

  Here, *msg* is the string to be displayed.

- The status window is a good place to give the user feedback about what is occurring in the applet, suggest options, or possibly report some types of errors.
- The status window also makes an excellent debugging aid, because it gives you an easy way to output information about your applet.
- Example of applet demonstrates **showStatus( ) is as follows**:

```
/*
    <applet code="SetStatusMessageExample" width=200 height=200>
    </applet>
*/
import Java.applet.Applet;
```

```
import Java.awt.Graphics;
public class SetStatusMessageExample extends Applet
{
    public void paint(Graphics g)
    {
        //drawString() shows message inside an applet
        g.drawString("Show Status Example", 50, 50);

        //showStatus() will displayed in a status bar of an applet window
        showStatus("This is a status message of an applet window");
    }
}
```

Output:

Fig. 6.7 : Example of show status

6.26 HTML APPLET TAG

- The HTML <applet> tag specifies an applet.
- It is used for embedding a Java applet within an HTML document.

Example:

```
<!DOCTYPE html>
<html>
 <head>
  <title>HTML applet Tag</title>
 </head>
```

```
   <body>
      <applet code="newClass.class" width="300" height="200">
      </applet>
   </body>
</html>
```

Here is the *newClass.Java* file:

```
import Java.applet.*;
import Java.awt.*;
public class newClass extends Applet
{
public void paint (Graphics g)
  {
     g.drawString("Hello", 300, 150);
  }
}
```

*   The HTML <> tag also supports following additional attributes:

Attribute	Value	Description
align	URL	*Deprecated* - Defines the text alignment around the applet
alt	URL	Alternate text to be displayed in case browser does not support applet
archive	URL	Applet path when it is stored in a Java Archive ie. jar file
code	URL	A URL that points to the class of the applet
codebase	URL	Indicates the base URL of the applet if the code attribute is relative
height	pixels	Height to display the applet
hspace	pixels	*Deprecated* - Defines the left and right spacing around the applet
name	name	Defines a unique name for the applet
object	name	Specifies the resource that contains a serialized representation of the applet's state.
title	test	Additional information to be displayed in tool tip of the mouse

...Conti

| vspace | pixels | *Deprecated* - Amount of white space to be inserted above and below the object. |
| width | pixels | Width to display the applet. |

6.27 PASSING PARAMETER TO APPLETS

- Parameters are passed to applets in NAME=VALUE pairs in <PARAM> tags between the opening and closing APPLET tags.

- Inside the applet, you read the values passed through the PARAM tags with the getParameter() method of the Java.applet.Applet class.

- Java applet has the feature of retrieving the parameter values passed from the html page. So, you can pass the parameters from your html page to the applet embedded in your page.

- The **param** tag(**<parma name="" value=""></param>**) is used to pass the parameters to an applet.

- For the illustration about the concept of applet and passing parameter in applet

- The applet has to call the getParameter() method supplied by the Java.applet. Applet parent class.

- Three methods commonly used by applets:

  ➢ **String getParameter(String name):** Returns the value for the specified parameter string

  ➢ **URL getCodeBase():** Returns the URL of the applet.

  ➢ **URL getDocumentBase():** Returns the URL of the document containing the applet

Example:

```
import Java.applet.*;
import Java.awt.*;
 /*<APPLET code="hai" width="300" height="250">
<PARAM name="Message" value="Hai friend how are you ..?">
</APPLET>*/
public class hai extends Applet
{
    private String defaultMessage = "Hello!";
    public void paint(Graphics g)
```

```
{
    String inputFromPage = this.getParameter("Message");
    if (inputFromPage == null) inputFromPage = defaultMessage;
    g.drawString(inputFromPage, 50, 55);
}
}
```

Output:

Fig. 6.8 : Passing Parameter to Applet

- You only need to change the HTML, not the Java source code. PARAMs let you customize applets without changing or recompiling the code.

- This applet is very similar to the HelloWorldApplet.

- However rather than hardcoding the message to be printed it's read into the variable inputFromPage from a PARAM element in the HTML.

- You pass getParameter() a string that names the parameter you want. This string should match the name of a PARAM element in the HTML page.

- getParameter() returns the value of the parameter. All values are passed as strings. If you want to get another type like an integer, then you'll need to pass it as a string and convert it to the type you really want.

- The PARAM element is also straightforward. It occurs between <APPLET> and </APPLET>.

- It has two attributes of its own, NAME and VALUE. NAME identifies which PARAM this is. VALUE is the string value of the PARAM. Both should be enclosed in double quote marks if they contain white space.

EXERCISE

1. What is Exception handling?

2. How can one handle Exception in JAVA?

3. Explain Nested try statement.

4. Explain Built in Exceptions in JAVA.

5. Explain Stream in detailed.

6. Explain Byte Stream and Character Stream.

7. Explain Applet life cycle.

9. Explain Applet Skeleton.

8. Write a short note on HTML applet tag.

9. Write a short note on Passing parameters to Applet.

10. Differentiate between Applet and Application Program.

11. How to create a thread?

12. How to extend thread class?

13. Explain Multithreading in detail.

SAMPLE QUESTION PAPER – I

End-Sem. Theory Examination

Time : 2 Hours   Marks : 50

1. (a) Explain the features of Object Oriented Programming.   [6]

   (b) Write short notes on   [6]

   (i) Function prototyping (ii) Call by reference.

OR

2. (a) What is inheritance? What are different types of inheritance?   [6]

   (b) What is operator overloading? Name the operators that cannot be overloaded in C++? How do you declare an overloaded stream insertion and extraction operator?   [6]

3. (a) Explain the features of JAVA.   [6]

   (b) Differentiate between C++ and JAVA.   [6]

OR

4. (a) Write a short note on Operator precedence and associativity.   [6]

   (b) Explain control statements in Java.   [6]

5. (a) What is Typecasting? Explain with example.   [7]

   (b) What is Array? Explain the types of Array.   [6]

OR

6. (a) What is Constructor? Explain the different types of Constructor.   [7]

   (b) Write a short note on

   (i) Garbage collection   (ii) Finalize method.   [6]

7. (a) Explain Package in detailed.   [7]

   (b) Explain Interface in detailed.   [6]

OR

8. (a) What is Exception? How to handle Exception in JAVA.   [7]

   (b) Explain the life cycle of Applet.   [6]

SAMPLE QUESTION PAPER – II

End-Sem. Theory Examination

Time : 2 Hours   **Marks : 50**

1. **(a)** Differentiate between C and C++.   **[6]**

   (b) Write short notes on :   **[6]**

   (i) Reference variable (ii) Scope resolution operator.

OR

2. **(a)** What is Constructor? Explain its types.   **[6]**

   (b) Example the different types of operator overloading.   **[6]**

3. **(a)** Explain the different Data types in Java.   **[6]**

   (b) Write a short note on Standard default values.   **[6]**

OR

4. **(a)** Explain command line argument with example.   **[6]**

   (b) Explain any five Mathematical functions in Java with example.   **[6]**

5. **(a)** What is Dynamic method dispatch?   **[7]**

   (b) Explain Package in detailed.   **[6]**

OR

6. **(a)** Differentiate between Method overloading and Method overriding.   **[7]**

   (b) Write short notes on   **[6]**

   (i) this keyword (ii) Recursion.

7. **(a)** What is Multithreading? Explain in detailed.   **[7]**

   (b) Write short notes on

   (i) Reading console inputs (ii) Writing console output.   **[6]**

OR

8. **(a)** Differentiate between Applets and Applications.   **[7]**

   (b) How to create simple applet? Explain with example.   **[6]**

◈ ◈ ◈